WENDY PERCIVAL's interest
the time honoured 'box of old
became the inspiration behind
novels and novellas.

Wendy shares the intriguing, sometimes shocking, discoveries in
her own family history on her blog and has had several
articles published in *Shropshire Family History Society*'s quarterly
journal and in *Family Tree* magazine.

She lives in South West England, in a thatched cottage
beside a thirteenth-century church, with her husband and
their particularly talkative cat.

The Esme Quentin Mysteries

Blood-Tied
The Indelible Stain
The Malice of Angels
The Fear of Ravens

Novellas

Death of a Cuckoo
Legacy of Guilt
*(*An Esme Quentin prequel – FREE to subscribers*)*

The
Indelible Stain
THE SECOND ESME QUENTIN MYSTERY

WENDY
PERCIVAL

OLD KEY PRESS

First published in 2014
by SilverWood Books

This edition published in 2021 by Old Key Press
Old Key Press
Worlington
Devon
EX17 4TT

ISBN 978-1-8380860-3-9

British Library Cataloguing in Publication Data A CIP catalogue record for this
book is available from the British Library

In memory of Moses Percival

Sentenced to 14 years transportation in 1831 for stealing a sack of barley

Acknowledgements

My thanks go to all those who have helped during the writing of this book. To Lorna Manton for her valuable input, and to my other beta readers, Liz Baber, Dawn Hudson-Vaux and Caren Denton for their enthusiastic feedback. Thank you to Willow Chaddock for permission to use an extract from her brilliant poem, which despite the very loose brief, tallied in spookily well with the storyline. Thanks also to Michelle Kelley for her conscientious editing. Finally, a huge thank you to Brian, my sound-board and reader-in-chief, who despite having to suffer spouse-in-author-zone syndrome, still manages to remain passionate about my writing and takes top slot as my biggest fan.

1

Esme Quentin's grim discovery that morning was shocking as much for its timing as its distressing nature. A cruel contrast to her carefree mood only moments before.

She'd had an uneventful journey to North Devon, arriving at the tiny historic port of Warren Quay earlier than anticipated for her meeting with Ruth Gibson, on whose farm she'd be staying. She parked her Peugeot beside some upturned boats and turned off the engine. It would be good to see Ruth again. Would they still recognise one another after thirty years? She climbed out of the car and stretched, savouring the smell of seaweed in the air as the breeze blew inland across the breakers.

She slammed the car door and headed for the small museum, a short way down the road to the harbour, where she'd agreed to meet Ruth. A poster on the door advertised the forthcoming visit of the *Mary Ann,* a replica nineteenth-century sailing ship, described as a 'Floating Museum on the History of Convict Transportation'.

As expected, the sign in the museum's window read 'Closed'. She checked her watch. Another hour before Ruth was due. A stroll by the sea would be the perfect way to pass the time.

She threw her sweatshirt around her shoulders and carried on down the hill towards the quay, winding her way between the hotel and the cottages, which in the nineteenth century would have housed labourers and their families who worked at Warren Quay when it was a busy port.

The hotel, like the museum, was not yet open for business. The outer door was closed and the curtains were drawn at the windows to the bar. Too early for guests to be at breakfast, though not too early for staff to be at work. She detected a distant clatter from the kitchen, suggesting the chef was already busy preparing food. She considered banging on the door to ask if coffee was being served but decided against it. Perhaps later.

She ambled along the path to the harbour wall, pausing to gaze across the still water of the harbour, encircled by the immense breakwater fashioned from granite boulders the size of a man to defy the ravages of the Atlantic Ocean beyond.

She continued down the steep stone slipway to the beach, pausing at the bottom to slip off her sandals and roll up her jeans.

Waves hurtled between the rock strata as though they were running late and she quickened her pace with them to reach the water's edge and splash in the shallows. As the wet sand oozed between her toes, she relished a bubble of excitement at the thought of spending the next few weeks in such a dramatic and unspoilt location. Not every day would herald the clear blue sky and sunshine of this particular August morning, of course, but childhood holidays had taught her that vagaries of weather rarely diminished the unique quality of this section of the Devon coast.

It had been a wise decision to seize the opportunity for a change of scenery and a new challenge. It was exactly what she needed right now. It would curb the restlessness she'd suffered in the months since Elizabeth's incident.

She looped the straps of her sandals together into one hand and paddled towards the opposite side of the beach. As she lifted her face to embrace the salted wind something flickered in her peripheral vision. She stopped and looked around. Was someone trying to catch her attention from the other side of the rocks?

She shaded her eyes with her hand. Debris was strewn along the tideline – tangles of orange binder-twine and bundles of bleached timber. And in the distance, something flapping in the wind from a bundle of brightly coloured fabric, like a heap of clothes left by a swimmer while taking to the water.

But no one was swimming today. The beach was empty. So what was she looking at?

She stood for a moment, deaf to everything but the snarl of the sea. It was just a pile of rags. That's all. But surely the colours were too vivid to have spent time in seawater? They'd be dulled, wouldn't they, if they'd washed up on the tide? A noose of unease tightened in the pit of her stomach. Perhaps she'd better take a look. Just to make sure.

She continued along the shoreline, turning inland before heading up the beach, annoyed with herself for not resisting the urge to satisfy her curiosity. Now she'd end up being late.

The unique strata of the cliffs loomed over the bay, like giant strands of folded toffee, eclipsing the early morning sun from the rocks and pebbles below. She stepped into the chill of its shadow and shivered. Two gulls screamed overhead. At the foot of the cliff she paused to gaze up at the tuft of green above then backed away, suddenly wary of unexpected rock falls.

The coloured cloth and littered tideline was out of sight now but she knew it was only a few steps beyond the jagged rock ahead. A quick scramble to the top, a quick look down and it would be done. With her fears dismissed and her buoyant mood restored, she could return to the quay to find Ruth.

The twist of apprehension tightened as she trudged closer. She reached the rock and paused to take a breath. Then she grabbed hold, launched herself up and peered over.

The scene hit her like a kick in the stomach. On the shingle below lay the battered and broken body of a woman.

Inertia gripped her. For a few seconds, she could only stare at the torn dress and the grotesque position of the body on the ground. A scrap of paper, lifted by the breeze, fluttered across the stones and settled in a rock pool.

The sound of a faint moan, barely audible over the rasp of the sea, jolted her out of her stupor and she half-fell, half-scrambled down to the woman's side.

'Don't move,' she said. What a stupid thing to say. How could the woman move? She must have broken almost every bone in her body.

Esme looked round, scanning the beach, willing someone to appear. But there was no one. No early morning surfers, no walkers, no day trippers. She was alone.

She leant over and spoke into the woman's ear. 'I'm going to get help. I'll be back as soon as I can.'

She threw down her sandals and turned to retrace her steps, sprinting down to the spit of sand where she'd paddled earlier. Easier to run here. A wave broke, hissing as it sucked at the shoreline. She darted out of the way, casting an anxious glance at the approaching tide. How long before the waves reached the woman's resting place?

On the other side of the beach she headed inland, splashing in and out of puddles at the base of the rocks. A ribbon of kelp caught her foot and she came crashing down on to her hip, grazing her arm on a colony of barnacles. She swore and got back to her feet. Keep going. Not far, now. She limped on.

The slipway to the harbour remained stubbornly distant but finally she reached the bottom. She slowed a little to catch her breath, preparing for the steep incline. Then, lactic acid surging through her calves, she drove up the slope, past the old lime kiln and on to the footpath where she'd ambled so casually only a short time ago.

By the time she reached the end of the path her lungs were raw and her chest ached. She stopped, bending double, hands on her thighs, and gasped for air. As breathing became easier she straightened up and looked around. The entrance to the hotel was still closed. She ran over and hammered on the door.

She heard movement from inside, heard the bolts being drawn back on the other side. At the same time, from behind, someone called her name. She stepped back and looked round. A woman with mouse-startled eyes and blond hair tied high in a ponytail hurried towards her. The familiar features of a girl, yet unfamiliar in a woman's face.

Esme stumbled towards her. 'Ruth.'

'Esme?' Ruth grabbed her by the arms. 'Are you OK? What on earth's happened?'

'Woman. On the beach. Need an ambulance…'

'Sit here,' said Ruth, steering her to a picnic table beside the entrance to the bar. 'I'll deal with it.' Esme sank on to the bench, breathing deeply, aware of someone emerging from the hotel, of urgent voices as her message was relayed.

That initial scene, as she peered over the edge of the rock, replayed over and over in her head like a jerky home movie – the tattered gaudy dress, the distorted angle of the woman's limbs and the sickly hue of her face in a frame of matted hair. She must have fallen from the cliff. What had she been doing so close to the edge? How long had she been lying there?

She flinched when she felt a hand on her shoulder and realised she was shaking. Ruth looked down on her with concerned eyes.

'Esme…'

'I ought to go back,' Esme said, standing up. 'Stay with her till the ambulance comes.'

'Not yet. Get your breath back first.'

'No, it's OK. I'm recovering a bit now.' She turned to Ruth. 'We need a blanket or something. Keep her warm.'

Ruth nodded. 'I'll get one. You go ahead.'

As Ruth hurried back to the hotel, Esme jogged wearily down the slipway and back across the sand, scrunching over the pebbles to where the woman lay. When she reached her, she knelt down, searching for signs of life in the woman's bleached-white face. Had death claimed her while she'd been away? But no – there was the discernable movement of shallow breathing.

'You'll be safe soon,' she told her, bending close. 'We've phoned for an ambulance.' She laid her hand on the woman's arm, disturbed by the chill of her skin. 'Take it easy. It won't be long, now.'

She wanted to ask her name. Wasn't that what paramedics did

13

when they reached a casualty? But she should rest, not talk, shouldn't she? First aid advice from courses taken long ago eluded her.

The sound of crunching gravel broke through the hissing of the waves. Esme looked up as Ruth appeared with a folded blanket under her arm. Ruth scrambled over the rock and froze. 'Oh my God.'

She dropped down beside Esme and together they laid the blanket lightly over the woman. It seemed a pathetic gesture, but there was little more they could do.

Esme looked back towards the quay for signs of help arriving. A futile search, knowing the emergency call had been made only minutes before, but it seemed to ease the torture of the seconds labouring by.

She felt Ruth tugging at her arm. 'I think she's trying to say something.'

'Are you sure? She must be in terrible pain.'

'No, it's not just that. Look.'

Esme bent down and hovered her ear near the woman's face. It was hard to hear with the sea smashing ever closer against the rocks. She felt the woman's frail breath brush her cheek.

'Perhaps you shouldn't try to talk,' she said. 'Just rest now. Help's on its way.'

But Ruth was right. The woman seemed intent on speaking. Her fingers clawed at the edge of the blanket, her lips moved and something akin to a gurgle escaped from her lips.

Esme gently took her hand and cradled it in her own. 'What is it?' she said. 'What are you trying to say?'

'Oh, poor, poor woman,' said Ruth, clasping her hands together. 'Surely it can wait, can't it?'

Esme lowered her head once more and the woman whispered two words. Then, with one pitiful exhale, her grip loosened and there was silence.

Esme stared down into the empty face. 'No! Hang on. They

won't be long…'

Ruth laid a hand on Esme's arm. 'I think she's gone.'

Esme sat back on her heels, blinking back hot tears which blurred her vision. She wiped them away with the back of her hand.

Ruth put her arm around Esme's shoulders. 'What did she say?'

Esme let the words echo in her head before answering. She turned to Ruth and repeated the woman's final words. 'She said, I lied.'

2

Esme wandered along the water's edge, staring out to sea. The pounding of the waves merged with the throbbing blades of the Devon Air Ambulance some distance away behind her. When the rhythm changed she turned to watch the helicopter lift into the air. It rotated, then pulled away from the coast and headed inland to the district hospital a few minutes flying time away.

The high visibility jackets of the emergency service personnel looked like psychedelic flotsam scattered across the beach, sporadically bathed in blue from the flickering light of the police vehicle parked on the slipway. She tucked a strand of her habitually wayward hair back in its fastening and turned her back on them, returning her gaze to the soothing rise and fall of the sea swell.

It seemed incomprehensible that she'd been standing on this spot less than two hours ago in a state of contentment, congratulating herself for the bold decision to seize the opportunity she'd been offered. Now her head was filled with troubled questions. How had the woman come to fall from the cliff? What had she meant by her final words?

She reached inside her pocket and pulled out a damp scrap of paper she had rescued from a rock pool near where the woman lay. A piece of torn photograph. One of many, she guessed, having seen a confetti of similar scraps fly across the beach, scattered by the helicopter's down-draught on its arrival. Too far flung by now to be gathered and pieced back together.

She sensed someone approaching and turned to see Ruth striding down the sand towards her.

'How're you feeling?' said Ruth, linking her arm through Esme's.

'Oh, you know. Bit shell-shocked. But don't worry about me.

I'll be fine.' She looked at Ruth's colourless face, devoid of the infectious smile she always wore as a child. 'How about you?'

Ruth merely shrugged and shook her head.

Esme looked back out to sea. 'If only I'd seen her earlier…'

'Esme,' said Ruth, in a tone she no doubt reserved for unruly children visiting her farm. 'I doubt it would have made any difference. I'm sure the outcome was inevitable. Goodness knows how long she'd been lying there. Stop torturing yourself.' She squeezed Esme's arm. 'At least she didn't die alone.'

'No. I suppose you're right.' Images of the woman's lifeless face swam in front of her eyes again. She forced them away. Ruth was right. No point in torturing herself.

'Not the best of ways to meet up after thirty years, is it?' said Ruth. 'You haven't changed a bit, by the way.'

Esme shot Ruth a sideways glance and rubbed her finger over the scar on her cheek. 'Apart from the odd, minor aberration.'

Ruth tugged her arm. 'Don't be silly,' she said, smiling. 'That's just so much grey hair. We've all got plenty of that.'

They stood in silence, staring out at the hazy shape of Lundy Island on the horizon.

'I saw you with the police,' said Ruth. 'Did you tell them what she said?'

Esme nodded. 'I'm not sure he was that interested, though. He told me someone more senior will come and talk to me. What did they ask you?'

'Nothing much. I just told them how I'd seen you coming up from the beach.'

'Did you mention the photograph?'

'No, I thought I'd let you do that. Come on,' she added, letting go of Esme's arm. 'Time to retreat before we get wet feet.'

They headed back up the beach, stepping in single file over the distinctive rock strata which stretched down the beach like the heads of protruding crocodiles standing in line. Esme looked ahead. A gaggle of early visitors stood on the quayside watching the emergency services in conference. Thank goodness it hadn't been later in the day or it would have made quite a spectacle. Then again, if it had been later she wouldn't have been on the beach at all but reminiscing with Ruth at Ravens Farm over childhood holidays spent there. Someone else would have found the woman's body.

She glanced round at Ruth, scurrying to keep up behind her. 'What d'you make of what she said?'

Ruth caught her up and plunged her hands into the pockets of her skirt. 'Her final confession, perhaps? No idea. Hard to know.'

'What do you think happened?'

'Fell? Jumped? Don't like to think about it too much.'

Esme gazed back up the beach. 'For a moment, I had the horrible idea that someone had pushed her.'

Ruth stopped walking. 'Pushed her?' She looked uneasy. 'Why would you think that?'

'I don't know. It just seemed an odd thing to say. As though she was trying to explain the circumstances.'

'Equally, she could have been trying to explain why she'd done it. Guilt, perhaps.' Ruth flicked her eyes towards the cliffs and back to Esme. 'She'd have said a name, wouldn't she? If someone had pushed her.'

'Unless she didn't know their name.'

'Then she'd say "someone pushed me", wouldn't she?'

'Yes, of course she would.' She smiled at Ruth's anxious face and shook her head. 'Sorry. I'm just trying to make sense of it.'

They carried on walking. When they reached the slipway Esme stopped to brush the sand off her feet and slip her sandals back on.

Ruth laid a hand on her arm. 'Look,' she said. 'You've had a horrible experience. Your perception of things is bound to be a little off kilter, right now.'

'You're probably right.'

Ruth smiled. 'Let's see what the police make of it, shall we?'

They climbed the slope and stopped beside the picnic tables. Esme leant against the sea wall and rubbed her hip where she'd fallen. It was beginning to stiffen. She tried not to think of the image the discomfort conjured up.

'Looks like that policeman's heading this way,' Ruth said, peering down the path towards the hotel. 'He'll be looking for you, I expect. I'll get out of your way. Rustle up some coffee.'

'You don't need to get delayed any more, Ruth. Aren't you meant to be working at the museum today?'

'Don't worry about that. One of the other volunteers can cover my shift. I'll phone from the pub. I'll catch up with you later and I can show you where you're staying. You won't recognise the place.'

Ruth hurried down the path, stopping to pass a few words with a tall grey-suited man with a chubby face and loosely cropped curly hair. Esme wandered to the end of the row of cottages which overlooked Quay Point, a mini-headland of rough grassland protruding out into the bay.

'Mrs Quentin?'

She looked round at the tall man Ruth had spoken to a moment ago. 'Yes, that's right.'

'Detective Sergeant Adam Collins.' He waved the customary ID and gestured towards the picnic table by the wall. 'Shall we?'

Esme nodded and sat down on the end. The sergeant perched on the opposite side, the tightness of his well-worn suit suggesting he was a man who enjoyed his food. She noticed his eyes, a vivid blue, were blood-shot. Working too hard or socializing too late? Or both?

'Rather a distressing experience for you, Mrs Quentin.'

She gave him a thin smile. 'I've had better starts to a day.'

He slipped his ID back inside his jacket. 'You've only just arrived in Devon, I understand, from Shropshire?'

'That's right.'

'On holiday?'

'A working holiday. I'm helping out a friend.' She jerked her head towards the cliffs beyond Warren Quay. 'I'm renting a cabin at Ravens Farm. Your officer's taken my contact details.'

'Good, good.' He studied her for a moment and she felt the usual discomfort as she braced herself to fence a reference to the scar on her face. But instead he said, 'You're a historical researcher, I understand.' He pulled at his ear lobe. 'That'd be people's family history? That kind of thing?'

'Sometimes. I do all sorts.' It was more like a chat at a bar, rather than any sort of police enquiry. For some reason it irritated her. Perhaps because her fraught nerves impeded such distractions.

He rested one arm on the table and rubbed his chin with his thumb. 'My colleague tells me the woman said something before she died.'

'Yes.' Now they were getting somewhere. 'She said, *I lied.*'

He nodded slowly, chewing over the information. 'Did she say what about?'

Esme frowned. 'She was hardly in a fit state to say anything, let alone give a detailed explanation.' She paused, surprised by the brusqueness of her tone, as though she felt the need to defend the woman, as if he was implying it had been her own fault that she was lying fatally injured on the beach. Perhaps it was the shock. If so, she shouldn't take it out on the sergeant. He was only doing his job.

'Look,' she said, with a sigh. 'When I first saw her she looked so badly injured I thought she was dead. When I realised she was still alive, I certainly didn't encourage her to talk. I thought she ought to conserve her energy.'

'Point taken.' He shrugged. 'So you have no idea what she meant.' It was a statement rather than a question.

'No.'

'And you didn't know the deceased.'

'No. I would have said, wouldn't I?' She bit her lip. There, she'd done it again. Was he really asking stupid questions or was she being hypersensitive?

She reached into her trouser pocket for the scrap of paper and slid it across the table. 'I found this. I'm not sure what to make of it, but it could be important.'

'And this was the victim's?'

'I saw it blow away into a rock pool. There were several smaller bits blowing around. She must have had this piece in her hand. '

He studied it and turned it over. 'Not a note, then.'

'Note? Oh, I see. A suicide note. No, I didn't find a note. Just this.'

'Doesn't tell us much.'

'Epson photographic paper. You can see the name on the back. So obviously a computer copy of something. The original image looks as though it was an old sepia photograph.'

He looked unconvinced. 'Could be damage from the salt water.'

Esme shook her head. 'No. Epson paper's much tougher than that.'

Collins's raised eyebrows disappeared under his fringe of curls. 'Quite the sleuth.'

She stared back. Was he patronising her or was she over reacting? Given her current state of mind it was hard to know. She decided not to rise to the bait. 'Do you think it might be significant?'

'In what way, exactly?'

'Well, I don't know. You're the detective.'

She saw one corner of his mouth twitch. At least it got a reaction. His languid tone was beginning to irritate her. Was it a deliberate tactic? She looked at his blood-shot eyes. Or maybe he was just tired.

'Do you know who she was?' she asked.

'Not yet. No ID. Someone will know her, though, if she's local. And if she's a visitor the place where she's staying will realise she's missing before too long.'

'She could be a day tripper.'

He smiled. 'We'll cross that bridge when we come to it, shall we?'

A uniformed constable strode down the terrace and hovered beside their table. Collins turned round. 'Yes?'

'A word, sir?'

Collins got to his feet. Esme stood up with him, snatching up the fragment of photograph from off the table. 'Aren't you going to take it with you?'

'We don't even know it belonged to the deceased, Mrs Quentin.'

She picked it up and held it out. 'Better safe than sorry. Her family might ask about it. You don't want to end up with egg on your face, do you?'

After a moment's hesitation he took it but she suspected it was out of politeness rather than because he attached any importance to it.

She walked with him towards the car park. 'What do you think she was doing up there?' she said. 'She wasn't out for an early morning hike, that's for sure. Wrong clothes. D'you reckon she fell over the edge last night sometime?' She glanced across at him. He was staring ahead, as though working something out.

They arrived at the end of the footpath.

'Well, sergeant?' she said, as they came to a halt. 'Any theories? Other than suicide, I mean.'

Collins turned towards her and inclined his head. 'Thank you for your information, Mrs Quentin. I'm sorry you've had such a harrowing experience. We'll be in touch if we need to talk to you again.'

She watched him walk away, irritated and frustrated by his evasiveness. And, she realised, with an inexplicable sense of loss.

3

Neave Shaw took a deep breath before knocking on the door of her boss's office and walking in. Janice was bent over the drawer of the filing cabinet flicking through files, a curtain of wispy grey hair hiding her face so Neave couldn't tell if her skin was flushed with her tell-tale signature of irritation.

She cleared her throat. 'You wanted a word?'

'Yes. Grab a seat, will you?'

Neave pulled out a chair and sat down, her hands pressed together between her knees. She gazed around the room, noticing the scuffed paint on the walls and the tired, dated office furniture, the fake veneer peeling off on the corner of the sagging bookshelf. Even the spider-plant on the top looked insipid and limp. But funds were tight and there was nothing extra for the luxury of an office makeover. In fact, nothing had changed since she'd sat in this room for the first time, five years ago. She'd not been a counsellor back then, of course. She'd been receiving help, not giving it.

Janice closed the drawer and sat down on the opposite side of the desk. She placed her palms down either side of the file in front of her and looked at Neave.

Neave avoided her gaze. 'Not a problem with Gail, is there?' she said, glancing down at the name on the folder. 'She seems to be coming out of herself a bit more, I thought. She even laughed the other day. So much more positive now. I'm really getting a good feeling about her, you know. It's amazing to think…'

'Neave.'

Neave swallowed. 'Sorry.' She tried a half-laugh in an attempt to break the tightness in her throat. 'Rambling again, aren't I?'

Janice looked at her, a mixture of concern and strictness in her eyes. 'I know it's not my usual style, but I think we've skirted around this for too long, now, don't you?'

Neave shuffled on her chair. 'I'm not sure I know what you mean.'

'Look, we have some really vulnerable individuals here.' Janice lifted her head and closed her eyes. 'God, listen to me. I can't believe I'm telling you that. You, of all people.'

'Sorry, Janice. I know what you're going to say and I know my fuse has been a bit short lately.'

'Non existent, some days, if we're honest. That new lad…'

'I did apologise to him. He was fine about it.'

'Let's hope so, for his sake.'

'You see, the thing is, I've had a lot on my mind, lately. But I'll put it all behind me and…'

'Ah, but that's just the thing, love. We've been here before. And I have to be honest, I really thought you'd sorted it. But lately, well, it's back to square one. So I can only conclude that you didn't sort it, at all. You just buried it. And as you know, if you plant something, there's a chance it might re-grow, for better or worse. Isn't that what we tell our clients?'

Neave studied her fingernails. She knew she owed Janice an explanation. She owed her much more than that, in reality.

Janice leant towards Neave. 'What's happened, Neave? What's triggered it?'

'I had…she wrote…' she began, grappling with the words, lining them up and re-ordering them in her head. But they refused to cooperate and remained in defiant disarray in a dark corner of her brain.

'She wrote to you?'

Neave managed a nod, the image of the letter swimming in front of her eyes, the instinct to back away.

'Saying what?'

Neave shook her head. How could she conjure up the bizarre claims, the near fanatical tone of the words, the panic they'd inflicted on her? The whole content was the work of a mad woman. Clearly the drink had permeated even deeper and with greater destruction than had been evident before. 'It didn't make any sense,' she said, eventually. 'I don't think she's in her right mind any more. I just want to forget about it.'

Janice sat back in her chair and sighed. 'Neave, Neave, Neave. You can't just leave it to fester. For God's sake, haven't you learnt anything while you've been here?'

Neave sat up straight and stared back, determined to hold her ground. 'I don't want to take the bait and I don't see why I should have to.'

'Bait?'

'Come off it, Janice. You know the tactics. Lies, remorse, false promises. I refuse to fall for them again. I can't do it. And I won't. Not any more.'

She looked away, conscious that Janice was perhaps the one person with the influence to change her mind. And she didn't want it changed. She wanted to stay in her bubble of control where she was Neave Shaw, independent woman, nobody's fool.

'But it's different now,' said Janice.

Neave threw her an alarmed glance at the way she was reading her mind. 'No, it's not.'

'That's the old Neave talking. The bright, confident and switched-on Neave I see on a daily basis can do this.' Janice reached out across the desk to Neave, spreading her fingers out towards her. 'Don't be scared you're not strong enough, because you are. I wouldn't suggest you try, otherwise. This is an opportunity. Don't miss it. Don't turn away or you might never resolve matters. And in the long run, it'll hurt you more. Believe me.'

Neave kept her eyes fixed downward. If only she could buy herself some time. Modify her behaviour, prove Janice wrong. She might back off and the idea would slip on to the back burner. 'OK. I'll give it some thought.'

25

'You've got leave owing. Take it, and go home.'

Neave shot up her head. 'What? No. I need time to get my head around it. I can't just go.'

'Yes you can. And you should.'

Janice stood up. 'I'll look at the roster and see who can cover for you. I can, if need be. You don't have to worry on that score.' She held out her hand. 'Good luck. Let me know how it goes.'

Neave could do nothing but stare at Janice. It was like someone had glued her to the seat.

'Go and put into practice what we encourage our clients to do,' said Janice, smiling. 'Call it Continual Professional Development.'

4

'Ruth, you've done a terrific job,' said Esme, gazing around the interior of the wooden cabin, determined to put the trauma of the past few hours behind her.

'Do you think so?' said Ruth, sitting down on the edge of the double box-bed. 'I saw a magazine article about a Swedish coastal cabin and fell in love with it but I wasn't sure if I could pull it off.'

'Of course you've pulled it off. It's fantastic.'

Once a humble hut, Breakers had stood overlooking the cliffs since before the Second World War, and was where Esme and her family had enjoyed numerous summer holidays when she and Ruth were girls.

'Well, the open-plan isn't what I would normally have thought to do and I was a bit worried that...'

'Ruth. It's perfect. I love it.'

'Good,' said Ruth. The broad smile which Esme had missed earlier was back on her face. 'It needed bringing into the twenty-first century, so hopefully there's everything you need.'

'I'm sure there is. And thank you. It's good of you to let me have use of it.'

Ruth shook her head. 'No, on the contrary. You're doing us a favour. You can be our guinea-pig before our first booking in September. I didn't bother to advertise it any earlier. There's nothing worse than mithering about it not being finished for the start of the season. You know how it is. These things always take much longer than you expect them to.'

Esme scanned the compact space, taking in the neat kitchen, dining area and comfy corner unit of the sitting room. 'I really can't believe it's the same place.'

Ruth laughed. 'Bit different from the tired old dump you used to come to before.'

'It wasn't a dump! Well, perhaps it was to some people but we didn't see it like that. It was all part of the big adventure. Anyway, how could you not love it, with a view like that?' She wandered through the open French windows out on to the narrow veranda and gazed across the field out to sea, lost in hazy images of running through the grass, their mother calling to take care by the edge. The memory shot her back to the present with a jolt.

'You thinking of that woman, again?' said Ruth, suddenly at her side.

'Hard not to, isn't it? But it's not our worry any more.' She moved back inside. Best not to think about it or she'd start wondering what the police were doing. They'd be in touch if they needed to talk to her. Though she wondered how likely that was. Not only had Sergeant Collins seemed to have already made up his mind, he didn't seem very interested in considering any other scenarios. Perhaps he was right.

Ruth perched on the corner of the bed. 'So what's this research you're helping Maddy with then?'

'Oh, nothing too onerous. It's in connection with a documentary she's putting together. She's a bit behind with things and she offered me a month's work to get her up to speed.'

'She's taking part in the Convict Ship Museum visit, isn't she?'

'Yes, she is. Which is partly why she's behind with her research.' Esme lifted her case on to the bed. 'You're not involved, then?'

Ruth laughed. 'Nice idea but it's so busy at this time of year with my B & B as well as doing extra hours at the hotel. Some of the other museum volunteers are, though.'

'I saw the poster earlier. Sounds interesting.'

'Yes, I'm looking forward to it. The idea's based on a similar project. A ship called the *Success* which had transported convicts to Australia. It was set up by a group of entrepreneurs in the late nineteenth century, apparently.'

'The crew all dress up in period costume, Maddy said.' Esme grinned. 'She enjoys a bit of play acting, does Maddy.'

'She's such an enthusiast, isn't she? We met her when she did the photos for our website a few years ago. She wasn't long out of college then. I hadn't realised until recently what a history buff she was.'

'That's how I got to know her. She's an expert on old photographs. Dates them, restores them. She's very good.' She thought of Sergeant Collins pocketing the piece of photograph the woman had held in her hand. If only she'd kept it, she could have asked Maddy for her opinion. But it had seemed so important at the time that the police use it in their investigation. Now she wasn't convinced they'd look any further than the ends of their collective noses.

She pushed the irritation away and unzipped the lid of her suitcase. 'Well, I suppose I ought to get myself organised,' she said, glancing round to appraise the drawers and cupboards.

Ruth jumped up. 'Anything I can do to help?'

'Oh, it won't take long. I travel pretty light.' She pulled out a skirt from the top of the case and shook the creases out. 'Probably left-over from when I was a bit of a nomad.'

'You must be pretty settled, these days, I would have thought?' said Ruth, handing her a hanger.

Esme looped the skirt on the hooks and hung it up in the wardrobe. 'I suppose I've put down a few roots.'

'Suppose? You don't sound very sure.'

'I've probably been too busy to give it much thought.' She gathered up her brush, make-up bag and toiletries and took them into the bathroom. Was the restless mood she'd been in before she'd left home an indication she was ready to move on? The image she had in her head of her Shropshire cottage sitting idle and lonely, waiting for her return, seemed to contradict that.

'Do you think the police have found out who she was, yet?' said Ruth, as Esme came back out.

'I thought you didn't want to talk about it.'

'I don't. I didn't. Well, it was so awful for you, when you'd just arrived. I suppose I wanted to pretend it hadn't happened.' She wandered over to the window and stared out.

Esme lifted out a pile of T-shirts and put them on a shelf in the wardrobe.

'What made you think she was pushed?' said Ruth.

Esme peered round the open wardrobe door, eyebrows raised.

'Yes, yes, I know I said you weren't thinking straight,' said Ruth, folding her arms. 'But I was thinking earlier, well…was it your investigative journalism antennae buzzing?'

Esme laughed. 'I was never a journalist, Ruth. Merely a researcher. Tim was the journalist.'

'Yes, I know not officially. But you and your husband worked as a team, didn't you?' She leant against the dividing post at the end of the bed. 'So it comes to the same thing in a way.'

'Perhaps.' Esme emptied the last clothes out on to the bed. She closed the empty case and zipped it back up. 'But that was years ago. I don't do that sort of thing any more.'

'What about Elizabeth?'

'That was different, she's my sister. What else could I have done?' She gave Ruth a quizzical frown. 'What are you driving at, Ruth?'

'You must have had a gut feeling about it, like when you and Tim worked on a case. That's all I'm saying.'

Had she? When Elizabeth was left in a coma, the urge to discover the truth had taken over the moment she knew the attack was no random assault. But had she sensed something from the start? She couldn't remember. Everything had happened so fast.

'So?' continued Ruth. 'Did something like that happen here? You seemed annoyed with the police. As if they weren't taking it seriously.'

Esme dropped down on to the bed. 'Stop worrying. The police will find out who she was, establish what happened, and that will be the end of it. I'm certainly not getting involved.'

Ruth smiled. 'Yes, of course you're right. It was when you said…well, it was a bit worrying. You don't like to think there's someone out there who…' She shuddered and shook her head. 'Don't mind me. I'm getting things all out of proportion. It's just another holiday tragedy. Goodness knows, it isn't the first and you can be sure it won't be the last.' She flapped her hand. 'But don't get me going on holiday makers leaving their sensible brains at home or you'll never hear the last of it.' She turned to go. 'Right. Now I shall leave you in peace. Come up to the farm when you're straight and say hello to everyone. We'll crack open a bottle of something.'

Esme nodded. 'Thanks, that'd be great. See you later.' She wandered to the open door and watched Ruth hurrying across the field towards the farm until she was out of sight.

Her gaze drifted north towards Warren Quay, the cliffs bold and imposing above the horizontal sea, and again the question of the woman's identity hung in her thoughts. She imagined the police arriving at the front door of the woman's family, braced to inform them of the tragedy. Would they suggest her death was suspicious? Would they ask about the photograph? Had Sergeant Collins's forensic colleagues discovered anything intriguing about it? Did they even care?

She gave herself a mental kick. Hadn't she just told Ruth that it wasn't her worry? She'd be busy enough doing her own job to worry whether the police were doing theirs.

31

5

'Well, well. Look what the cat's dragged in.'

To her dismay, Neave felt herself flushing. 'So am I invited in?' she said, staring back at her grandmother. 'Or is that your way of saying I ought to stay on the doormat?'

Gwen Preston scoffed, turning away to shuffle back down the hall. 'Not exactly a regular visitor, though, eh?'

'And hardly likely to, with a welcome like that.'

'I suppose not. Cuppa? I've only got the real McCoy. None of your fancy brew.'

'They're just herbal teas, Gran. Not witches' potions. Ordinary's fine.' She followed Gwen into the small kitchen at the back of the house her grandmother always referred to as the scullery, a hangover from Neave's great-grandmother being in service, apparently. It was certainly basic. Gwen said she'd no time for new fangled gadgets. Neave recalled her regarding her first fridge with suspicion. Sometimes Neave wondered how she, Neave, had ever been sufficiently prepared to escape into the twenty-first century, having spent so much of her childhood indoctrinated by the culture of the 1930s.

Having switched on the kettle and set a tea-tray – tea drinking was an event in the Preston household – Gwen leant back against the sink and folded her arms.

'They haven't smartened you up, then, I see. Though your hair's a bit tidier than last time.'

Neave self-consciously tucked a short strand behind her ear. No long tresses to hide behind any more. Wasn't that the point of the change of style? Face the world for better or worse? Having marched into the stylist as some sort of challenge to Janice's accusation that she wasn't addressing her "issues" she was now feeling shorn and exposed and wasn't yet used to the neat, clipped cut which finished at her chin. The sudden realisation of the irony that the style was more 1930s than contemporary alarmed her. But at least it meant that her gran approved and she'd need Gwen's backing if this leave which Janice had insisted upon was to prove fruitful.

'So, has your mother been similarly honoured by your presence?' added Gwen, turning to the boiling kettle.

'She wasn't in. I thought she may be here. Not that I wouldn't have called anyway,' she added hastily. 'I want to talk to you too, Gran.'

'Do you now. Well, there's a thing.' Gwen picked up the tray. 'We'll go into the parlour, shall we? I might even find a spot of Dundee cake. Unless you're one of these diet fanatics. Not developed an eating disorder, I trust? They were on about them on *Woman's Hour* last week. Can't see the point of it, me-self. These kids don't know they're born. You didn't get that sort of thing in my day. Glad of whatever we could get, we were. We knew what it was to go hungry.'

'There's a bit more to it than that, Gran.' Neave went ahead and opened the door to the front room.

'So they say. Have some of them where you work, do you? Along with the rest of them that never learnt how to get their lives in order.'

Neave walked into the room and dropped down on to the battered armchair beside the beige glazed-tiled fireplace. 'So how's Mum?' she said, eager to change the record.

'Why you so keen all of a sudden? You didn't want to know last time.'

Neave looked around the room, noticing how faded the wallpaper had become. 'I can change my mind, can't I?'

Gwen tossed her head and gave a dismissive harrumph. 'I'll get that cake.' She disappeared, leaving Neave to close her eyes and slump against the back of the chair. This was going to be more difficult than she'd expected. No, not expected. Hoped. Wanted.

33

Would love to be. Was her gran aware of what had been in the letter? Information had been hinted at but nothing Neave could understand. She recalled the wording, but there was no suggestion of revelation or secrets told. In fact, the past hadn't been mentioned at all, quite the opposite. The letter was upbeat and enthusiastic about the future. Optimism flew from the page. The word atonement featured somewhere in her mother's ramblings. It may have been that which tipped the balance and made Janice's reprimand ring true. 'An opportunity not to be ignored', she'd reminded Neave as she'd left.

Gwen arrived with a round cake tin, an image of the Royal Family embossed on the lid. She opened it and handed it to Neave. 'Help yourself. I've cut a couple of pieces.'

Neave took a slice, the rich smell of fruit transporting her back to Sunday afternoons at Mrs Felton's a few doors down. At least her gran could cook a decent fruit cake. Mrs Felton's were always dry and over-baked. Neave would pick out the raisins and push the cake crumbs to the side of the plate. Whether Mrs Felton was hurt by this most obvious of rebuffs to her cooking, she never said. She was all coos, smiles and patting of heads. Perhaps she just assumed Neave a finicky child. Either way she never held it against her.

'Lovely, Gran,' said Neave. 'You're a good cook.' She licked her sticky fingers. 'You were about to tell me about Mum.'

'Was I? I don't recall. You were about to tell me why you've dropped in unannounced on the doorstep, more like.'

Neave wiped her mouth with the back of her hand. 'Mum wrote to me.'

'About what?'

'You didn't know, then.'

'Why should I? I dare say she doesn't think to tell me about every piece of correspondence she puts in the post.'

'It wasn't in the post. She e-mailed me.'

'Did she now? Now that is news. Didn't know she did that sort of thing. Here, have your tea before it goes cold.'

'She must have said something.'

'Is that right. And what makes you think that?'

'It was an odd letter. As though she'd reached a decision. Surely she'd have told you?'

'Was I surprised to see you?'

'Yes, but…'

'Then that's your answer. She no more told me she'd written to you as she's told me what she's gallivanted off to Devon for.'

'Devon? Why Devon?'

'I just told you, didn't I? I wasn't party to that decision, either. So looks like we're both in the dark. Best we can hope for is that she's planning to put us in the picture when she gets back.'

'Does she have friends there? Family I know nothing about?'

'You know as much as me, love. And sounds like you know more, if she's contacted you.'

Neave put down her cup and leant over the arm of the chair. 'How's she been, lately? You know, how's the…'

A loud rap at the front door made them flinch.

Gwen scowled. 'Someone's determined.' She made to get up but Neave was there before her.

'Don't worry, Gran. I'll go. Probably doorstep selling. I'll get rid of them.'

She hurried out of the front room and down the hall. A distorted shadow through the opaque glass shifted close to the door and backed off. She turned the latch, pulled open the door and peered out.

A uniformed policeman stood on the step, a younger fresh-faced female officer beside him. It was the woman who spoke.

'We're looking for Mrs Gwen Preston.'

'That's me,' said Gwen's voice from down the hall.

Neave spun round. Her grandmother stood on the threshold to the front room, her hand on the doorpost. 'What d'you want?'

'May we come in, Mrs Preston?' said the young officer,

35

glancing at her colleague.

As Neave stood back to let them pass, something gripped her insides as she saw the grim expression on the woman's face. It was bad news.

6

The incident at Warren Quay made *The Western Morning News*. Esme was sitting on the veranda, wallowing in the idyll of living with a sea view and sipping her breakfast orange juice, when she spied Ruth on her way across the field, carrying a newspaper.

'You're mentioned,' said Ruth. She dropped the paper in Esme's lap and collapsed into the other deckchair. 'Well, indirectly, anyway.'

'Have they found out who she was?' said Esme, picking up the paper. The headline read, FATALITY AT WARREN QUAY.

Ruth nodded. 'Woman from Reading, apparently.'

Esme stood up. 'Orange juice?' she said, raising her glass.

Ruth shook her head. 'Not for me.'

Esme went inside to fetch her reading glasses before retrieving the folded newspaper from the deckchair and sitting down to read.

The body of a woman, believed to be that of Bella Shaw, 46, was found at the base of cliffs near Warren Quay yesterday. The Devon Air Ambulance was deployed but the woman was declared dead at the scene. A holiday maker staying at nearby Ravens Farm found the woman while walking on the beach.

She looked at Ruth over the top of her glasses. 'I don't remember seeing any reporters around yesterday, do you?'

Ruth shook her head. 'No. Perhaps they came later and talked to the hotel. Or the police issued a press statement or something.'

'No one's phoned the farm, then?'

'Not while I've been in but I haven't checked the answerphone today. I assume you're incommunicado, should anyone ask?'

'Yes, please.' She glanced down at the newspaper report. 'Was she was on holiday with anyone else?'

'Doesn't say. Read the next bit.'

'*Ms Shaw,*' read Esme, out loud, '*made the fatal mistake of taking a cliff top walk after dark, losing her footing and plunging on to rocks below.*'

'Word has it, she probably wasn't sober, neither,' said Ruth.

Esme looked up from the newspaper. 'She'd been drinking?'

'Had a skinful the night before as well, apparently. According to the bar staff at The Red Lion.' She nodded her head in the direction of Warren Quay. 'Seems she came by the hotel, too, at one point.'

Esme dropped the paper on to her lap. 'So an accident, then,' she said, taking off her glasses. 'Not suicide, like the sergeant suggested.'

'Well, it's a relief in a way,' said Ruth. 'At least we know there isn't someone out there pushing tourists off cliffs.'

'I guess it'll be down to the inquest to decide.'

'Goodness knows when that'll be. They seem to take forever in this part of the world.' Ruth took the newspaper from Esme and refolded it. 'So what d'you think? You still feel there's something else?'

Esme shrugged. 'Oh, I don't know. It's like you said, yesterday. The shock of finding her. Her last words. It felt so horrible. But if the police think everything adds up, there's no point in making more of it.' She stood up. 'Well, I'd better get a move on. I'm supposed to be at Maddy's in an hour.' She was grateful she had something to take her mind off Bella Shaw's distressing death.

*

Maddy Henderson lived in a tiny Bideford back-street behind St Mary's Church. Esme parked along the quay in front of the police station which sat high above the road, looking down across the River Torridge. As she waited for the machine to print her ticket, she gazed up at the commanding brick building with its parapet gables and multi-paned windows. Was anyone in there dealing with Bella Shaw's case at that moment? Probably not. She understood that these days its function as a hub for police activity had waned, despite its size suggesting otherwise. She wasn't even sure it was manned every day.

She locked her Peugeot and crossed the road, heading through the arch under the historic but inelegantly situated Tantons Hotel and right along Prisoners Walk, so called because of its position behind the old magistrate's court. She continued past the church and its burial grounds, raised above the alleyway by the vast number of bodies interred there over a period of 600 years.

Maddy's tiny terraced house was tucked away along a pedestrian route just beyond the church, towards the market. Esme walked up the short path and banged on the front door. The handle rattled and the door was flung open. Maddy was dressed in grey cropped leggings and a bright green baggy T-shirt, her raucous copper hair knotted on the top of her head.

She held a copy of The Western Morning News in her hand.

'Esme! You poor thing,' she said, giving Esme a hug. 'You found Bella.'

'Bella?' Esme took a step back to look at her. 'You knew her?'

'I did,' said Maddy, with a frantic nod. 'She was a client. It's really odd.' She stood back and held open the door. 'Come on in. I'll tell you everything.'

7

Maddy's narrow hallway was piled high with cardboard archive boxes. She showed Esme into the front room, equally as cluttered.

'Sorry about the state of the place,' said Maddy.

'You mean this is all *Safe*'s stuff?' said Esme, gaping at the boxes.

Safe was the name of the local charity whose archives Esme was helping Maddy sort and catalogue. 'Literally, a safe haven for young people who've slipped off the rails,' was how Maddy had described it over the phone.

Esme gazed around the room. Towers of boxes filled every corner. 'I didn't realise there'd be so much of it.'

Maddy pulled a face. 'And this isn't all of it, either. There's more back at their HQ.'

'I shall be here for a year, not a month.'

'Well, they've been around for a long time. Hence the documentary. Don't worry. I don't expect you to do it all,' said Maddy. 'I shan't abandon you completely.' She rummaged around amongst the papers on the table. 'Here you go. You can read about what they do while I get the coffee on.' She handed Esme a folded leaflet picturing smiling young people, horses and a view of the sea. 'Dan Ryder runs it, these days. I'll introduce you later. An ancestor of his set up the charity about 100 years ago. Inspired by her grandmother who was a transported convict, so the story goes.'

'He'll be interested in the Convict Ship visit then,' said Esme, scanning the flier.

'Not sure history's his thing, actually.' Maddy waved her arm around the room. 'Take a seat. I'll go and kick-start the coffee pot. Move something if you need to,' she added as she disappeared down the hall.

'That include a cat?' Esme called after her, noticing a large ginger tom on the sofa and a tabby kitten curled up on a pile of papers on an armchair.

'Sure, they're quite friendly.'

Esme didn't like to disturb the kitten purring away happily in his sleep and, despite Maddy's assurances, she wasn't keen on challenging the ginger tom for his place on the sofa, either. He had a warning glint in his eye. She pulled out a dining chair, instead. Another cat, black with yellow eyes and a striking resemblance to Slinky Malinki from the children's book she recalled reading ad nauseam to a friend's five-year-old, blinked back at her from the table.

'How many cats have you got?' she asked, as Maddy arrived with two mugs and a steaming cafetiere.

'Seven. I hope you don't mind black. I'm clean out of the white stuff.'

'No, that's fine. How did you end up with seven?'

'I don't know. They hear on the feline grapevine I'm a soft touch and seek me out.'

'What happens when you go away?'

'Mrs B, next door, looks in on them. She loves them as much as I do. There's probably as many in her place at the moment as in here.' She plonked the coffee and mugs on a pile of magazines in the middle of the table next to Slinky, before gathering up Ginger and dropping down on to the sofa with him on her lap.

'So tell me about Bella Shaw,' said Esme, leaning forward.

'Well, it's an interesting one. She commissioned me to restore an old photograph. I was busy as hell but she wanted it doing, like yesterday. Said she was only around a few days. I presume she needed it to show someone.'

'Someone down here in Devon?'

'Well, that's what I assumed. So I did a rush job on it.'

'Have you spoken to the police about this?'

Maddy shook her head. 'Not yet. I only saw her name in the

paper a few minutes before you showed up. Saw Ravens Farm mentioned and called Ruth. She filled me in. So what happened?'

Esme related the events as dispassionately as possible, though with Maddy watching closely, her face reflecting empathy with Esme's unwelcome experience, it was impossible not to conjure up the distressing images of Bella's damaged body striving to speak her final words. By the time she'd finished, she felt drained.

'What could she have meant?' said Maddy. 'Lied about what?'

'You've more chance than me of answering that,' said Esme.

'I doubt it. She didn't give much away.'

'Is there a clue in the photograph? What was it of? It was all in pieces and scattered to the four winds when I saw it.'

Maddy put down Ginger and went over to a desk in the corner on which a computer sat, a printer-scanner alongside. She opened the drawer of the filing cabinet underneath the desk and flicked through the files.

'I'll show you my copy and see what you think.' She pulled out a manilla envelope and slammed the drawer closed with her hip. 'Like I said, she wouldn't tell me anything about the photo, just wanted to know how quickly I could do the job.' She leant against the edge of the desk and fished inside the envelope, pulling out a print which she handed to Esme. 'That's the restored version. Taken around the mid 1850s, judging by their clothes.'

Esme took it eagerly. There was something she loved about old photographs. An intimate conduit to the past, a testimony to the actuality of the subjects' existence. She studied the image. A family group. The mother was seated, wearing a full-skirted dress with a V shaped bodice which finished in a point at the waist. The daughter, possibly around twelve years of age, her solemn face framed with ringlets, stood beside her and the father in waistcoat and necktie, bearded as the fashion of the time, grown under his chin, standing behind his wife.

'What happened here?' said Esme, pointing to the blurred right hand edge.

'Another mystery she wouldn't enlighten me about,' said Maddy, delving into the envelope once more. 'Here. This is the original.'

'She didn't keep it?'

'I'm sure she intended to, but she was in such a hurry she went off without it. And without the little velvet bag it came in. I'd been trying to get hold of her ever since. Now I know why she never called back.' She nodded towards the picture in Esme's hand. 'That's not the true original, by the way. What I mean is, it's probably a reprint from an earlier daguerreotype or ambrotype image.'

'That's the glass plates they used?'

'Ambrotypes were glass, yes. Daguerreotypes were silvered copper-plate. They came first. The ambrotype method was quicker and cheaper. Most family photos are on printed cards which became popular around the 1860s.' Maddy leant over and pointed to the corner of the mount. 'The photographer who printed this one, fortunately for us, embossed his name on the front and I've managed to track him down. He operated in the 1860s to 70s in Sydney, Australia.'

'Australia?' Esme looked up. 'How fascinating. I wonder why Bella wouldn't tell you any more.'

'Frustrating, isn't it? Like, what does it matter who's in the photo, after all this time?'

'Perhaps she didn't know.'

'Then why not come right out and say so. Can you see what's wrong with that edge bit, now?'

Esme held it away from her and squinted at it. 'It's been torn.'

'I reckon there was another person on this side of the photograph and someone's ripped them off.'

'Why? And when? Not recently.'

'No. Doesn't look like it.'

Esme turned it over. In the smooth dark grey on the reverse, she could just make out faint pencil lines. 'There's something

43

written on the back.'

'Is there? Too much to hope it's a name, I suppose.'

Esme took it over to the window where she could look in better light. 'It might be a name.' She tipped it back and forth to illuminate the cursive script. '*Liberty*...No, wait a minute. It's not a name at all.' She stopped, puzzled. 'What d'you suppose that means?' She said, handing the photograph to Maddy. 'It says, *Liberty or Death*.'

8

At Warren Quay, the pub was buzzing. Esme pushed through the crowd, eager to find Maddy and hear the police's reaction to the photograph. She found her at the bar, in conversation with a man on the other side. He looked thirty-something with tangled hair framing a tanned, weathered face. Clearly a man who enjoyed being outdoors.

'Ah, Esme,' said Maddy sliding off the bar stool. She nodded at the barman. 'This is Dan Ryder. He helps run *Safe*, when he's not pulling pints in here.'

Dan reached across and shook Esme's hand. 'Ah,' said Esme with a smile, making the connection. 'The man responsible for Maddy's cluttered hallway.'

Dan held up his hands, surrender style. 'Guilty as charged.' He winked at Maddy. 'Her idea, though. She thought a documentary might give us some useful publicity.'

'Yeah, I should learn to keep my mouth shut. I had no idea so little was catalogued.'

'Maddy tells me your charity was founded by one of your ancestors.'

'So they tell me. You must come up to the farm sometime. Find out what we do.'

'I will, thanks.'

'You're into this sort of thing all the time, then?' said Dan, resting his hand on the beer pump handle.

Esme smiled. 'Oh, I'm a glutton for browsing through old documents.'

'History's lost on me, I'm afraid,' he said, grinning. 'I just muck-out horses and play football with disadvantaged kids.'

'One day you might get into it. When you're a bit longer

in the tooth.'

A wiry man holding two empty glasses knocked into Esme. He backed off apologising, while looking round to see who, in turn, had bumped into him.

'Busy, today,' said Esme, acknowledging the man's apology with a brief smile.

'Yeah, bit more than usual.' Dan pulled a face. 'Morbid curiosity about the accident, I reckon.' Esme wondered if he knew about her part in the drama. He must do and she was glad he didn't ask any questions.

'Shouldn't complain, mind,' Dan added. 'Good for trade. Can I get you ladies something?'

When Dan had served their drinks, Maddy suggested they convene outside. They manoeuvred their way through the throng and out on to the terrace. The last dregs of the day's sun were sliding into the sea as they commandeered a table, vacated by a harassed couple with four lively children.

'So, what did the police say about Bella's photo?' said Esme as they sat down.

'To be honest, they didn't seem that interested. I guess it's only the likes of you and me who think a photograph taken in Australia 170 years ago is intriguing.'

Esme frowned. 'But she was so furtive about it. You would have thought that might have stirred some interest. You'd think they'd want to check there wasn't a connection with what happened to her.'

'Well if they did, they didn't tell me.'

'What about the words on the back?'

Maddy looked at her from under her brow. 'What do *you* think?'

'No. OK. I get it. If they weren't moved by what you'd already told them, a pencil scribble of an obtuse phrase won't change things. I'm sure I know it, though I can't think where it's from.'

'I told them to let Bella's family know I still had the photo and

46

to pass on my details. I assume they'll want it back.' She lifted up a patchwork tote bag from the floor beside her and dumped it on the table. 'Meanwhile, I think I might know who's in the picture.'

'Really?' Anticipation replaced disappointment. 'Now that sounds more like it. How?'

Maddy dug deep into the bag and pulled out a faded blue velvet pouch and laid it on the table.

'Oh, isn't it gorgeous,' said Esme, rubbing the soft fabric with her finger. 'Is this what the photograph came in?'

'Yes, but there was something else in it, too.' She untied the frayed strings of the pouch and pulled out a small piece of linen folded into a two inch square. She opened it up and laid it out on the table, smoothing the fragile material flat so Esme could see it clearly.

'An embroidery sampler,' said Esme, leaning across. 'Wow, it's beautiful.' Tiny embroidered letters of the alphabet, stitched in neat rows, first in lower case then in capitals, adorned the scrap of fabric. Faded now, even grubby, but still legible. Underneath the alphabet was an exquisitely crafted verse. She felt a tug back in time. 'Think of the time and patience which went into creating such a thing. I remember doing something similar at primary school but nothing so intricate. We made a handkerchief pouch. Not on your list of must-haves, these days.'

'There's a name at the bottom,' said Maddy.

Esme looked at where Maddy pointed. '*Sarah Baker, 15 April 1827. Aged 8. Devon.*' She looked up. 'And you think she's in the photo?'

Maddy delved back in her bag and pulled out a copy of the sepia photograph of the family group and laid it down next to the embroidery. 'One of these guys must be Sarah Baker. What d'you think?'

'That has to be the Devon connection, surely.' Esme reached down and pulled out a notebook from her bag. 'If she was eight years old in 1827, her birth year would be about 1820. I'll see what

I can track down. It might explain what Bella was doing here.'

'And we need to know because...?'

Esme dropped her notebook back in the bag. 'No, you're right. Sorry, I was getting carried away then. I've enough on my plate with all those boxes. Can't afford to get side-tracked.'

'This has got you buzzing, hasn't it?'

'Of course it has. I told you I was ready for a change of scene.'

'No, not *Safe*. This.' She tapped the bag with a forefinger. 'I can tell you've done this sort of thing before.'

'Oh, don't you start,' said Esme, frowning. 'You're as bad as Ruth. She seems to think I've got some sort of sixth sense left over from when I was Tim's researcher.'

'And do you?'

'No, of course not.' She looked away, her gaze drifting dangerously towards the beach. 'Finding a woman's body splattered across rocks is more than adequate to stimulate the other five, thank you very much.'

'But you've got suspicions.'

'I didn't say that, did I? I'm just interested in the story behind the photograph, that's all.'

'So what's Ruth's problem?'

Esme played with her glass, lining the edge up with a blemish on the wood grain. 'She's just jumpy, that's all. She'll be happy when it's all sorted and explained away. Then she can forget about it.'

'Poor Ruth. Probably worrying about the effect on tourism.' Maddy cradled her glass. 'You don't think she has a point, though?'

'About what?'

'About her assumption that you've sensed something in this.'

'Maddy...'

Maddy leant across the table. 'Don't tell me you can't see how odd it is. Bella's evasiveness with me, the mystery of the chopped photograph, her last words, what she was doing late at night on

48

the cliff path…'

'Are you priming me?'

'Are you pretending you're not the teensiest bit intrigued?'

'I'm trying not to be.'

'Why?'

Esme was prevented from answering as Dan came out of the bar and began collecting up dead glasses.

'Hey, Dan,' Maddy called.

'If it's waiter service you're after, I'm afraid you're going to be disappointed,' he said, loading a tray with the empty glasses.

'The other night when that woman went over the cliff?' said Maddy, grabbing his sleeve. 'She'd been drinking in here, apparently. Were you working?'

'Yeah. Should've been my night off but Jen was off sick.'

'And did you see her in the bar?'

Dan rested the tray on their table. 'Difficult not to. All dressed up flash, like. High heels up to her elbows.' He looked at Esme. 'Well, you'd know 'bout that, o' course.'

Esme nodded, thinking of the bright chiffon which had attracted her attention in the first place. 'Not your usual walking gear.'

'Was it busy?' said Maddy.

'Heaving. Bit like now.' He began to back away but Maddy hadn't finished.

'Was she drunk? Rumours were she could put it away when she chose.'

Dan pulled a face. 'Didn't look drunk to me.'

'If you were busy, maybe no one really noticed how bad she'd got,' suggested Esme.

Dan shook his head. 'I served her about ten-ish. She seemed fine then. Perhaps she hid it well? Or maybe went on drinking somewhere after she left here?' He gathered up the last few glasses and hurried away.

Dan's words lingered on the sea breeze. 'Where else could

Bella have gone drinking, on foot?' Esme said, after a while. 'There's not another pub for miles.'

'Someone's house?' suggested Maddy.

'Could be. Maybe that explains why the police weren't interested in the photograph. They already know the full story.'

'Ah well. If no one wants to know who Sarah Baker was, that's it, then,' said Maddy, downing her drink. 'End of.'

Esme looked down at the velvet bag and chewed her lip. 'Be interesting to find out, though, wouldn't it? From an historical point of view, I mean.'

'Something to tell the family?' suggested Maddy. 'Assuming they don't already know, of course.'

'Well,' said Esme, reaching in her bag for her notebook. 'No harm in having a dig around the archives, is there?'

9

Esme sat at Maddy's dining table browsing internet genealogy sites on her laptop, looking for a record of Sarah Baker's birth, watched by the tabby kitten. She hoped by the time Maddy got back with their fish and chips she'd have something significant to tell her.

The name had thrown up over ten thousand hits for Sarah Bakers born in England between 1818 and 1820. Not surprising with such a common name. Limiting the search to Devon, England reduced the number to less than 700, still a sizeable figure, but on closer inspection she noted that the US based website had included New England in its trawl and the relevant data only extended to two pages. Easy then to find Sarah Baker, baptised in Hartland parish in 1819 to parents Jeremiah and Mary. She made a note of the details, including from where the information had been sourced.

Unfortunately, there the trail went cold. She wasn't completely surprised. The International Genealogical Index, or IGI, had been compiled by The Church of Jesus Christ of Latter-Day Saints, or Mormons as they were more commonly known, from existing parish records. Historically, as permission to access such records had not always been granted by certain members of the clergy, the database wasn't comprehensive. She'd need to take a trip to North Devon's record office for more information.

When her mobile phone rang out, she was gazing out at St Mary's church, admiring the castellation on the tower and reflecting on her findings. She answered automatically without looking to see the caller. The sound of Detective Sergeant Collins's voice at the end of the line hauled her brain away from genealogy with a jolt. Was he phoning to announce that they'd discovered something about the incident which merited further investigation?

But nothing so dramatic. Bella Shaw's daughter, Neave, had asked if it would be possible to meet the woman who had comforted her mother in her last moments.

'Of course you are under no obligation, Mrs Quentin,' said the sergeant.

'Not at all, I'd be only too pleased to see her,' said Esme, and adding before she could stop herself, 'she didn't give any explanation of her mother's final words, did she?'

A pause. 'I'm afraid I couldn't say.'

'And the photograph?' She stood up and wandered over to the window. A figure jogged around the corner and headed up the street.

'What about it?'

'Maddy Henderson had recently restored it for her.'

'So I believe…'

'Well, we've since come up with a name. Sarah Baker. We think she might be in the picture. It was taken in Australia, so Maddy says.'

She heard him sigh. 'Mrs Quentin, I understand that to a family historian such things are fascinating…'

She felt her face redden. 'That's completely beside the point. Just because the photograph was taken a long time ago doesn't mean it isn't relevant.'

'We do have to look at the facts, Mrs Quentin, and our enquiries have revealed nothing to suggest that Mrs Shaw's death was in any way suspicious.'

Her grip tightened around the phone. 'How do you know, if you've no idea where or how that photograph fits in?'

'Mrs Quentin,' he said, with exaggerated patience. No doubt it was a manner he employed with small children or senile pensioners. 'I do sympathise that, given your unfortunate and distressing involvement, you might have a tendency to see things through different eyes than the objectivity of a police enquiry. But, as I said, we have no reason to believe that Mrs Shaw's death…'

'Was in any way suspicious. Yes, so you said. And if anything else comes to light to suggest otherwise?'

A short silence in which she imagined him closing his eyes and counting to ten. 'We would, of course, appraise any further information should it come to our notice.'

'Good. Thank you for your time, Sergeant. If I learn of anything, I'll be in touch.'

She lobbed her mobile on to the table with a growl as the front door opened and Maddy burst into the hall along with the blissful aroma of battered fish and vinegar.

'Who was that?' she said with a grin, coming into the room and dropping the steaming bundles on to the table. Esme closed her laptop and made space for their meal.

'Police. Bella's family want to meet me.' She slammed salt, vinegar and a roll of kitchen roll into the middle of the table.

'Understandable, under the circumstances,' said Maddy, pulling out a chair and sitting down at the table. She looked at Esme. 'That a problem?'

'No, no, not at all. It's just…' She shook her head, annoyed at herself for saying too much to Collins. Why couldn't she leave it alone? 'No, it doesn't matter. Perhaps I'm expecting too much. I thought they'd be more proactive, you know? More suspicious. Where's their need to know?'

'Not as finely tuned as yours, obviously. Or perhaps the burden of the inevitable bureaucracy has killed it off. Now get stuck in before it goes cold.'

She sat down too and unwrapped her parcel. Perhaps Ruth was right and finding Bella had affected her ability to see things rationally. She tore off a piece of battered fish. 'I didn't do myself any favours, either. I'm sure Sergeant Collins has me down as a meddlesome and irrational pest with a sepia photo fixation.'

Maddy doused more vinegar on to her chips. 'That's his

problem. Forget it and eat your chips.'

'I told him I'd get back to him if we found anything to change his mind,' said Esme, popping the fish into her mouth, chewing and swallowing. 'These are heaven, by the way. Oh, and I've found Sarah Baker. But short of establishing her birth in Hartland and her parents' names, I've drawn a blank. I thought I'd try the record office next.'

'Hey, I almost forgot.' Maddy fished something out of her joggers pocket and handed it to Esme. 'They had some fliers in the chip shop about the ship arriving.'

Esme licked her lips and took the leaflet. 'That's good. Word's getting around, then.' A soft focus image of the *Mary Ann* in full sail graced the front. Inside were pictures of the crew in period dress and details of when the museum was open to visitors. 'Looks pretty impressive. Who owns it?'

'Don't know. Felix, the curator cum captain, is coordinating everything but he's not the owner. Some rich celeb is supposed to be involved but no one's saying who. Perhaps we'll find out on press day. Oh, and I've wangled you a visitor pass, by the way. Hope you packed your glad rags.'

'Ruth told me there'd been something similar years ago, in Australia.'

'Yes, there was. A dilapidated old sailing ship supposed to have been used to transport convicts to Australia. Not that it ever had. That was just a marketing ploy. This is more authentic. It has its own archives, apparently. Ships' logs, criminal records, that sort of thing.'

'Hang on a minute.' Esme tore off a piece of kitchen towel and wiped her fingers. 'Just had an idea.' She reached for her laptop and opened it.

'What are you thinking?' asked Maddy.

'Sarah Baker,' said Esme, typing in a web address. 'What if that's the Australian connection? It would explain why I can't find any records other than her birth. She doesn't show up on the censuses. There could be a gap in the records of course, but even so…worth a check.'

The website opened. She typed Sarah Baker into the search engine, adding Devon as a key word. Then she clicked on the magnifying glass symbol. The page refreshed and offered two Sarah Bakers.

'There,' said Esme, tapping the screen excitedly. 'Got to be her. Convicted at Bideford Assizes and transported to New South Wales on the *Henry Wellesley* in 1837.' She swivelled the laptop around so Maddy could see the screen. 'I wonder what crime she committed.'

10

Esme was late. She'd forgotten how long it took to walk to Clovelly harbour through the village. She should have driven down the back road instead but it was always difficult to resist the unique atmosphere of the steep cobbled street. She gazed down at the sea below, debating whether it was better to retrace her steps to the car park or continue on foot. Fortunately the village was still quiet, most visitors still in the visitor centre at the top, drinking coffee or watching the video of the village story before tackling the steep descent to the harbour. Probably as quick to walk, now she'd gone this far, despite the risk of ricking an ankle on the uneven cobbles.

She hurried down the hill, as brisk as she dare, weaving her way among the small number of early walkers, past the New Inn, the post office and the galleries. Even on a summer morning the smell of coal burning in the cottages' stoves hung in the air, and stayed with her as she wound round the bend and under Temple bar, where the cottage's kitchen bridged the street. Momentum propelled her down the last slope and she arrived at the quay gasping, her knees shaking uncontrollably.

She paused to catch her breath before continuing under the arch to The Red Lion, where she was meeting Neave Shaw and Gwen Preston, Bella's daughter and mother. Maddy had also arranged to be there to return the photograph and embroidery.

She opened the latch of the heavy wooden door into the snug. The place was empty but she could hear voices from the other side of the bar. She wandered through the interconnecting rooms and saw Maddy in a far corner, next to a window seat overlooking the harbour. She'd swapped her usual sports attire for a pair of pale cream trousers with matching linen jacket and was talking to a willowy young woman with short dark hair. Bella's daughter, presumably. The elderly lady sitting beside her must be Gwen Preston, Bella's mother.

As Esme approached, Maddy saw her and stood up to make the introductions. Esme glanced at the empty coffee cups on the table in front of them and apologised for her late arrival.

'I'm so sorry for your loss,' said Esme, glancing at both women in turn.

'Thank you,' said Neave. Mrs Preston, a thin woman with short limp grey hair, nodded her acknowledgement. Her complexion matched the hue of her hair, as though tears shed at the loss of her daughter had washed away all her colour.

'I'll get some fresh coffee,' said Maddy, heading for the bar.

'Thank you for coming,' said Neave, focusing on Esme with steel blue eyes. She rubbed her hands down the thighs of her cropped jeans.

'No, not at all,' said Esme, sitting down on the stool opposite. 'It's really no trouble.'

Neave pressed her palms together and slid them between her knees. 'Maddy says you never met my mother before…'

'No, I'm afraid not. Did she have friends down here?'

Neave glanced at her grandmother and shook her head. 'We've no idea, have we Gran? We're not completely sure why she was here at all. Gran thinks she came to see a solicitor in Bideford. Cooper, we think? Could that be it?'

Esme shook her head. 'I'm sorry, you'll have to ask Maddy about that. I wouldn't know. I don't actually live here.'

'Oh, right.'

Gwen pressed her lips together. 'Hardly matters now, does it? She's gone and that's that.'

Neave tucked a strand of hair behind her ear. 'The photograph is a mystery, too. I've certainly never seen it before.'

'And you don't have any links to Australia, that you're aware of?' said Esme.

Neave shook her head.

Gwen had turned towards the window and was watching the activity out in the harbour as though trying to distance herself from the conversation. 'Do you know anything about it, Mrs Preston?'

Gwen looked round, gripping the handbag on her lap. 'I'm sorry you had to find my daughter, Mrs Quentin, and I thank you for all that you did for her. As does Neave.'

'I'm sorry I couldn't do more,' said Esme.

'Neave knows as well as I do that something like this was always going to happen.' She glanced at Neave as though challenging her to disagree. 'Well, you can't wander along a cliff path two sheets to the wind and not come a cropper. You know what she could be like.'

'That's as may be, Gran, but why was she there? That's what we want to know. Don't you?'

'I've given up trying to work out your mother's way of thinking years ago, love. Thought you had, too.'

Maddy returned with the coffee, setting down the cups while giving Esme a querying look.

'Where's the Ladies?' said Gwen, looking around.

'Across the way,' said Maddy. 'I'll show you.'

Gwen stood up and Maddy guided her to the door.

'I'm sorry about Gran,' said Neave, when they were out of earshot. 'It's just her way.'

Esme held up her hand. 'No need to apologise. This can't have been easy for her.'

'Gran says she lost Mum a long time ago and that she's done all the grieving she's going to. But I don't really believe that.'

'It probably won't have hit her yet. You might need to be prepared for a kick-back reaction.'

'I'm sure you're right.' Neave looked down at her lap and fiddled with her fingernails. 'Gran always used to tell Mum she'd drink herself to death. Of course she was talking about her liver.

She could never have imagined anything like this.'

Esme watched Neave pick at a thread on her jeans, lost in thought. Perhaps she was revisiting a childhood memory, hearing her grandmother's voice echo her warnings.

'Things must have been difficult in the past. For both of you.'

Neave nodded. 'Yes, they were. But we got through it.'

Again she tucked a strand of hair behind her ear. 'What Mum said…at the end. Are you sure those were her words?'

Esme nodded. 'I've asked myself the same question but I'm positive. They don't mean anything to you? Or your grandmother?'

Neave sighed. 'I don't know what to think. Mum wrote me a letter recently. In it she said…things.' She shook her head. 'It doesn't matter what. But Gran thinks that's what she was trying to say. That she'd lied in the letter.'

'It must be a help to be able to talk it over with your gran.'

Neave lifted her head and laughed without humour. 'I wouldn't say we'd talked, exactly.' She gave Esme a wan smile. 'Gran lives by the "least said soonest mended" philosophy. Trying to get answers about anything in our family was always an uphill battle.'

'Could that explain why she's not said anything? If she was tracing her family history and knew your grandmother wouldn't approve, she might have kept it quiet.'

Neave shrugged. 'I don't see Mum sparing Gran's feelings on the subject. And to be honest, I can't imagine Mum being interested in family history, anyway. It's not her sort of thing.'

'Maybe she stumbled across the photograph,' suggested Esme, 'and it sparked an interest. It can happen like that sometimes. Suddenly it becomes important.'

The door at the other end of the bar opened and Maddy reappeared, Gwen close behind her. When they'd taken their places again, Esme held out the photograph to Gwen. 'We were just speculating as to whether Bella had started researching her family history, Mrs Preston. Do you think that's possible?'

'If she was, she never said nothing to me,' said Gwen, snatching up her coffee cup and draining it down.

'There's Mum's laptop,' said Neave. 'I suppose if she *was* searching for family, there might be clues there.' She frowned. 'Though why she'd come down here to do it, I don't know. Mum was born in London. That's where Gran's family come from, don't they, Gran?'

'Most families have a London connection at some point in their history,' said Esme. 'That doesn't mean they don't have roots elsewhere, too.'

'What about your father's side of the family?' suggested Maddy.

Neave shot a glance at her grandmother before answering. 'My father left my mother before I was born. I never knew him.'

Gwen Preston made a noise, something between a scoff and a snort. Neave rounded on her grandmother. 'And what's that supposed to mean, exactly?'

'You know what. It means, that's just as well.'

'Why, Gran? Why shouldn't I know?'

Gwen scowled at her granddaughter. 'What's there to know, eh? He deserted your mother when you were hardly a lump in her belly. Isn't that enough? Nothing no photo's going to add to, that's for sure.'

Neave narrowed her eyes. 'You know something about the photograph.'

'I've never seen it before.' Gwen pressed her lips together and avoided Neave's gaze.

Esme swallowed, feeling like an intruder on a conversation she shouldn't hear, and yet she felt she'd been instrumental in starting it. She glanced at Maddy. Perhaps it was time to draw the meeting to a close. They seemed to have hit an impasse, in any case.

But Neave hadn't given up on her grandmother yet, it seemed. She took Gwen's hand and squeezed it. 'Come on, Gran,' she said, her anger abated. 'This is important to me. It could have something to do with what she said in her letter.'

'It's just an old photograph, lovey.' Gwen looked at Neave, her eyes pleading. 'It's not going to bring her back.'

'But it might help me understand, don't you see?'

Gwen snatched her hand out of Neave's grasp. 'All right, all right. Have it your own way.'

They fell silent, waiting. Gwen smoothed her skirt, her mouth working as she stared at the floor. Esme wondered what was going through her mind. Perhaps she'd kept the words locked away for so long she'd forgotten how to say them.

Eventually Gwen sighed and looked at Maddy. 'You said it was taken in Sydney, love.'

Maddy nodded. 'That's right.'

'Well, then. It must have been his.'

'It was my dad's?' whispered Neave. 'Do you mean my father was…?'

'Yes. That's right. He was Australian.' She stood up. 'So now you know. And if you're harbouring any thoughts at finding out any more, then forget it. You'd be best to leave well alone.'

11

Bella's funeral was a quiet, slightly surreal affair with a disparate group of people, most of whom were Gwen's friends who'd come to support her, rather than in any deference to her daughter. From what Neave could work out, Bella's friends were a large buxom woman who sobbed throughout the service in the crematorium's small chapel and a wiry little man who polished off Gwen's plentiful supply of sandwiches and cake back at the house afterwards. Neave wondered briefly if he was a habitual mourner, who attached himself to funeral parties for the food. Although he came up to Gwen and offered his condolences, his apparent knowledge of Bella went no further than what he could have gleaned from the minister's thin eulogy. She considered wandering over to cross-examine him as he vacuumed up the last few chocolate brownies on the table but she found she didn't really care enough to deprive him. Besides, if he didn't eat it, they would be facing the leftovers all week. Gran never threw food away.

Eventually, the mourners drifted home and Neave closed the door on the last one, resting her back against the glass panel and bracing herself for the battle ahead. It was even more imperative that Gwen gave up her secrets, having discovered that access to Bella's laptop was only via a password that she didn't have and hadn't yet stumbled over by chance or guesswork.

She went in search of Gwen in the kitchen and found her washing up the plates and teacups. Neave snatched a tea towel from the hook on the back of the door and began drying.

'I'd hoped one of Mum's friends would have known what she was doing in North Devon,' said Neave, wiping a side plate and adding it to the pile on the worktop. 'But apparently not.'

'Well, that was her business and now she's gone. It's no concern of ours.'

'We don't know that.'

Gwen responded by agitating the washing-up water. Neave ignored the implied message and pressed on.

'Why are you so secretive about my father? You must be able to tell me something about him?'

'It's always been the same with you, hasn't it? Questions, questions, questions.'

'That's because no one would give me any answers. Perhaps if they had done, I wouldn't be so desperate to know everything.' She took a teacup and dried it, cautioning herself to slow up. Dropping her gran's best china wasn't likely to improve her mood or her cooperation. She tried to keep her voice steady. 'Seen but not heard doesn't wash any more, Gran. I'm not a child you can send out of the room because there's something you don't want me to know.' She put down the cup and turned her head to look into her grandmother's face. 'You still haven't told me about the legal matter you told the police Mum had gone to Devon for. What was it about?'

Gwen dropped the brush into the water and turned to Neave. 'I don't know what it was about. How many more times?'

'Don't you want to find out?'

'Is it going to bring her back?'

'What are you afraid of?'

'Don't you start talking in that sort of a tone.' She pressed her lips together and leant on the edge of the sink. 'Look, I know you're finding her going hard, on account of her writing to you, but that's something you'll just have to get used to. It wasn't meant to be, and that's that. Let's say no more about it.'

Neave sighed. Perhaps today wasn't the day to pursue matters. Her grandmother was still raw from the funeral. Maybe in a day or two she'd be more amenable. She took up another piece of crockery. 'I suppose I'd better clear out her flat tomorrow. I didn't

63

much take to the landlord. He wasn't particularly cooperative. Sooner the better, he said and that there wasn't much in there so it wouldn't take long. I'll bring it all back here, shall I?'

'I've no room for furniture, so don't think I'm taking that. One of those house clearing outfits can get rid of it.'

'Perhaps a charity shop would take a look. I'll ask around.' She wiped the last plate and threw the tea towel over her shoulder. 'What about personal stuff?' she said, picking up the plates and putting them back in the wall cupboard. 'I assume you'll want to go through that.'

Gwen shook the suds off her hands and tipped out the water from the bowl. 'Pack them up in a box and you can shove it in the loft.'

Neave paused and glanced over her shoulder. 'You'll want to sort through it, first, won't you?'

Gwen grabbed a towel and dried her hands. 'Another cup of tea, love, or have you had enough?'

*

A morning of negotiations with the landlord and liaising with a recycling charity for the collection of Bella's few sticks of furniture left Neave emotionally drained. She dumped a pile of cardboard boxes in the middle of the floor and sat on the edge of the bed, paralysed as to where to begin, trying to rationalise her grandmother's apparent indifference to Bella's personal belongings. Perhaps Gwen was simply tired. Or having been released from worrying about her daughter's messy life, she needed time to adjust, to withdraw and lick her wounds.

Neave stood up and gave her head a shake. This wasn't going to get things done. And her grandmother was unlikely to change her mind and offer to help. Neave felt a twinge of sadness. The task might have brought them closer together, had she done so. But maybe Gwen didn't want to share her inner demons with anyone. She clearly didn't want to share them with Neave, insisting it was to protect her from what she didn't need to know. Neave closed her eyes and let out a sigh of exasperation.

She snatched open a drawer and emptied its contents into one of the cardboard boxes. And another. And another, ever more frantic. When one drawer load missed the target and cascaded over the floor, she slumped down on the floor on her knees and allowed herself the luxury of tears. Were they because of her grandmother's attitude to the truth? That she never got to speak to her mother before she died? That their relationship had deteriorated so badly? Or that she didn't understand the circumstances of her mother's death? Probably all of those things.

She wiped her eyes with the heel of her hand, took a moment to collect herself and then gathered up the offending chaos of papers. She would have to go through this lot eventually, she supposed, as she piled everything into the box. Most of it could probably be discarded. It wasn't as though it was full of valuable mementoes or letters. It was junk – leaflets, booklets about garden openings, bin-day collections, Save the Children address stickers, charity draw-tickets which had never been sold. But if she started sorting it now, who knew how long it would take. And having seen the more agreeable side of the landlord when she'd turned up to begin clearing, she decided she couldn't cope with the inevitable row if she now told him it would take longer than she had said. She kept going.

With the living room done, she turned her attention to the bedroom, encouraged by her progress. The bedside drawer was stiff and as she tugged, it came out completely, landing on her foot. She cried out, taking out her frustration on the drawer as she shoved it back into the carcass. But it wouldn't go all the way in. Something was caught at the back. She knelt down and reached in, her fingers fumbling to catch the edge of the folded piece of paper. When she pulled it out and looked at it, she knew immediately it wasn't any ordinary piece of paper. It had a feeling of quality, and although folded, she could make out green hatching and the watermark. A marriage certificate.

She dropped back on her heels and unfolded the document. She stared down at her mother's name. How many times had she accused Bella of fantasy, of not really knowing who her father had been, of lying about their being married? And yet here it was; the evidence to dispel such accusations. Why had Bella never shown her? Why, when she could have laid it in front of her daughter and said, there you are, I'm telling you the truth, look at it, had she not done so?

There was a loud rapping on the front door and a loud voice on the landing. 'Hello? We've come to take your furniture, lovey. You in there?'

Neave shoved the certificate in the back pocket of her jeans and jumped up.

'Yes, hang on. Coming.' And she hurried into the hall to let them in.

12

Esme was at the cabin at Ravens Farm unloading her boot of two of *Safe*'s archive boxes from Maddy's hallway. Between the two of them, they should be able to work their way through the box mountain, or at the very least, make a sizeable inroad into the stack of records which had gathered in the years since Dan's mother's last inventory.

When she'd stored the boxes away behind the sofa in the cabin, she sat outside on the veranda browsing the literature Maddy had given her about the convict ship museum arriving the next day. She was reading about the notorious Captain Brookes, who'd kept his Dublin prisoners in cramped and insanitary conditions to allow room for the wine and spirits he planned to trade, when she heard someone call her name. She took off her reading glasses and looked across the field towards the farm to see Neave on her way towards her, waving. Esme put down her book and went to meet her.

'Wow, what a place,' said Neave as they came round the front side of the cabin. Neave wandered out into the middle of the field. 'I wouldn't mind living here,' she said, gazing out to sea.

Esme smiled. 'Pretty perfect, isn't it? Wild in the winter, mind. Difficult to imagine now, with the sun out and the warm sea breeze.'

'How did you find it?'

'Oh, I've known it for years. We used to come here for family holidays. Rather less stylish in those days, mind. More of a hut, really, and very basic. Cheap but cheerful, my dad used to say. I think my mother had her own words for it. Me and my sister thought it was the best place on earth, of course.' She smiled. 'But then we weren't the ones who had to empty the chemical loo.'

Neave laughed. She dropped down on to the grass, resting back on her elbows and crossing her ankles, her eyes focused on the seascape ahead. Esme sat down beside her.

'We never really had family holidays,' said Neave. 'I often used to wonder what it must be like. To have a brother or sister to play with. The kids at school used to talk about where they'd been, what they'd done. I'd hang on their every word, storing it up to dream about later.' She threw a brief smile at Esme. 'I may have even regurgitated one or two memories and put my own stamp on them, so I didn't feel left out. Pathetic, eh?'

'No,' said Esme with a sympathetic smile. 'Understandable.'

'We did have one holiday. In a hotel. Somewhere in Wales, I think. Didn't stay more than a couple of days. I think Bella'd disgraced herself in the bar one night and we were asked to leave. That was the last of our little adventures.'

'You didn't go anywhere with your gran?' asked Esme. She thought of the security of her own childhood and knew she was lucky. So very different to that of Neave's.

'No. Gran could never see the point of spending money on holidays. That's what she said, anyway. More likely she couldn't afford them and was too embarrassed to say so.' She reached over and tapped Esme's arm. 'Now don't go feeling sorry for me,' she said, smiling. 'I can make up for lost time, now, can't I?' She scrambled to her feet. 'Anyway, I didn't come to off-load on you. I came to ask you something.'

They climbed back up to the cabin and Esme fixed them cold drinks while Neave made herself comfortable in a deckchair on the veranda.

'So how are things?' Esme asked, handing Neave a glass of elderflower cordial before sitting down on the other deckchair.

Neave cocked her head to one side. 'So-so. And I've made progress, of sorts. I found my parents' marriage certificate.' She set her glass down on the floor and dragged her bag on to her lap. 'Seems strange seeing my mum's name next to a man I've never heard of. And yet he's my father.' She pulled out a document and passed it to Esme.

'Declan Patrick Shaw,' read Esme, scanning the information on the form. 'Irish descent, I assume?' She handed it back to Neave. 'I take it your gran didn't give you this?'

Neave shook her head. 'No. Found it amongst Mum's things. But in a way, it explains Gran's attitude. She wasn't invited to the wedding.'

'Do you know why?'

'She didn't approve of him and made no bones about it. Well, you're not going to invite someone with an attitude like that to put a damper on the day, are you?'

'Sounds like she's opened up a bit more.'

Neave pulled a face. 'By Gran's standards, she probably has.' She leant forward and rested her elbows on her knees. 'She told me it was a whirlwind romance. That Mum thought he was wonderful and that their relationship was passionate. Gran had her own word for it, she said.' Neave smiled at Esme. 'I told her I didn't want to know. I'd rather keep my own interpretation and not have it unpicked by Gran's distorted perspective.'

Whatever happened between Neave's parents, Esme understood why Neave needed to see their story as something positive.

'If Mum was so passionately in love with him,' Neave continued, 'it might explain why Mum fell apart when he left. Gran's attitude wouldn't have helped. Thank God and goodbye, she probably thought.'

'You must have relied on your gran a good deal, when your mum was struggling.'

'She pretty much brought me up. Mum was out of it most of the time. She promised so often to…well, there were moments when I hoped she'd…Perhaps if Gran *hadn't* been on hand, maybe she'd have turned it around for me but…' She shook her head. 'Ignore me. I'm not making any sense. It doesn't matter.' She went

69

back to her bag. 'I've come to a decision. I wondered if you might help me.'

'Of course, if I can.'

Neave pulled out a crumpled piece of paper. 'My father,' she said, handing Esme a dog-eared photograph. 'Not that you can see him too well. I thought Maddy might restore it for me.'

'I'm sure she'd be happy to. Where did you find this?'

'With the certificate. It was taken on the day they got married, in Brighton. Gran told me that much.' She smiled. 'After a bit of persuasion.'

Esme studied the picture, its image faded and the edges torn. The happy couple. Heads pressed together, laughing into the camera. He wore a fringed leather jacket, she a blue halter-neck dress and ribbons in her hair. Esme gazed at the young woman's face, willing the smiling image to displace the one which still haunted her. But it was hard to believe they were the same person, even given the time gap.

Esme handed the photo back to Neave. 'I'm glad she's thawing a little. She must realise that it's important for you to know these things, even if she and he didn't get on.'

Neave sighed. 'I don't think she's going to be quite so chilled about my decision, though.'

'What decision?'

Neave leaned closer. 'I don't just want to know more about him, Esme. I want to find him. I want to find my father.'

13

The excitement was palpable amongst locals and tourists alike, as the resplendent *Mary Ann* arrived at Warren Quay. Crowds stood on every available vantage point, watching it sail majestically into port. Esme mingled amongst the onlookers on the quayside, watching the ship as it progressed slowly round the end of the breakwater, the sound of distant voices of the young crew shouting instructions as the magnificent sails were lowered and gathered in. Finally the vessel was expertly manoeuvred into the harbour and came to rest against the old quay wall.

As the tall ship appeared in front of them, she caught her breath at the stunning sight close up, lifting her head to track the towering masts to the top where the ensign flapped in the breeze.

A walkway linking the ship to the shore was hurriedly slid into place and secured. Felix Anderson, the museum curator, a deeply tanned man with scruffy blond hair tied back in a ponytail, stepped off the ship and jumped up on to the harbour wall to address the crowd and the posse of journalists gathered at the front, holding up cameras and voice recorders. With his shirtsleeves rolled back to reveal a snake tattoo (acquired for deliberate effect, according to Maddy) and with a twang of the antipodes in his accent, he introduced the project and its aims, pledging to tell the story of The System – the transportation of England's criminals to the colonies – and promising that visitors would experience some sense of the atmosphere of those times when stepping on board his ship.

When he'd completed his oratory, Esme made her way to the ship's gangway, flanked either side by crew members dressed in period costume. She showed her pass and was welcomed aboard with a curtsey from a fresh-faced girl with a wide smile, wearing a mop cap.

She accepted the customary glass of champagne and wandered around the deck. Everywhere was burnished timber and thick rope, coils of which hung rank and file along the sides of the ship. Three giant masts dominated the deck, ever more imposing at close quarters. She tried to imagine surviving a four month voyage to Australia in such a space. However generous the deck felt accommodating the small social gathering while in port, it would become tiny and insignificant once surrounded by a vast ocean. Gales, churning seas and cold torrential rains would pummel the ship in the Atlantic. Hot, stifling and airless discomfort would create misery in the tropics.

The deck slowly filled with people, as invited guests were ushered on board. Esme moved aside as Maddy joined her from across the deck. They stood against the rails of the ship, out of the way of the shuffle of people.

'Love the outfit,' said Esme, appraising Maddy's lace-trimmed sky blue dress and cotton cap.

'That's as maybe,' said Maddy, running a finger between her chin and the strap of her bonnet. 'But this is going to drive me mad all day. Perhaps I've got it too tight.'

'Are you meant to be anyone in particular?' said Esme, sipping her drink.

'Elizabeth Fry. Or one of her cronies, anyway.'

'What's in your bag?' A Hessian bag dangled from Maddy's fingers.

'A sewing kit, like the ones they gave the women prisoners to give them something to do on the voyage. Keep them out of mischief.'

'Oh, I remember. Sarah Baker would have appreciated that. We know she was a sewer, from the sampler.'

She imagined Sarah and her fellow prisoners standing on deck, watching in awe as Elizabeth Fry and her entourage of well-to-do ladies dressed in their silk finery, were welcomed aboard by the captain. Over a period of twenty years, the Quaker reformer visited more than 100 ships transporting women prisoners before they set sail. Esme hoped Sarah's ship had been one of them. The girl would have welcomed the gift of needles, threads, thimble and patchwork pieces. She may also have been able to read the bible that each of them would have been given.

'You have to hand it to them,' said Maddy, plucking at her skirt. 'Can't have been easy clambering in and out of a small boat in this garb. And they went out in all weathers, apparently.'

Esme turned round and leaned over the side of the ship. 'Neave said she'd come today,' she said, scanning the quayside. 'I thought you might swing it for her to get aboard.'

'Yeah. No problem.' Maddy took a sip of champagne. 'It was always going to be pretty odds on that she'd want to find her dad. Gwen's just going to have to live with it. I'll get on with that photo of him as soon as I can. It might come in handy for her.' She wrinkled her nose and held up the glass to examine it. 'Why do people go mad for this stuff? I don't get it.'

'You're cheap to run, then,' said Esme, with a grin.

Maddy put the glass down on a passing tray. 'So are you going to help track him down?'

Esme shook her head. 'No. I've put her in touch with a colleague of mine, Kim Weller. People finding's much more her area of expertise than mine. But I did warn her he might not want to be found.'

'I guess if he'd wanted to be in touch he'd have done so before now. Unless he thought she wouldn't be interested with him doing a bunk.'

'He may've not known Bella was pregnant and not know that Neave even exists.'

Esme glanced at her watch and looked down on to the quay again. 'Look, there she is,' she said, pointing into the crowd.

Maddy manoeuvred her way back to the top of the gangplank and after a brief negotiation with the steward Neave was allowed on board. She declined champagne and brought over a glass of orange juice.

'I've spoken to Kim,' she told Esme, when they'd raised a glass to the success of the ship visit. 'She said tracing a father was by far the commonest request she had.' She glanced between the two of them. 'But don't worry. I'm not naïve. I do understand the risks. He might be indifferent to me. Hostile, even. Especially if he's in a relationship with someone who knows nothing about me or Mum. I'm prepared for that.' She looked at Esme. 'I'd like to find out more about Sarah Baker, too. See where she fits in. If my father doesn't want to know me, there may be family overseas who do.'

'OK,' nodded Esme. 'I'll put out some feelers to my Australian contacts, if you like.'

'Thanks, that'd be great.' She turned to Maddy. 'And I've spoken to Jack, too.'

'Jack?' said Esme.

'Jack Munroe. Works at the records office,' explained Maddy. 'Techno wizard. Going to take a look at Bella's laptop. See if he can't crack the password.'

'If there's anything useful that Mum's got on there,' Neave told Esme, 'I'll pass it on.'

'Hey, watch it!' said Maddy, as the crowd shuffled backwards. She yelped as a foot crushed her toes. A man with a paunch and thinning hair looked round and scowled at her before turning away to say something to the woman with a wide-brimmed hat. She laughed and they moved away.

'He might have said sorry,' said Esme.

'I doubt it's in his vocabulary,' said Maddy, rubbing her bruised foot.

'That sounds like the voice of experience,' said Esme. 'Who is it?'

'Giles Cooper. Solicitor. One of his clients invited him, probably. His firm represents half of Bideford.'

74

'Horrible man,' said Neave.

Maddy frowned. 'You've met him before?'

Neave glared at the man's back. 'Yes, unfortunately.'

'Cooper?' said Esme. 'Isn't he the one you said Bella went to see?'

Neave nodded. 'Mum had an appointment with him the day she died. I was hoping he'd tell me what about.'

'Don't bank on it,' said Maddy, pulling a face. 'Not unless it's in his interest, anyway.'

'Yeah,' said Neave, continuing to stare at Cooper's back. 'Tell me something I don't know.' She walked over and tapped him on the shoulder. 'Excuse me.' Cooper turned round and glared at her.

'What's she doing?' said Maddy, looking at Esme.

Esme shrugged, her eyes focused on Neave. 'No idea.'

'So sorry to bother you,' said Neave, in a voice heavy with sarcasm. She held out her hand. 'We met before. I'm Neave Shaw. You knew my mother, Bella.'

Cooper shrank back, pulling his shoulder away from her. 'You must be mistaken. Now, if you'll excuse me.' He turned his back on her.

'You won't get rid of me that easily. You saw my mother the day she died.'

Esme went over and took Neave's arm. 'Neave, perhaps this isn't the right place. Better to make an appointment...'

'I already did. He told me she never showed up.'

'Well, then...'

'But she did. I know she did.'

Neave's outburst had attracted attention at the back of the group. Esme steered Neave away from their gawping faces and back to Maddy.

'Hey, come on, girl,' said Maddy, putting her arm around Neave's shoulder. 'You'll only come off worse if you tackle Cooper in public. He's got friends in high places.'

'I'm sure there's a simple explanation why your mother didn't make the meeting,' began Esme.

Neave looked up at her with wide eyes. 'You don't understand. She did make it. I spoke to Cooper's receptionist. She definitely remembers her.' Neave pulled away from Maddy and stared back down the ship at Cooper. 'So why's he lying through his teeth?'

14

3rd July 1837. Esme sat at the microfilm reader in the North Devon Record Office in Barnstaple and read through the meticulous and hand-written record of the Midsummer Quarter Sessions at Bideford's Guildhall. First the list of those on the Grand Jury, followed by the swearing in of each individual and then the fascinating part – details of cases heard. The 3rd July session began with those inhabitants hauled up before the court for allowing '*offensive privies and dung pits*' to overflow on to the public highway and become a nuisance to their neighbours. It seemed to be a common complaint, judging by the number of offenders. Esme imagined the difficulty of keeping such waste in check within a small urban back yard. In the twenty-first century we took our civic sewage system for granted.

She wound the reader further along a few more pages to the neatly recorded summary of Sarah Baker's trial. The indictment against her was for '*feloniously stealing a gold watch of the value of £10 of the property of Mr Thomas Ashgrove while in his service*'. Sarah had pleaded not guilty but the jury concluded that the evidence against her was irrefutable. She was pronounced guilty and sentenced to be transported to '*such a place as his Majesty should think fit for the term of 7 years*'.

Esme assumed 'his' majesty was a slip of the pen. Victoria would have become queen two weeks earlier on the death of William IV. Maybe the clerk didn't consider the young queen worthy of the name until her coronation, a year away. More likely he'd merely forgotten. It had been over 120 years since England had been ruled by a female monarch.

As for the place she should 'think fit' to send her convicted felons, Australia had been a penal destination for fifty years and would continue to be so, officially, for another thirty. The final transport ship would deposit its last convict cargo in Western Australia in 1868, following a long campaign against the policy, backed vigorously by the country herself objecting vehemently at being used as a dumping ground for England's criminals.

The year of Sarah's conviction would see the first step in this change to England's penal policy with the convening of the Molesworth Committee, its subsequent report testifying to The System's failures. Four years after Sarah's indictment, transportation to New South Wales, though not all of Australia, would cease.

Esme pencilled her notes on Sarah and browsed the records for other unfortunates who had found themselves the victim of the system; eleven-year-old Mary Ann Cutliffe, transported for seven years for stealing money in Barnstaple market and accomplices Elizabeth Leverton, William Litson and William Morris for blackmailing a 'respectable inhabitant' for his alleged homosexuality.

Ruth had told her the story of a local girl, Jane Willis, found guilty of stealing a quantity of silk and calico. Jane had railed against her conviction and escaped from Bideford prison with the help of her family. The local paper recounted with relish the tale of her being tracked down by the district's first policeman and his posse, and returned to custody. From here, she was conveyed, as Sarah Baker would also have been, to the hulks of London's Woolwich, the fate of all Devon's female prisoners as they awaited a ship to transport them 'across the seas'.

Esme imagined Sarah arriving at the ship in the obligatory black carriage, its windows boarded, a target for catcalls and jeering, even stone throwing as it passed by. At least, thanks once again to the persistence of prison reformer Mrs Elizabeth Fry's lobbying of parliament against the practice, Sarah would not have had to suffer the indignity of an open cart, when the ravages of weather, missiles and hecklers would have made the journey even more repugnant. Even so, Esme imagined the stifling and disorientating confinement of the darkened transport would wreak its own terror.

She looked up to see Neave bounding across the room towards her and she took off her reading glasses.

'Result?' she asked as Neave dropped down on to the vacant chair beside her.

'He's not back from his coffee break yet. Bout five minutes.'

'And he was quite hopeful he could crack your mum's password?'

'Yeah. He said most people have crappy passwords.'

Esme wrinkled her nose. 'That makes me nervous. Perhaps I'd better get Jack to check mine are as good as I think they are.'

'And let's hope Mum's *is* a cinch or we're back to square one.' She inclined her head towards the microfilm reader. 'Got anything on Sarah?'

Esme slipped her reading glasses back on. 'Yes, quite a bit.' She pointed to the appropriate passage and gave Neave a quick summary.

'Who was Thomas Ashgrove, do we know?' asked Neave.

'Someone she worked for, I assume, being as the entry said *in his service*.' She wound back the film and removed it from the machine, returning it to its box. 'Jack should be back by now?' she said, glancing up at the clock.

They headed over to reception as the swing door opened and a skinny man with a blond stubbly beard, wearing rimless glasses, strode inside. He was clutching a laptop and looking pleased with himself. He gave Neave a thumbs-up and indicated an empty table space across the room beside a tall filing cabinet which served as a room divider.

'Jack, I assume?' said Esme.

'Yes. Looks hopeful.'

'I'll take this back and catch up with you,' she said.

Neave hurried after Jack and Esme returned the box to the

79

front desk.

'Any luck?' said the archivist, peering over the top of a pair of heavy rimmed glasses which looked over-large on her narrow face.

'Yes, very useful, thanks.' She described what she'd discovered.

'Ah, the Ashgroves,' said the archivist.

'Well known family?'

'They were at the time your young convict was transported, anyway. Had a rather grand place over Hartland way, if memory serves.'

Esme nodded. 'That'd make sense. Sarah was born in the parish.'

'If she stole a watch, sounds like she was a household employee.'

'Yes, I thought the same. She learned to sew at an early age. She could have been a seamstress.' She glanced over to Jack and Neave, where Jack was explaining something in great detail. Had the mystery of Bella's Devon trip been solved? Esme thanked the woman and excused herself before wandering over to join them. The laptop lay open on the table.

'That's really great, Jack,' Neave was saying. 'Can't thank you enough, honestly.'

'There's no password set at the moment so I suggest you set one. A strong one, this time.'

'Sure, thanks. I will,' said Neave, sitting down.

Jack stood back, nodding. 'Well, I'll leave you to it then. Let me know if there's anything else I can do for you.' He acknowledged Esme with a nod and strode off across the room where an elderly couple accosted him to answer a question on a document the woman waved in front of him.

Esme turned to Neave. She pulled out a chair and sat down. 'So what have we got?' she said, a bubble of anticipation in the pit of her stomach.

Neave stared at the screen, focusing. 'Nothing yet. No files

80

called family or family history anyway.' She chewed her lip for a moment before clicking with the mouse. 'Let's have a look at her e-mails. I'm so looking forward to presenting the nauseating Giles Cooper with the evidence that he's lying about her appointment.' She stopped, frowning, and stared at the screen.

'What is it?' said Esme. 'What have you found?'

Neave slumped back in her chair. 'I don't get it. There's nothing here.'

'What d'you mean, there's nothing there?'

'No files, no e-mails, nothing.' Neave looked at Esme with wide eyes. 'It's all been wiped.'

15

Back at her cabin, Esme took a glass of water outside on to the veranda, her thoughts on the disconcerting matter of Bella's laptop. Had Bella wiped the files? Given her secrecy with Maddy, it was possible. But why so cautious? What had she discovered? Perhaps she'd saved them somewhere. On a disk or a memory stick. But why delete her e-mails too? Even assuming she had e-mails she'd rather not be read by others, why delete *everything*? It seemed to go beyond caution. The more likely scenario was that someone had hacked into her computer and had cleared everything in the interests of speed and effectiveness. Whether such an anomaly would make the police take more interest, though, was a moot point. It wasn't her prerogative to bring it to their attention, it was Neave's.

She dropped into a deckchair and gazed out to sea. A small sailing boat bobbed about in the distance. She watched it for a while. It didn't seem to make much progress. Lack of wind or the ineptitude of the sailor? Maybe they were practising their tacking skills. Or perhaps they were simply enjoying the view back to the shore.

Her father had once taken her and Elizabeth out in a boat. Nothing as sophisticated as the one she could see now but a simple rowing boat. Had Ruth come with them that time? She recalled Ruth being agitated, complaining about her feet getting wet. But surely the boat hadn't capsized, had it? No. Now she remembered. It was Elizabeth who'd been uneasy, shrieking at every slight sway of the boat and they eventually had to give in to her anxiety and return to shore. The incident when they'd got wet feet was when they'd climbed across the rocks to explore caves and misjudged the tide. She smiled at the image of Ruth stomping up the beach, grumbling about something. Was it because she was wearing new sandals, that day? Esme couldn't recall.

She went back indoors and put her empty glass in the sink. Leaving aside the worry about the laptop, the visit to the record office had proved positive. The little information they'd found about Sarah Baker seemed to have buoyed Neave and she was keen to learn more. What had been Gwen's response to Neave's intentions, Neave hadn't said and Esme hadn't asked.

Esme had promised to look into what happened when Sarah had reached Australia. For the mother country, transportation was the end of the story, symbolizing the ethos behind the penal policy. England's establishment not only wished to be rid of the 'criminal class' but forget it once its inhabitants had left her shores.

But Sarah Baker didn't cease to exist once she'd been banished across the seas. So what sort of life had she lived? She'd obviously married, as the photograph suggested. Was he a fellow convict? Who were the family members in the photograph? Who had been torn from the picture? And, more intriguingly, why?

Esme took her laptop out of its case and set it up on the table. Grace, her contact in Australia, would have started the search by now, though it was too early to hope for more than the sketchiest of information. She booted the machine and felt a ripple of anticipation when Grace's name popped up in her Inbox. She clicked on the e-mail impatiently.

'Might be a link with your Declan back to an Irishman called Connor Shaw,' Grace wrote. 'Transported to New South Wales in 1801 and involved in the Castle Hill rebellion of 1804. Waiting for someone to get back to me. Meanwhile, something to be going on with. Will be in touch when I've got some more.'

Below, Grace had listed Declan Shaw's immediate family. His father Padraig, mother Niamh, sister Colleen, and paternal grandparents Brendan and Sinead. Esme smiled at the roll of Gaelic names. Clearly a family with a pride in their Irish heritage.

She wondered if Neave's grandparents were still alive. Had Declan returned home to Australia? No doubt Kim Weller would help Neave establish that. Esme's role was to find the link to the photograph.

Esme replied to Grace's e-mail, thanking her and saying she looked forward to the next instalment. As she sent the e-mail winging off into cyber-space, she looked again at the roll call of names and Grace's information. Her gaze settled on the words, *Castle Hill Rebellion*. Of course. That was it. Now she knew why the words on the back of the photograph were familiar. Why had she been so slow?

At the time Connor Shaw arrived in Australia, there was much to embitter the Irish. A surge in numbers of transported Irish dissidents planted fear of revolt in the minds of the authorities, resulting in harsher treatment of the Irish compared to other prisoners. This and high death tolls on ships sailing from Ireland convinced the Irish of a conspiracy against them. Anger and hatred finally erupted in the Castle Hill Rebellion. But poor communication, bad planning and betrayal resulted in fiasco. The uprising failed and the ringleaders were hung in chains as a mark of disgrace, their corpses left rotting where they died. 'Liberty or Death' had been the Irish battle cry.

But as Esme enjoyed the satisfaction of solving the riddle of the enigmatic words, she remembered that Maddy had dated the photograph at around 1850.

So why would someone pen those words half a century after the event?

16

Safe's headquarters lay about half a mile in from the coast. Esme drove down the bumpy track to Dan Ryder's farm and pulled up in front of a series of barns around a large courtyard. A fence separated the yard from a paddock next door and the end barn had been converted into an office. The seaward boundary hedge beyond was punctuated with stunted and bowed trees. Fields of rough yellow-green pastureland stretched either side into the distance and in a dip in the land she could see the muted blue of the sea.

She climbed out of her car and walked towards the yard as Dan emerged from the corner building with a broom in his hand.

'Esme,' he said, walking over to meet her. 'Glad you could make it. Welcome to Kernworthy Farm.'

'Thank you. Good to be here.' She handed him a bundle of leaflets. 'Instructions from Maddy – please pin up, give out or otherwise distribute to whoever will take them. We need to spread the word of the museum ship's visit as far as we can.'

'Cool. I'll give them to the lads.'

'Great location you've got here,' said Esme, looking around at the stone and slated buildings which enclosed the courtyard.

Dan propped the broom up against the fence. 'Let me show you round while it's quiet. The lads are out exercising the horses and Mum's out at the accountant's.'

They toured the stables where 'the lads' learnt to care for the horses, as part of their rehabilitation. One set of barns had been converted into modest bedrooms, a large games room and a lounge area with sofas and a TV. There was even a small snug boasting a shelf packed with books. On the ground floor was a kitchen, in the middle of which stood a huge farmhouse table with benches down either side.

Back outside they crossed the cobbled yard to the office at the end of the building group and Dan showed her into what he termed 'the centre of operations'.

'Fancy a coffee?' he asked.

Esme nodded and he went over to a small kitchenette in one corner of the room to put the kettle on while he told her about their plans to start holidays for younger children.

'Aimed at city kids who'd never normally get the chance to experience coast and countryside,' he said, handing her a coffee. 'Space to let their hair down, a break from pressures they have to deal with in everyday life. Domestic abuse, alcoholic parent, drugs, that sort of thing.'

Esme thought of Neave and her dreams for a family holiday. She would have benefited from such a scheme.

Dan nodded to a display board on the far side of the office. 'There's some of the feedback we got back from the pilot we ran last year,' he said. 'Makes it worth all the effort.'

Esme cradled the mug in her hands and wandered over to look at the crayoned pictures of smiling faces, seascapes and lollipop trees, photographs of children on ponies, or decked out in lifejackets waiting to jump aboard a dinghy for a trip across the bay. Beside the display was pinned a large ordnance survey map, a large swath of land outlined in red ink.

'Is the surrounding land all part of your farm?' she asked, sipping the steaming coffee.

'I wish.' He gave her a wry smile. 'Part of Kernworthy Farm, yep. Ours, no.'

'Oh, sorry. I didn't realise. I assumed you owned it.'

'Belongs to the estate. Be great if we did. It'd give us more flexibility, not to mention security, but we're tenants. Have been since we set up here.'

'You must be fairly secure, though, I would have thought, being here for several generations?'

86

He pulled a face, shaking his head. 'Actually we had hoped to buy it, once. Almost did, in fact. But that was when the old lady was still alive. She was a supporter and patron right into her nineties. But she died before anything could be sorted.'

'Shame. So what about the new owner?'

'Not a cat in hell's chance. Edward Ashgrove isn't the world's most cooperative individual at the best of times.'

'Ashgrove?' The name of the family Sarah Baker was accused of stealing from.

Dan pushed his hand through his hair. 'You know him? Trust me to put my foot in it.'

'No, not at all. The name came up in some research I was doing. A young girl from around here was transported for stealing a watch from a Thomas Ashgrove in the 1830s. The archivist said the Ashgroves were a well known family then. For some reason it never occurred to me that they might still live in the area. She told me they had a big house near here.'

He nodded. 'Kernworthy Manor.'

'Ah, I see. Same name as your farm. Could explain why they don't want to sell, perhaps?'

Dan snorted. 'More likely cos he and Cooper like to get their kicks squeezing us for yet another rent hike.'

'Cooper, the solicitor?'

'Come across him before, have you?'

'Sort of. He was at the ship Open Day. Not a candidate for the most charming citizen award, from what I saw.'

Dan gave an ironic laugh. 'No, you're right there.'

'So he's the Ashgrove's solicitor.'

'In common with half the county.'

'Yes, that's what Maddy said.'

'It's his father's legacy, though. He was all right. Trouble is, people round here...' He made a gesture of hopelessness with his hands. 'Well, they don't like change, do they? So they stick with the firm, even though the son's a waste of space. Same with the

Ashgroves, I guess. They've been clients since forever.'

'What's he like, this Edward Ashgrove?'

'Obstinate bugger, in my opinion. But then I've only got his attitude towards the farm to go by.' He shrugged. 'I've never actually met the guy. Keeps his head down. Don't reckon he's the sociable kind.'

17

A session in the North Devon record office furnished Esme with a rudimentary history of the Ashgrove family. At the time of Sarah Baker's indiscretion, Thomas Ashgrove lived at Kernworthy Manor with his wife Catherine and their children – William, the eldest, daughters Phoebe and Emma, and younger son James. William Ashgrove, though, born in 1818, had not inherited on his father's death and from what she could work out, the estate had passed to his younger brother, James. What became of William, however, Esme failed to discern. She could find no record of his burial in the parish records. Neither did his death show up in the relevant list following civil registration in 1837. Though registration, particularly in its infancy, wasn't to be relied upon. At the time not everyone was aware that all births, marriages and deaths were required to be registered, whether or not they were also recorded by the church. Others looked at the system with suspicion, considering it an invasion of their privacy. An attitude compounded by the introduction of the first census to include personal data, four years later. Either of these reasons, or simply clerical error, could explain why William seemed to have disappeared without a trace.

His younger brother, James, meanwhile, had gone on to marry and have one daughter, Eleanor, born in 1885. This would be the 'old lady' Dan mentioned, who was a patron of *Safe* and died in her nineties. She found no marriage for Eleanor and no children, implying that the Ashgrove line had ceased at that point. Yet Dan had confirmed an Ashgrove lived at Kernworthy Manor. A distant relation, she assumed. Perhaps Ruth would know.

*

'What do you know about the Ashgrove family who live at Kernworthy Manor?' she asked Ruth when she stopped by at the farm to collect her post.

Ruth was at the sink, up to her elbows in soapy water. 'Don't know as I know anything about them. Never met them, far as I'm aware.'

'Sounds like not many people have.'

Ruth picked up a towel off the rail on the range and dried her hands. 'Not like in the old lady's day. Very community minded, she was, Eleanor Ashgrove. Always out and about, involved in everything that was going on. Right to the last.'

'Dan mentioned that she was a supporter of theirs.'

'That's right. Lovely old dear. Do anything for anyone.' Ruth took Esme's post from off the dresser and handed it to her. 'Message there from that young Neave, too. Been trying to get hold of you. Said your mobile was off. Told her it'd more likely be the poor signal. City folk don't seem to understand that.'

'Thanks, I'll give her a call.' Esme wondered whether Kim had located Declan Shaw. She looked forward to passing on what she'd learnt about the early branch of Neave's family tree. Hopefully it wouldn't be long before she'd link up everything else.

'So why d'you want to know about the Ashgroves?'

'That photograph. We've identified her as a servant girl we think worked at the house in the nineteenth century, and was transported to Australia. Pity Eleanor Ashgrove's not still around, she might have known the story.'

'You mean the photograph the dead woman had?' Ruth looked worried.

'That's right.' Esme smiled. 'Turned out it belonged to Neave's father, who was Australian. She's asked me to find out a little about her.' Ruth's expression hadn't changed. 'What's the matter?'

'Should you be doing that, d'you think?'

90

'Why ever not?'

'Well, weren't you thinking the photograph had something to do with what happened to her mother? Sounds like you could be stirring up a can of worms, to me.'

'*Opening* a can of worms, Ruth,' said Esme, laughing. 'Not stirring. That's a hornets' nest.' The disquieting analogy registered only briefly but she didn't dwell on it. 'Look, the poor girl's lost her mother in tragic circumstances. She's quite keen to know a bit about her family history, that's all. It could help her, don't you think? Find her father's relatives, perhaps.'

'Yes, I suppose so. Poor maid. Must be difficult for her.' Ruth seemed to relax. 'Yes, it's a shame about Eleanor. She would have been only too happy to help. Tell you what. Have a chat with Phyllis Hodge. Used to be a teacher at the local primary school before she retired. She knew the old lady quite well. She might know a thing or two.' She opened a drawer and fumbled around inside. 'I've got her number around here somewhere. Give her a ring. She'd be delighted to have a chat, I'm sure.'

*

Back at the cabin, Esme returned Neave's call. As the phone rang out she realised she'd forgotten to ask Ruth about the current Ashgrove living at Kernworthy Manor. And what relation they were of the old lady. Neither had she found out where the manor was. Perhaps it was open to the public and she and Neave could visit next time Neave was in North Devon.

But all such niceties went out of her mind the moment she heard Neave's voice.

Esme gripped the handset. 'Neave. What's happened?'

'He's dead, Esme,' said Neave, her voice breaking. 'My father's dead.'

Esme sank down on the corner of the bed. 'I'm so sorry, Neave. I guess this was one of the scenarios Kim said you had to

91

be prepared for.'

'But you don't understand. He died, here, Esme. Here, in North Devon.'

And before Esme could fully grasp the significance of that fact, Neave delivered the final unpalatable truth. 'He was murdered.'

18

Neave clutched the insignificant posy of cornflowers against her and pushed open the iron gate to the churchyard. When she smelled the newly mown grass she hesitated and looked around. But she saw no one and heard no sound of machinery so she relaxed and let the gate swing shut behind her.

Ahead of her the modest village church regarded her benignly and she wandered towards the front porch along the cracked path, where tufts of grass dislodged the ageing concrete. She looked around her, scanning the gravestones as she walked. *Elizabeth, wife of Thomas Ellisdon, died 5th December 1849. William Brownlow, taken from this life 23rd March 1815. Hannah, daughter of Ann and Joseph Hillier, fell asleep 16th July 1855, aged 2 months. Now in the arms of Jesus.*

But she was wasting her time looking for her father's name. Declan Shaw's grave was unmarked; her mother apparently too distressed to commission a headstone and her gran, Neave surmised, content to allow his existence to fade into obscurity.

She started as the deep sound of a heavy door banged closed nearby. A lean, freckle-faced man with a receding hairline and dressed in a surplice, strode out of the stone porch, almost crashing into her. He stumbled to a halt.

'Oh, I am so sorry. More haste, less speed, eh?' He stepped back and smiled. 'Can I help?' He glanced down at her posy of flowers, gripped tightly against her chest and she suddenly felt foolish.

'Well, I...' She felt an overwhelming urge to make something up. To say that Thomas Ellisdon was her great-great something and she'd come to put some flowers on his grave. But she didn't have the mental capacity to calculate how many 'greats' that would be, had Thomas been her legitimate ancestor. Besides, only a short while ago she'd censured her grandmother and mother for hiding the truth of her father's death. How could she stand on that moral high ground and lie to this man of the cloth, now?

'Thank you but I doubt it,' she said, looking down at the posy, wilting now from her tight clutches. 'I think I was being a bit optimistic.'

'Oh?'

Neave looked around. 'There's no stone for who I'm looking for. Perhaps I'll leave these on another grave instead.'

'Are you sure there's no stone? I'm fairly familiar with all my residents. Perhaps I can guide you in the right direction.'

Neave avoided his gaze. She looked across the churchyard and focused on the boundary wall, moss and lichen covered. 'It's good of you but it's not that I've searched and not found. There literally is no stone.'

The vicar spun on his heel and pointed down the path. 'There is one unmarked grave. The ladies who do the church flowers occasionally leave a token on there. You should be able to make it out. The mound next to the marble headstone. And if you need water,' he added, indicating with his other arm, 'there's a tap around the back of the church.'

She thanked him and he inclined his head before striding off, his shoes clicking on the concrete and the folds of his black surplice flapping around his legs.

Neave continued down the path to the marble grave the vicar had indicated. Beside it, a hummock of ground indicated its significance as a resting place by the small glass vase on top, containing shrivelled carnations. She removed them, emptying out the grubby water on to the grass before walking to the tap to refill the vase. She placed her posy in the fresh water and returned the vase to the grave. Her contribution looked forlorn, sitting crooked on the uneven ground. Were his Australian family aware of where he lay? Did they even know he was dead? And how he died?

Now it seemed even more imperative that she find that link

back to his family. Her family. To someone who could tell her more about who she was and from where she'd come.

Why had she never insisted on knowing more while she was growing up? Why had the evasion and diversionary tactics she'd encountered at every question not spurred her to push harder? She could have searched before, had she taken a moment to stop and think. Why had it never occurred to her to conduct her own investigation?

She heard a sound behind her and she spun round. Gwen was coming along the path towards her, her walking stick tapping the concrete. Neave watched and waited, her jaw clamped tight against the swelling anger and words of reproach in her mouth. All this time her grandmother had known of this place. All this time she'd deliberately kept it from her.

But when Gwen reached her, Neave found she was unable to speak. Gwen looked down on the cockeyed display on the ground and laid a hand on Neave's shoulder.

'I never wanted you to be hurt,' she said, squeezing Neave's shoulder. 'Who wants to know their father's been murdered? Sometimes I wanted to tell you there'd been an accident. A car crash, something of that nature. At least you'd know he was never coming back. But your mother wouldn't hear of it. Insisted we say nothing. I thought she'd tell you the truth one day. When you were old enough. So I kept my mouth shut.'

Neave reached out and grasped her grandmother's hand but emotions were too close to the surface for her to risk speaking.

'I s'pose it let me off the hook, in a way,' Gwen continued. 'But it was wrong. I should've spoke up.' Gwen shuffled closer. Neave slipped her arm through her grandmother's and laid her head against Gwen's shoulder, tears spilling out of control now.

'That damned photograph,' said Gwen. 'Like a bad penny. Never knew she still had it.'

Neave lifted her head and looked into her grandmother's face. 'You said you'd never seen it before.'

Gwen shuffled. 'Well, how could I have said anything? It would've all come out, wouldn't it?'

Neave frowned. 'What would have come out?'

Gwen pressed her lips together, her eyes fixed on the sad little bouquet nestled in the grass. 'He had it on him, didn't he?' she said, waving her stick at the ground. 'He had the photograph on him when he was killed.'

19

Esme stood on the cliff where the path veered close to the edge. Ahead, the dark sea was a flat blue with sporadic white horses, the sun throwing spangles of light on to its surface. She gazed down at the faded floral tributes wrapped in cellophane, torn and fluttering in the sea breeze, marking the point from where Bella had fallen.

She kicked at the rough tufts of grass with her toe. Easy to stumble in the dark if you strayed from the path and lost your bearings. Especially if you were in a hurry. *Had* Bella been in a hurry? Was she meeting someone and was running late? Running or fleeing? From where? From whom?

She stared down, mesmerised by the rhythm of the incoming tide as it breathed in, was sucked back, came in, out, in, out. She pulled back from the edge, her heart thumping. *Nothing to suggest Mrs Shaw's death was in any way suspicious*, the police had said. Would they change that opinion if they knew about the photograph coincidence?

She'd not made too much of the missing laptop files. If the inquest eventually concluded Bella's death was suicide, it could be argued she'd cleared them herself, not wanting whatever it was to be seen by her family. But the matter of the photograph was different and taken along with the deleted files, more so. She had to persuade Neave to tell them.

She heard footsteps across grass behind her and spun round.

'Sorry,' said Neave, looking alarmed. 'Didn't mean to startle you.'

Esme shook her head and smiled. 'No. My fault. Deep in thought.'

'Was it OK to call you? I'm sure you're busy as hell.'

'It's fine, Neave,' said Esme. 'Honestly.' She gestured towards the flowers on the grass. 'Some kind words.'

Neave nodded and crouched down, fingering a card attached to one of the bouquets. 'Odd how people do this, though, isn't it? It's not like they even knew Mum.'

'A gesture of sympathy, that's all.'

Neave stood up. 'Isn't there something ghoulish about it, though? As if they want to be a part of it.'

'Isn't that what empathy is all about? Isn't that what you do as a counsellor?'

Neave wrapped her arms around herself. 'It's not always like that, though, is it? Sometimes people just enjoy a salacious story to liven up their dreary lives. Like at the record office.'

'Why? What happened at the record office?'

Neave reached inside her pocket. 'I went and looked it up in the archives like you said.' She pulled out a folded piece of paper and handed it to Esme.

'What's this?'

'The front page of *The Bideford Gazette* for Thursday 18th February 1982.'

Esme opened the sheet out and read the bold and pithy headline. AUSTRALIAN MAN MURDERED IN STREET. Neave's father.

'He was found in a side street in Barnstaple with stab wounds,' said Neave.

Esme scanned the article. There was no photograph, but Declan wasn't a Devon man; perhaps a local weekly paper wouldn't have the inclination or the resources of the national dailies to resource one. No internet and e-mail connections back then.

She passed the copy back to Neave. 'What d'you mean about it being a salacious story?'

'No, not the article. Jack Munroe.'

'Jack? Why?'

'He was going on about how he was a kid at school at the time,' said Neave, a scowl driving the colour from her face. 'How it'd happened in one of the alleyways they used as a short cut. How it'd scared the girls rigid and they wouldn't go down there for ages after. And how the lads used to dare one another to show their macho credentials.'

'Neave, you can't blame him for that. It would have shocked the whole town. Everyone has their own way of coping. I'm sure he wasn't sensationalising for the sake of it.'

'And he had the nerve to accuse his brother-in-law of milking the story all his life.'

'His brother-in-law?'

Neave shrugged. 'He'd been the mortuary attendant or something. Made a thing of being involved in a murder ever since, trying to make out there was something suspicious about it. His fifteen minutes of fame. You know what I mean.'

Esme laid a hand on Neave's arm. 'Look, he obviously didn't realise your connection or he'd have been more sensitive.'

'He did back off pretty quick when the penny dropped.'

'Well, there you are then.' Esme put her arm round Neave's shoulders. 'I'm sure he'd be horrified to think he'd upset you. Come on. Let's wander back now, shall we?'

'Did they get anyone for it?' asked Esme, as they rejoined the path.

'There was a gang of lads in the area at the time but I don't think they could pin it on any of them.'

'And no one saw anything?'

'The police were keen to talk to a woman as a possible witness, apparently, but she never came forward.'

They passed sheep grazing amongst a swathe of taller grasses, eying them warily and keeping their distance as they moved on to another patch of tasty fodder.

'It's weird after all these years, finally knowing what happened to my dad.' She chewed at her lower lip. 'I still don't understand

99

why she never told me. Gran said it was to protect me. And she might have been right to, I guess. If people knew, I'd be a figure of fascination, wouldn't I? Being talked about, pointed out in the street. Maybe they made the right decision after all. And it explains a lot about Mum, doesn't it? She couldn't cope, could she? That's why she buried herself in a bottle. She was angry with him, Gran said.'

'That's not unusual with grief in any circumstances,' said Esme. She should know. She'd felt the same when Tim died. She smiled at Neave. 'But knowing the full story helps understand things, doesn't it? For you, I mean. It helps you understand your gran, for one thing.'

'I think Gran thinks he got his just deserts.'

'Why was she so against him? It can't be only because of the whirlwind romance, surely?'

Neave shrugged. 'It's not so uncommon, is it? Boyfriend not good enough for your daughter. I wonder what my granddad would have made of him. Mum was quite young when he died and then it was only Gran and Mum. Perhaps that was a factor, too. Gran saw him taking her little girl away from her and leaving her alone.'

Esme reflected on the sad fact that Declan's going had not returned Bella to Gwen as she would have hoped. She'd simply lost her in a different way.

'I had a really stupid thought yesterday,' continued Neave. 'That if he'd stayed he'd have been there for me, understanding what I was going through, helping me deal with Mum.' She looked at Esme and gave a wistful smile. 'But if he'd been around, she'd have been fine, wouldn't she?'

'I suppose so.'

'Gran said him being murdered made it worse for Mum. That he was cruelly taken when they had their whole lives ahead of them. Perhaps if he'd simply walked out, she might have been able to forget him and move on. I'm sure Gran blames him for getting himself murdered and wrecking her daughter's life. Like it was his own fault.' It certainly explained Gwen's hostility. It seemed they'd both been angry with him.

'What was he doing in Barnstaple?' asked Esme.

Neave shook her head. 'No idea.'

'Odd that both your parents had that photograph. Have you mentioned it to the police?'

Neave stopped walking and looked at Esme, frowning. 'You think I should? Why would they be interested?'

'It's a coincidence which needs further investigation, I would have thought,' said Esme. 'And they won't make the connection, unless someone points it out.' Neave chewed her lower lip.

'You'd want them to know about it, wouldn't you?' Esme prompted. 'If it was important?'

'Important how?'

'A link with what happened to your father, perhaps? Explain what your mother was doing here?' Esme knew she'd want to know everything if it was her parents. But perhaps Neave had already learnt more than she could cope with.

'What's more important to me at the moment is learning about my family. And you've already told me more than I've ever known before.'

They resumed walking and Esme told Neave about Phyllis Hodge. 'Ruth's given me the name of someone who knew Eleanor Ashgrove, the old lady who used to live at Kernworthy Manor. She might know something about your Sarah Baker. Do you want me to go and see her? We could both go, if you like?'

Neave smiled. '*My* Sarah Baker. Sounds good, doesn't it?'

'That's assuming she *is* yours. We've got to find the evidence yet. Which is why it might be useful to speak to Miss Hodge.'

They came to the gate where the path joined the road down to Warren Quay. As they passed through on to the grass verge, Esme stopped and turned to Neave. 'So, what do you think?' she said.

Neave climbed on to the grass bank and looked down across

the bay. 'I would certainly like to find out more.' She looked back at Esme. 'But I know you're busy and I have to go back to work.'

'Not too busy to squeeze in something important like that. And Grace is doing her bit too, with what she's already given us and I'm expecting more information any day.'

Neave nodded. 'OK, then. If you're sure. You go and see this lady. And I'll think about telling the police about the photograph.'

20

Phyllis Hodge, the primary school teacher who'd known Eleanor Ashgrove, lived a short distance inland from the dramatic coast at Coombe Mill. Esme tucked her car into a niche on the crossroads, which Miss Hodge said she'd find in the lane below her cottage, and leant back in the driver's seat.

She tilted the rear view mirror and checked her face. Her eyes were a give-away of lack of sleep, but she decided it wasn't too bad. She'd looked worse. A modest dab of foundation concealed her scar enough for it not to alarm. It was a practice she adopted when she met clients for the first time, though face-to-face consultations were less common now with the increase in electronic communication. She realigned the mirror and climbed out of the car, checking her location by the traditional fingerpost on the junction. Then she walked up the lane to the gate to Miss Hodge's cottage.

Miss Hodge was in the garden. Watering can in hand, she was attending to a collection of flowering pots adorning the flagstones above the fast moving stream which ran past the cottage. She turned at the click of the gate and put down her can to greet Esme. Short and stout, her ample bosom had no doubt comforted scores of young children from playground scrapes and grazes during her years as a primary school teacher.

She bade Esme sit at the cafe table on the lawn and bustled off indoors. The sound of sawing wood could be heard somewhere in the direction of the cottage. Esme strained her neck to peer down the path running along the side. An elderly man in baggy blue overalls was sawing timber on a rickety old sawhorse. He paused and looked up, nodding at Esme briefly before returning to his work.

Miss Hodge emerged from the cottage with a jug of lemonade and glasses. 'Home-made,' she beamed. 'One of the joys of retirement, having time to indulge in the little niceties of life.'

Esme acknowledged this with a smile, suspecting that making home-made lemonade was something Miss Hodge had always done, retired or not. Miss Hodge set down the tray and poured out three glasses. She handed one to Esme. 'I must give Walter his,' she said, taking a second, 'and then we can talk.' She shuffled off down the garden.

Esme picked up her glass and looked around. With the coast so close she guessed the stream must run into the sea over the dramatic waterfall which defined the end of the valley. Even though it seemed a long way down from the level of the lawn, she wondered if it ever came up high enough to flood the garden or even the cottage itself.

She leaned back in her seat and sipped her drink, letting the perplexed thoughts of recent days melt away in the sound of the burbling stream. The sight of roses on the cottage wall and bedding plants tumbling out of the clay pots on the flagstones made her think wistfully of her own garden back in Shropshire, but she had to admit that sitting in this tranquil setting, sipping home-made lemonade on such a pleasant summer's day, was hard to better.

'There we are,' said Miss Hodge, returning to the table. 'Walter's mending the rail alongside the stream around the back there. It's so rotten now it was becoming quite dangerous. I'm lucky to have Walter to give me a hand. He only lives up in the village and he can turn his hand to anything I might need attending to.' She chuckled. 'I'm afraid woodwork isn't my cup of tea at all.' She took a long draught of lemonade. 'Now then, how can I help?'

'As I mentioned on the phone,' said Esme. 'The Ashgrove family cropped up during some research I was doing and Ruth said you knew more than most.'

'I expect it's the scandal you'll have heard about,' she said, her eyes twinkling.

'Scandal?'

'Oh yes. So very romantic. Sadly not with the story book happy ending, though.' She put her glass down on the tray. 'Young William Ashgrove fell in love with a young servant girl called Sarah.'

'Sarah Baker?'

'Yes, that's right. You've come across her name, I see.'

'Yes, but I didn't know anything about her and William. How intriguing.'

'Naturally the family didn't approve. The story goes that they used to meet secretly in the garden summer house.'

'I assume they were found out?'

Miss Hodge nodded. 'Inevitable, I suppose. Anyway, the story goes that William refused to give her up and was packed off to relatives to some far flung wilderness north of the border.'

'So what happened to William? From what I read in the records it was James who inherited the estate.'

'Yes, that's right. As for William…' She inclined her head, her expression wistful. 'Died of a broken heart, perhaps? He never came home, certainly.'

'His father must have been incensed to take such a severe step.'

'Quite so. A scandal of mammoth proportions in those days, of course. Bed the girl, perhaps – we all know that sort of thing went on – but contemplate marriage to one of such low birth? I think not.'

'And then Sarah was convicted of theft and transported to Australia. Poor girl. Lost her sweetheart and her freedom.' An idea popped into Esme's head. 'Do you think the incidents are linked? Perhaps she took the watch to raise money to go to Scotland after him?'

'It's possible, I suppose. I hadn't thought of that.'

'Strange, in a way, though. You would have thought that once she'd been transported and was out of the way, William's father

105

would have relented enough to bring his son back into the family.'

'I understand he was a strict and stubborn man. Once he'd barred William, he would see it as a weakness to go back on his word.'

'Did you learn all this from Eleanor Ashgrove?'

'Oh yes, I knew Eleanor for a number of years.' She retrieved her glass and sat back in her chair. 'She was on the school board of governors at the school where I was teaching. That's where we first met. Wonderful lady. Passionate about holistic education. "Education is more than jumping academic hoops, Phyllis," she used to say. "Society ignores that to its cost." She was ninety-seven when she died, you know.'

'Shame she never married,' said Esme. 'Clearly, children meant a lot to her.'

'There was a cousin on her mother's side for whom she held a candle. Alas her affection wasn't reciprocated and he married someone else.'

'Oh, how sad.'

'There was never any bitterness, though. His children used to spend their summer down here at the manor, as did his grandchildren. And then of course, she left the estate to his great-grandson.'

'And he owns the manor now?'

'Yes, that's right.'

'Do you know him? Someone said he's rather a recluse.'

'I met him as a child on several occasions, during his visits to the manor. He used to join us at the primary school for the last few days of the summer term. Of course that was back in days when attitudes were more relaxed than they are today.' She laughed. 'Oh, yes. I remember Little Leonardo. That's what we called him, on account of his mirror writing. Not uncommon in left-handed writers, of course. But he wrote poetry. Very good poetry for his age. There was one about the coast that impressed me, I recall. It had a particularly poignant part in the middle. Let me think. I've never forgotten it. Yes, that was it. '*Cries for help, for guidance, shrouded by the sound of white horses' footsteps.*' Quite deep for one so young, I thought. Wonderful allegory.'

'Yes, isn't it?' Esme's thoughts drifted to the sight of Bella, lying broken and defenceless on the rocks. Had her cries for help been 'shrouded' by the sound of white horses' footsteps?

'Is everything all right, my dear?' said Miss Hodge.

'Yes, sorry. I was thinking about the accident on the cliff.'

'Oh yes, what a tragedy. I'm sure it was that which prompted my memory of the poem. Quite uncanny, don't you think?'

Esme nodded and smiled. She didn't want to reveal her role in the drama and have to retell her story. She cleared her throat. 'So does Little Leonardo still write poetry?' Perhaps it accounted for his reclusive existence.

Miss Hodge shook her head. 'I've no idea. Our paths have never crossed, I'm sad to say.'

'So you've never met him as an adult?'

'No, dear.' She held up a finger. 'Though that's not entirely true. I encountered him not so very long ago while I was walking across the golf course one agreeable Sunday afternoon. His golfing partner was one of my former pupils and I stopped to talk to him. He introduced us.'

'Did he remember you from his visits to your school?'

She smiled. 'He said not, but I think he just felt a little self-conscious. Perhaps he thought I might embarrass him in front of his friend with some tale of a childhood misdemeanour.' Then her smile faded and she frowned, deep in thought. 'Strange, though…'

'What is it?' said Esme, watching the old lady's anxious face. When there was no response, she reached over and touched her arm. 'Miss Hodge? Is everything all right?'

Miss Hodge blinked, as though forgetting for a moment where she was. 'I'm so sorry, my dear. Don't know what got into me. Something flittered past, you know, how it does.'

'What sort of thing?'

'I don't know. Something not quite right but I can't...' She laughed and shook her head. 'Take no notice. The muddled head of an old lady, nothing more. It's gone now, whatever it was. Now my dear, more lemonade? And then there's a photograph I'd like to show you.'

*

Esme blinked while her eyes adjusted to the dim interior of Miss Hodge's cottage, a tidy but cluttered retreat, reminiscent of a well-stocked antique shop. Miss Hodge cleared the polished table and fetched a sepia photograph from the dresser drawer. She set it down on the table and pulled out a dining chair, gesturing for Esme to do the same.

'Here we are. This is Eleanor's family home. Kernworthy Manor.'

The photograph was of the front elevation of an elegant Georgian house. A portico framed the front door and the house walls were cloaked with climbing roses in full bloom.

'It's beautiful,' said Esme. 'When would this have been taken?'

'Early twentieth century. Eleanor's parents would both still be alive, then, of course and Eleanor about fifteen or sixteen years of age. Eleanor's mother was a great gardener. Much of the grounds as they are today reflect the work she did.'

'Is it open to the public?'

'Sadly no. The gardens used to be. Charity events, that sort of thing. But not any longer. A real shame. It was a marvellous garden. Quite an achievement to create such a horticultural gem, given its position.'

'Its position?'

Miss Hodge sat back and regarded Esme soberly. 'Yes. It's on the cliff a short distance away from Warren Quay. Near where that poor lady fell off the cliff.'

21

Esme checked her watch for the third time in two minutes and continued pacing along the path in front of the hotel. Where was Neave? Perhaps she'd gone back home early, after all.

The telltale beep, beep of a reversing vehicle shook her out of her thoughts and she moved out of the way as a delivery lorry crawled its way backwards between the hotel and the buildings opposite.

Dan appeared from inside the pub to open up the cellar doors. He shouted to the driver and walked to the back of the wagon, where he caught sight of Esme.

'All right?' he said with a nod, pulling on a pair of gloves. The driver unlocked the chains on the rear flap and jumped up to unload the barrels on board.

'You haven't seen Neave at all, have you?' she called over to Dan, wary of getting hit by a wayward barrel.

'She was here earlier.' He pulled the cuff of his glove back and looked at his watch. 'About an hour or so ago. She's not back yet, then?'

'I was supposed to meet her.' Esme shrugged. 'I wonder where she's got to.'

'She seemed a bit pissed off, to be honest. She was asking about the manor.'

'The manor?' Esme walked a little closer, concern tightening in her stomach. 'As in, the Ashgrove's manor?'

'Yeah. Reckoned she'd got an ancestor as used to work there, or something?'

Esme nodded. 'That's right. That's who I was researching when I came across the name Ashgrove.'

'Oh, yeah. You said. Seems to have got it into her head they might tell her something about it.' He bent down and tipped a barrel on to its side.

'Did you tell her how to find the manor?'

'Yeah, sure. And I told her what I told you, too,' he said, rolling the barrel towards the cellar hatch. 'That she'd be wasting her time getting anything out of Ashgrove.'

Esme thanked him and glanced up at the road which wound up behind the hotel and led to the cliff path. Why hadn't Neave waited? She would know by now that Kernworthy Manor was only a short distance from where Bella fell because Dan would have told her when he gave her directions. Had she learnt something from her visit to the police which had prompted her to go in search of answers?

Dan said she'd only been gone about an hour. Perhaps she intended merely to take a gentle stroll along the coast path to look at the manor. Maybe there was a chance to catch her up.

Esme hurried back to her car and fetched a rucksack from the boot. After calling at the shop for water and an OS map, she climbed back up the steep road away from the harbour. At the top of the hill, she turned left through the gate to join the South West Coast Path, firmly demarked from centuries of pounding footsteps. She glanced towards the edge of the cliff where she'd met Neave the other day, before continuing down into the narrow valley and up the other side. Of course there was no way of knowing whether Neave had come this way or changed her mind and gone elsewhere. But she'd have waited at Warren Quay, otherwise, wouldn't she?

As the summit of the next rise came into view, so did the chimneys of Kernworthy Manor to her right, tall and bold above well maintained boundary hedges.

By the time she reached the top, she was hot and tired. She sat down on a tussock of grass to get her breath back. Sarah Baker might have walked past this very spot regularly. Perhaps she came this way on those rare days when she was released from her duties and could visit her family. Esme imagined her hurrying along, eager to get home to share her news and hear what had happened at home in her absence. Maybe she'd have a month's wages wrapped up in a handkerchief, a contribution to the family household. They'd be looking out for her, perhaps. Younger siblings might run to meet her as she got close to home. What stories would she tell, as they sat in their cottage for those precious few hours, before her return, of life at Kernworthy Manor? Had Neave had similar thoughts as she'd walked along?

She dug around in her rucksack for the bottle of water and took a long draught while she decided what to do next. A bridle path turned off the coastal path and led inland. Were there any signs that Neave had passed this way? How could there be? There must be many a walker who used the main coast path. The next part of the journey might tell, though. If it only served the manor, there may be evidence of a recent visitor. She returned the bottle to her rucksack, threw it over her shoulder and took the bridleway in the direction of the Manor.

The path ran in a direct line inland. To the right hand side was a high dry-stone boundary wall, clothed in lichen. Clumps of red valerian sprouted out from the base of the wall across the path, amongst a variety of tall grasses. As she got closer, the house became obscured by large shrubs on the garden side which over hung the wall, creating a tunnel as they merged with the upper branches of scrubby blackthorn trees on the left hand side. She pushed her way on. As she'd surmised, this wasn't a path used very often, though whether anyone else had walked this way recently was difficult to tell.

Eventually the house came back into view and she stopped for a moment to appraise which direction to take. There was no obvious entrance from the cliff path side, it looked like she would need to walk all the way around and approach the house from the main drive, off the highway. She carried on, bypassing the house itself, and arrived at a fork in the path. One way turned left, towards the corner of a field. In the other direction the path appeared to peter out but she saw she'd arrived at the back of the outbuildings at the rear of the property.

She pressed on through the long grass until she arrived at a high weather-beaten gate with warped wooden planks. She put her eye to a crack between them and peered through to a cobbled yard. In the distance a narrow path led around to the front of the house. If she followed the boundary around to the drive, she could approach the house by the front entrance. But if the gate was open, she could take the side path and access the front door from here and save herself an unnecessary detour.

She took the large iron ring in her hand and turned it. Good. Not locked. To her right a range of outbuildings bordered the yard opposite the main house. She turned left, cutting across the courtyard and taking the path which ran beside the main house. As she approached the gable end, she noticed a glazed door standing ajar.

She stopped. Was there someone inside?

'Hello?' she called, peering round the door.

The room appeared to be a study cum library. Book-lined walls surrounded an antique pedestal desk in the centre on which stood a Victorian style lamp, an ancient typewriter and an old faded photograph of a young girl in a silver frame.

Esme reached out and tapped gently on the glass. 'Hello?' she called again.

As she stepped over the threshold, someone grabbed her from behind.

22

Instinctively Esme kicked out, achieving a modicum of satisfaction when she made contact and heard a grunt of pain.

'Sergei!' shrieked a woman's voice.

Esme was thrust back outside and her arms released. She stood upright, rubbing her left arm and turned towards her attacker, a burly individual with thick lips and a nose like a car jack.

'She just walk in,' he growled as an elegant woman, wearing sunglasses, white cotton jeans and a silk shirt, marched across the yard towards them. 'Is my job, no?'

The woman ignored him and addressed Esme directly.

'I'm so sorry,' she said. 'Are you all right?'

'What the hell does he think he's doing?' said Esme, flexing her arm to test for damage. 'And I didn't just walk in, I knocked. And I called out. What's his problem?'

'I'm afraid Sergei only knows one strategy,' said the woman. She pushed her sunglasses up on to the top of her head to reveal ice-blue eyes. Her thick, expensively cut hair shone a glorious rich mahogany, a shade which Esme had yearned for as a teenager, in preference to what she saw as her own bland colouring. 'I've tried my best to train him but he seems utterly incapable of learning social graces.'

'So sack him.' Esme glared at the big man. He stared back, feet apart, arms hovering by his sides as though expecting her to rush him.

'Thank you, Sergei,' said the woman. 'That will be all.' He stayed put. A muscle twitched in his jaw. 'Well, off you go,' she said, flapping her hand at him. 'I hardly think this lady constitutes a threat of any sort, do you? Now away with you.'

Sergei scowled and retreated to one of the outbuildings along the rear wall of the courtyard.

The woman turned back to Esme and smiled. Her teeth were intensely white and even, her mature face rather too smooth not to have encountered the surgeon's scalpel. The hair too probably benefited by colour enhancement. 'I'm so very sorry about that,' she said, holding out a hand jangling with bracelets. 'Rohesia Ashgrove. How can I help you?'

'Esme Quentin.' She winced as a pain shot down her arm.

'Oh dear. Did he hurt you?'

'He's not exactly the gentle touch is he?' she said, massaging her shoulder. She wondered about Neave and realised she was shaking. 'Is he like that with everybody who pauses to admire your house?' she said, looking around, half expecting to see Neave emerge from somewhere.

'I do apologise,' said Rohesia. 'Security is Edward's idea. We do seem to attract our fair share of interest. Especially being so close to a public right of way. He frets about trespassers, particularly at this time of year with tourists using the coast path.'

'And in what way, exactly, does he think we tourists are such a threat?'

'Oh, please don't take it personally. He once came across a group of people wandering in the grounds under the misapprehension we were open to the public. He resented both the presumption and the intrusion.' She made a resigned gesture with her hand. 'So now we have Sergei.'

As they walked back along the path towards the courtyard, Esme wondered if Rohesia Ashgrove's defence of her husband implied that she agreed with the need for Sergei's employment or whether she merely indulged him.

Esme paused to gaze up at the house. Its ornate chimneys loomed above, creating the illusion that they were tilting and about to fall. She looked at Rohesia. 'An impressive building like Kernworthy Manor will always attract interest,' she said, as they continued walking. 'I'm sure your husband values its heritage appeal.'

Rohesia lifted her chin. 'Edward also values his privacy.'

Esme smiled. 'Of course.'

They arrived back at the edge of the courtyard. A tantalizing glimpse of the garden beckoned through an archway in the wall.

'Oh, your garden looks delightful,' Esme said, peering through the arch to the lawns beyond. 'Quite a challenge to garden so close to the coast.'

'I'm afraid I can't take the credit for its creation. The garden was laid out in the mid nineteenth century.'

'It did used to be open to the public in days gone by, didn't it?'

'I believe so.' Rohesia glanced back at the house and seemed to come to a decision. 'Perhaps you'd like to have a short tour?'

'I'd love to, yes. If you're sure it's not inconvenient.'

Rohesia inclined her head and smiled. 'Not at all.'

But despite the confident words, Esme sensed unease as Rohesia gestured towards the arch. Unsurprising, perhaps, given Edward Ashgrove's attitude towards visitors. Maybe Rohesia feared Esme might make a formal complaint of Sergei's assault and hoped her offer might pour oil on troubled waters.

They emerged on to a sweeping lawn bordered with a high stone wall, the other side of which Esme had walked along earlier. To their left were several mature shrubs, some of which Esme recognised though many were unfamiliar. Specimen varieties probably, chosen for their rarity. The Ashgroves must employ a gardener to tend such an unusual range of plants. She wondered briefly if he or she was local. Perhaps they would have their own take on the background of the Ashgrove household.

'Rohesia is an unusual name,' said Esme, as they strolled along the path.

'Popular in the thirteenth century, I'm told. And the name of one of my ancestors.'

'Oh, so you've an interest in genealogy?' This sounded promising.

But Rohesia slid her sunglasses back in place and shook her

head. 'It's merely something I was told as a child and, I'm ashamed to say, is the limit of my knowledge.'

'What about your husband's family? I understand the Ashgroves have been here for many generations.'

'You obviously take a keen interest in history yourself, Ms Quentin.'

'Esme, please. Yes, I'm…' Something stopped her from revealing her professional role. 'Quite an enthusiast.' She paused. 'Actually, a friend of mine believes her ancestor was a servant here in the nineteenth century. She was planning to contact you.'

Rohesia inclined her head but offered nothing. Neither confirmation that Neave had visited nor encouragement that she'd be welcomed if she did so.

'I think she hoped you might have some information,' Esme prompted. 'Some estates keep their old records of former household staff.'

'I suppose previous occupants might have done. I'm not aware of any.'

The shrubbery parted to reveal the rear of the manor house, its elegant windows watching them as they sauntered along the edge of the lawn. Esme stopped and gazed up at the rear elevation. Was she expecting Neave's face to appear behind the glass of one of the windows, gesturing to Esme that she needed rescuing? Suddenly Esme felt the absurdity of her suspicions. She turned to Rohesia. 'I'm always curious about people who live in a house like Kernworthy Manor,' she said. 'Whether they do so willingly because they have a genuine love of history, or whether such responsibility is thrust upon them.'

Rohesia kept her gaze trained at the manor's stern walls. 'Do we have a choice? If history requires us to take on our liabilities, then so we must. We can't change history to suit us. We merely act upon the consequences of what's gone before.'

She stepped on to the lawn, pausing in the shade of a large camellia to indicate a ramshackle building in the corner. 'The old

116

summer house. Not that there's much of it left these days.'

Clearly once a centrepiece of the garden, the ruins of the summer house now sagged into the hedge behind. Evidence remained of its stone base but the rest was a tangle of ivy and blackthorn. They stood under the canopy of the trees and gazed at the pitiful structure now almost devoured by nature.

'To restore?' said Rohesia. 'Or allow it to die a graceful death?'

'Restore, surely?' Esme pictured William and Sarah stealing across the lawn to their rendezvous. 'It might have a part in the story of the manor.' But she couldn't read Rohesia's expression. Her eyes were hidden behind the veiled lenses of her sunglasses.

'Edward feels…' Rohesia stopped and gazed towards the house, as though she'd seen something.

Esme watched her, wondering at the hesitation. Had she been about to utter some indiscretion? Was she assessing whether they were being observed? The sun slipped behind a cloud and Esme shivered. Suddenly the shadow of the enigmatic Edward Ashgrove and his obsessive need for isolation felt uncomfortably close. She wrapped her arms around herself and turned back to the summer house.

Rohesia glanced round and smiled. 'Sorry, I've lost my train of thought.' She held out her arm. 'It's this way.'

They walked across the lawn and rejoined the path, crunching along the gravel towards the house where the garden swept around the side of the manor and merged into a laurel lined drive at the front.

'The gardens are quite extensive,' Esme said. 'I assume you don't tend them all yourself.'

'Goodness no. We have someone who comes from Exeter regularly.'

'You haven't found anyone locally?'

'Edward prefers it that way.'

Esme smiled to herself. Of course Edward would. She wondered why he chose to be so detached from those around him. She supposed it wasn't uncommon. And if she'd interpreted Rohesia's earlier remarks correctly, his inheritance of the estate and the responsibility which came with it had been foisted upon him. Perhaps it was resentment of that legacy which spawned his reclusive and fractious existence. Then why not sell and move on? As a distant relative, he didn't have the same connection as a child who'd grown up at the manor. Was there another reason which tied him to the estate? Had it been a condition of Eleanor Ashgrove's will, perhaps?

They continued down the drive to the end where a wide gated entrance met a narrow lane winding back inland. The same lane, she assumed, on to which she'd emerged from the bridle path and which served the courtyard and garages at the rear. She wondered if the main entrance was ever used. The gates showed no signs of having been opened for some while. She halted, and looked expectantly at Rohesia.

Rohesia gestured towards the thick foliage on the edge of the grass. 'There's a short cut to the cliff path through here,' she said, stepping ahead of her and disappearing amongst the bushes. Esme followed and was surprised when they emerged between two flanks of overgrown stone walling, directly above the cliff path.

'Amazing,' said Esme, drinking in the vision of Lundy Island on the distant horizon. 'What a spectacular view.'

Rohesia stood for a moment beside her, staring out to sea. 'Magnificent, isn't it?' she said. 'I couldn't imagine living anywhere else in the world.'

'Magnificent and treacherous,' said Esme. 'A woman fell from the cliffs near here last week.'

'Yes, I heard. Dreadful story.'

'You didn't see her along here that night, then?'

Rohesia shook her head. 'I only wish I had. I could have warned her of the dangers. Walking the cliffs in the dark is a fool's errand in any condition and I understand she'd been drinking.'

'You didn't know her?'

'Know her? Of course not.' She frowned. 'A strange question to ask.'

Esme flushed. She guessed the question hadn't sounded as nonchalant as she'd assumed. 'Well, there are so very few houses around here. If she was visiting…'

'Oh, of course. I see your point. But no. I didn't know her.' Rohesia held out her hand. 'Well, I must say goodbye. Good to meet you, Esme.'

'Likewise. And thank you for the tour.'

Rohesia smiled fleetingly. 'I'd be grateful if you didn't mention it to anyone. If word got around…'

'You'd have a queue of people on your doorstep. Don't worry. Your secret's safe with me. I appreciate your breaking the rules on my account.'

Rohesia inclined her head, then turned and walked away.

Esme stood for a moment from the elevated grassy bank, watching the white horses on the sea. Rohesia clearly adored living in such a beautiful location, but what other emotion was concealed behind her eyes? Loneliness? Frustration? Oppression? So Neave hadn't come to Kernworthy Manor after all. So where was she?

As she stepped to the edge of her vantage point, ready to clamber back down on to the cliff path, something made her turn and look back at the front façade of Kernworthy Manor. Suddenly the temperature of the warm sea breeze plummeted to a chill. Someone was watching her from the shadow of an upstairs window.

23

Esme's phone rang as she stepped off the coast path back on the road down to Warren Quay.

'Where on earth have you been?' she said, her words exploding when she saw Neave's name on the screen. 'No, hang on,' she added, when Neave's garbled reply became a series of burps and whistles. 'You're breaking up.' She climbed up on to the bank. 'Where are you now? I'll come to you.'

She disconnected and hurried down the hill. Neave was waiting at the bottom. When Esme rounded the corner she was talking to Ruth outside the hotel.

'Sounds like she's succeeded where the rest of us have failed,' said Ruth, smiling. 'I tell her she should be honoured.'

'I'm sorry?' said Esme.

'Got Mrs Ashgrove talking, she says.'

Esme turned to Neave. 'You met her?'

'Yes. Lovely lady. We had a really nice chat.'

'I'll leave you to it, then,' said Ruth. 'Must go and rustle up some dinner for the lads. They've started on some walling today. They'll be ravenous. See you later, Esme.'

'Yes, right,' said Esme blinking after her. 'OK.' She turned back to Neave. 'I came after you. And I met Rohesia Ashgrove. She said nothing about seeing you. I asked her.'

'Did you?'

'Yes, I did.' Esme glanced up. A coach party was streaming in front of the hotel on its way to the *Mary Ann*. 'Come on,' she said, steering Neave away. 'You can tell me what happened.' They made their way on to the rocky promontory which pushed out beyond the row of cottages into the sea and sat on the bench overlooking the harbour. The coach party joined the harbour teeming with visitors, occasionally stopping to admire the majesty of the tall ship, pointing and taking photographs.

'First things first,' said Esme. 'What did the police say about the photograph connection?'

Neave shook her head and looked down at her hands. 'I decided not to go in the end. They'd only think I was looking for excuses because I couldn't face the unpalatable truth. It's not uncommon, you know. I find it a lot at work. People in denial. It can be what tips them over the edge. I don't want to go there.'

Esme recalled the sergeant's comment about her own perspective as a family historian and found she didn't have the confidence to contradict Neave's assumptions.

'And then I suddenly thought,' Neave was saying, 'why not just go up there and ask? All this cloak and dagger stuff. Why make it more complicated than it really is? Anyway, I'm glad I did.'

'Did you meet the delightful Sergei?'

'No? Who's he?'

'Security. He's a bit keen.' She rubbed her shoulder.

'Oh no. Poor you. What happened?'

Esme shook her head. 'He grabbed me as I arrived, that's all. You obviously missed out on that pleasure.'

'I never saw him. I saw Rohesia in the front garden and stopped to speak to her.'

'So you didn't go up to the manor itself?'

'No, we went for a walk along the cliff path.'

'So why on earth didn't she say she'd seen you?' said Esme. 'She couldn't have misunderstood who I meant because I mentioned you were hoping to contact her and why. Odd that she didn't say anything?'

Neave shrugged. 'Perhaps she was just being discreet. She wouldn't know whether I minded people knowing my family history, would she?'

Esme sighed. Perhaps Neave was right. Rohesia didn't know Esme. Why should she share confidences about Neave's family history? And perhaps talking with Neave on the cliff path, rather than at the manor, was significant. Rohesia's caution might be coloured by her husband's bordering paranoia. Maybe once out of his sight she enjoyed a freedom she couldn't experience in his presence. There was only so far he could see from an upstairs window.

'You know, it's weird,' said Neave. 'But I found myself telling her all about Mum. Rohesia's obviously one of those people you meet sometimes, you know? Really genuine. You feel you've known them for years when you've only just met. A bit like Janice, my boss. I have a lot to thank Janice for. She picked me up off the floor and helped me find myself. She's the reason I'm here at all, finally uncovering the truth about my family.'

'So did you ask Rohesia about Sarah Baker?'

'Yes, I did. She was really interested.' Neave laid her hands palm down on her knees and leaned towards Esme, her eyes shining, as though about to impart something of great secrecy. 'And guess what? You won't believe it, honestly. Rohesia knows of someone who's already researched the Shaw family in Australia, so she's going to ask them for me. Isn't that just brilliant? She thinks there might even be a connection with the Ashgroves.'

'Yes, brilliant,' said Esme without enthusiasm. She was still trying to equate Rohesia's declared disinterest in family history to her with the excited picture she'd painted to Neave. But perhaps following Sarah Baker's trail and her connection with the Shaw family might be good for both Neave and Rohesia. With her husband being such a recluse, Rohesia might benefit from Neave's company. And if Rohesia was true to her word, links might be established with Neave's Australian family.

'I'm really grateful for you starting the ball rolling, Esme,' said Neave. 'And you must let me know what I owe you, by the way, for what you've done so far.'

Esme shook her head. 'No, there's nothing. I'd hardly really got started.' She hesitated. 'I guess you might uncover something which helps understand what happened to your mum?'

A shadow passed over Neave's face and she turned away, focusing towards the ship where a queue of visitors was forming beside the gangway. Esme cursed herself for bringing the subject back to Bella's death, when Neave's mood was so positive.

'I wonder whether we're making too much of things. I knew my mother, Esme. You didn't.' She looked round. Esme could see the pain in her eyes. 'Falling after drinking too much is a scenario which, sadly, fits all too well. I'd be kidding myself trying to see it any other way.' She pushed a tendril of hair off her face. 'Her letter implied things were going to be different. That she'd somehow stumbled upon...oh, I don't know...Shangri-La, the answer to everything.' She swallowed. 'I have to face up to the fact that it was the same old story. Another ruse to portray herself as something more than the damaged woman she'd become. That I've only ever known, despite my wanting it to be different.'

'But what about her laptop and the deleted files and e-mails?'

Neave shook her head. 'A virus maybe? Or maybe she deleted them herself?'

'Why, though?'

Neave stood up. 'Don't ask me to rationalise her behaviour, Esme. I never could while she was alive and I guess I'm not going to manage it now she's dead.' She held out her hand. 'Thanks for everything. I'm around for a couple more days so I'll fill you in if I learn anything. I know you'd be interested.'

'Yes, I would, thanks.'

She watched Neave head back into the hotel and tried to discern what was niggling her. That there were still unanswered questions which she'd now not get to solve, perhaps? She gave her head a shake. Well, that's the way it went sometimes. No point in dwelling on it.

She stood up and stretched. A walk along the shoreline perhaps? She hadn't been near the beach since she'd found Bella. Perhaps it was time to climb back on the horse.

She looped one strap of her rucksack over her shoulder and marched off the promontory on to the path down to the beach. Most of Warren Quay's visitors were heading for the ship so the slope down to the beach was almost deserted. At the bottom, where concrete and stone gave way to sand and boulders, she heard her name being called. She looked round to see Maddy waving at her from the top of the slope, her camera around her neck.

They wandered down to the water's edge as she filled Maddy in with Neave's news and decision to switch allegiance to Rohesia's promises to help with Neave's research. It was comforting to share a walk and conversation, distracting her from dwelling on the nightmare of her previous sortie along the sand. She was shocked when she worked out they were already half way through the ship's visit, which meant it was over two weeks since Bella's death.

'That's a shame,' said Maddy, turning back to take a shot of the *Mary Ann* across the beach. 'I'd tracked down the quote on that embroidery sampler, too. Do you think she'll be interested, still?'

'Didn't realise you'd been looking out for it,' said Esme, slipping off her trainers and tying the laces together.

'Thought it might be a clue. Behold, the daughter of innocence how beautiful is the mildness of her countenance. You feel it ought to be significant, don't you?'

'And is it?'

'Not that I can see. It's a line from some eighteenth-century publication extolling the virtues of womanhood. Or,' she added with a grimace, 'declaring what virtues and duties were expected of a woman of the times. Written by some guy called William Kenrick. A bit rich coming from him. Someone referred to him as the most despised, drunken and morally degenerate writer in late eighteenth-century London.'

Esme looped her trainers over her rucksack. 'Typical. Do as I say, not as I do.'

'*She frequenteth not the public haunts of men,* was one bit,' said Maddy. 'Ironic, given the ordeal awaiting Sarah when she arrived in Australia. Paraded on deck along with all the other women to be picked out by randy militia men or free settlers.'

'Picked out?'

'Sure. Better someone else feed and house them than at the government expense. And Sarah, poor kid, would have attracted a lot of attention as a young girl.'

Esme splashed along the edge of the sea, watching the water encircle her ankles. 'And a pretty one, too, to have caught William's eye.'

'Did you ever find what happened to William after he'd been banished to Scotland?' said Maddy, heaving her camera on to her shoulder.

'Don't know. I couldn't find any marriage or death record for him and he didn't show up on any censuses. So I don't think he stayed there.'

'He never came back to Devon, though, did he? Or his brother James wouldn't have got his hands on the pile. Perhaps he went to London to drown his sorrows and live the same debauched sort of life as our friend Mr Kenrick.'

'That's an idea,' said Esme. 'Maybe I'll take another look.'

'I thought you'd been sacked?' said Maddy.

'Oh, thanks for that. No need to rub it in.' Esme kicked out at a wave, spraying water up her leg. 'Doesn't mean I can't take a look for my own satisfaction, does it?'

*

Back at Breakers, Esme booted her laptop. She supposed she should let Grace know she didn't need to continue with the research for Declan Shaw. She checked her e-mails. There was one entitled *Re: Shaw Family Tree.* Well, no harm in reading it. She might as well pass it on to Neave anyway. The e-mail came from an enthusiastic Australian family history buff called Greg, a descendant of the Connor Shaw that Grace had mentioned.

Greg, it seemed, had spent a lifetime collating information on his great-great-great-grandfather. He confirmed that Connor Shaw had been transported for dissent and she shuddered when she read the name of the notorious ship on which he'd arrived from Dublin – the *Hercules*. Appalling conditions resulted in the death of many, convincing the Irish that the English had adopted a deadly policy against them, an accusation strongly denied by the authorities. Hatred and resentment of the English would continue to pervade the psyche of the Irish Australian even after the penal system was a long distant memory.

She replied to Greg, thanking him. As she sent the e-mail on its way, her laptop pinged to announce the arrival of another, from Grace. There was nothing about Declan Shaw this time, though. Only a puzzled message concerning a UK client of Grace's. 'It was weird,' wrote Grace. 'One minute she's pushing me to find this guy as a matter of urgency, e-mailing every day to find out how I'm doing and then not another thing.' Esme sympathised. There were always clients who proved to be more than a little eccentric. Everyone had them and had to deal with them as best they could. In this case, however, eccentricity had not been the issue. The client had died.

Esme browsed the rest of the message, wondering why Grace was telling her all the details. Until she got to the end of the e-mail. 'Strange thing is, though,' Grace wrote, 'it was near where you're staying. Do you know anything about it? Apparently she fell off a cliff.'

24

The time difference between the United Kingdom and Australia meant Esme had to wait until the following day for Grace's e-mail reply to confirm that her deceased client had indeed been Bella Shaw. Grace was more than willing to share her information, on the assumption that Bella's search was connected with Esme's own hunt for the Shaw family on Neave's behalf. Esme felt only a minor twinge of guilt for not admitting that Neave had since dispensed with her services.

Bella had commissioned Grace to track down a man called Ted Marsh, believing he lived in Australia. But Grace confessed to finding no evidence of him and had e-mailed Bella but received no reply. According to Grace's information, Ted Marsh's last known address, albeit many years ago, was in Exeter. Had Bella received that e-mail before she came to Devon? Had this been the reason for her trip? But why had she come here, to North Devon? Why not go directly to Exeter? Who was Ted Marsh and why was Bella looking for him? Other than assuming a family connection, Grace had no idea.

By the end of the afternoon, Neave had still not responded to the message Esme had left on her phone and Esme decided to go looking for her. She tidied up the contents of the archive box she was currently working on and headed across the field to the coast path and Warren Quay Hotel. But when she got there, the girl behind the bar said Neave had checked out.

Esme ambled along the path towards the harbour, debating what to do next. There was little she could do, she guessed, until Neave picked up her messages.

Visitors were thinning out along the quayside as it drew towards closing time at the *Mary Ann*. She picked up her step and headed towards the ship museum. Perhaps Maddy had seen Neave before she left Warren Quay.

A sign saying, 'Sorry, we're closed' hung on a thick rope across the gangway. Esme could see Felix on deck manoeuvring an exhibition stand into position. She unhooked the rope and called over to him as she came aboard.

'Hi, Esme,' he said, standing back from the display board. 'How you doing?'

'Good, thanks.' She looked at the display of the records of Devon's transported prisoners, collated by the county's archivists especially for the *Mary Ann*'s visit. 'You seem nicely busy. Always a queue on the quay whenever I look down this way.'

'Yeah, it's going well,' he said, nodding. 'Can't complain. After Maddy, are you?'

'Yes, is she around?'

'Below deck.' He nodded towards the captain's cabin. 'Grab yourself a coffee. I'll let her know you're here.'

As he strolled away Esme lingered at the display, her eye drawn to the line of mug shots of Victorian criminals, some in black and white, others in sepia. Old faces, young faces, a girl clutching a shawl around her shoulders, women with matted hair and torn clothes, men with dirty neckerchiefs. Some cradling a black board with their details chalked up in looped cursive script. Some perplexed, some resigned, some terrified. And in the final row, faces to haunt your dreams, archetypal images of the most hardened of criminals, leering back at her, scowling and defiant.

She shivered and turned away to cross the deck to the captain's cabin which, according to Maddy, had been set up to illustrate the disparity between the comfort levels of the ship's master and the cramped, squalid conditions of the prisoners. The cabin was spacious, large enough for a sizeable dining table, sideboards and shelves. The convicts' quarters, on the other hand, comprised of an area six feet square, shared between four prisoners. They were housed on the orlop deck – one deck above the bilge, where the stench of sewage and dead rats sloshing about in stale seawater permeated through the boards, inches from their faces as they slept.

The images of their faces, conjured up from the photographs she'd witnessed moments before, filled her thoughts as she reached the cabin and found the door closed. As she grasped the brass doorknob she hesitated when she heard raised voices from inside.

'Can't I trust you to do anything?' said a woman's voice, none too gently. Esme frowned at a familiarity she couldn't place. A deeper voice answered but it was muffled through the polished wood.

As she backed away, the door burst open and Giles Cooper stormed out of the cabin. He paused long enough to hurl a scowl of disdain at her before marching across the deck and off the ship.

Esme peered round the open door, faltering as she recognised the woman inside. Rohesia Ashgrove stood beside the table, her hand resting on the back of a dining chair.

'Rohesia,' said Esme, flinching as she spied Sergei in the corner. He stood feet apart and arms folded, appraising her.

'Hello Esme,' said Rohesia, standing up straight. If Rohesia was as surprised to see Esme as Esme was to see her, she didn't show it. Any brief agitation she'd shown to Cooper dissipated and she smiled. 'Are you looking for Neave?'

'I did want a word with her, actually...' Esme said, flicking another wary glance at Sergei.

Rohesia gave Sergei a brief nod of her head. He dropped his arms by his side and with a guarded glance at Esme, strode out on to the deck.

'She'll be along shortly,' said Rohesia, joining Esme outside.

'Sorry, I didn't mean to interrupt...' Esme began, her brain racing to work out the significance of Rohesia's presence.

'Nothing to interrupt. Giles and I were having a difference of opinion on some logistical matter, that's all. How are you enjoying your stay?'

'Er…very much, thank you.' She tried to remember what she'd told Rohesia when they'd met and wondered what Neave might have added since. 'Are you…?' She ground to a halt, not sure what she was about to ask. *What are you doing here,* sounded impertinent.

'Naturally, you wouldn't be aware that this is my venture.'

'Yours?' She shook her head. 'No, I didn't know. So you're the mysterious sponsor?'

'Hardly mysterious. Merely private.'

'Your husband prefers it that way,' said Esme, recalling the silhouette of Edward Ashgrove, watching her from an upstairs window. It explained why Rohesia didn't attend public events.

'What do you think of our project?'

'Impressive,' said Esme.

'It's been a life-long ambition of mine to tell the convict story,' continued Rohesia, as they wandered along the deck. 'Prisoners' stories usually end with their banishment. I wanted to look beyond their sentence. Reveal their fate once they stepped on board the transport ships. For good or evil.' They came to a halt by the wheel and Rohesia grasped it with one hand, dropping back her head to look upward into the melee of ropes and folded sails above. 'Isn't she beautiful?'

Esme followed Rohesia's gaze. 'Stunning,' she agreed, becoming dizzy as the far reaches of the masts swayed slightly with the harbour swell. 'I'm looking forward to seeing her in full sail again. What made you choose the *Mary Ann* as your replica? Was she built as a convict ship?'

'No ship was ever built specifically to transport convicts. Merchant ships were commissioned and fitted out for the purpose.' Rohesia's grip tightened on the wheel, her knuckles white. 'And with disastrous results in the early days. The abolition of slavery had forced slave transporters to look elsewhere for trade, you see. They were amongst the first to take on contracts to deliver the prisoners, bringing their atrocious practices with them.' She turned towards Esme. Her ice-blue eyes looked more intense today, darker and deeper. 'You'll have seen the leg irons displayed below?'

'Yes,' said Esme, grimacing as she recalled the shackles which bound the convicts' ankles. 'The prisoners weren't able move.'

'"At the risk of both legs being broken", to quote a horrified ship's visitor of the time,' said Rohesia. 'But to answer your other question, the *Mary Ann* transported many of our Devon convicts. Though not the young woman that you're interested in, I understand. Sarah Baker.'

'Yes, possibly Neave's ancestor. Neave said you knew someone who could help her find out more about her?'

'Yes, in fact,' Rohesia dropped her arm from the ship's wheel, her bracelets rattling. 'Neave has something rather exciting to tell you.'

'Oh?'

Rohesia laughed. 'Oh, I wouldn't dream of spoiling her surprise. Now if you'll excuse me, I must speak to Felix.' She waved a hand and walked away. Esme watched her heading for the hatch which accessed the lower decks, reflecting at what Rohesia was hinting. Neave had reached the end of her search.

The sound of her name being called broke her thoughts and she turned to see Neave hurrying across the boards towards her.

'You have some news, Rohesia tells me,' said Esme, going to meet her. 'Did you get my message?'

'Yes and I wanted to see you anyway,' said Neave, excitement clear in her voice. 'Rohesia's friend found the link between Sarah Baker and me.'

'That's great news, Neave. Tell me more.' She steered Neave to a bench, placed along the side of the ship for the benefit of museum visitors.

'Apparently,' began Neave. Her face was flushed and she couldn't sit still. 'Sarah Baker married another convict out in Australia, called Nathan Shaw.' She grinned and placed the flat of her hand against her chest. 'And I'm their descendant. Isn't that fab?'

'It's brilliant. Well done.'

Neave held out her hand and began counting on her fingers. 'Now, let me get this right. She was my great-great-great-great…grandmother.'

'So do you know any more about their story?'

Neave shook her head. 'Not all of it. But Rohesia says there's plenty of time. We're going up to London to the National Archives and see what else we can find out. I've never done anything like that before, it's really exciting. I can see now why you enjoy your job, Esme.'

'There's nothing quite like following a trail, I must admit. I thought you were due back at work, though?'

'Oh, we can fit it in before I have to go back.' She turned to Esme, her eyes bright. 'Look, thanks for everything, Esme, I appreciate it. And I mean it about that bill for what you've done.'

'Don't be silly, there's no charge. I've already said. But before you dash off…'

'Oh, sorry, yes. You wanted to talk to me, right?'

'Yes, you might be able to answer a question for me, now. Have you come across someone by the name of Ted Marsh?'

Neave frowned and shook her head. 'No, I don't think so. Should I have?'

'Well, your mum was looking for him. In Australia. Or at least she'd engaged my contact, Grace, to do so.'

'So did she find him?'

'No. Grace thinks he's still in the UK. Or was. Last known address, Exeter, apparently, about thirty years ago. I just wondered if his name had come up in what you've discovered. It might explain why your mum was searching for him. Perhaps he's also linked to your family.'

'Well, it hardly matters now, does it? I've found my Australian link and solved the photograph riddle. The man would be Nathan

Shaw, Sarah's husband.' She smiled and stood up. 'Don't worry, Esme. I can see you're really keen to know more, so I'll keep you in the loop, I promise. Now I'd better go and find Rohesia.'

Esme watched her hurry across the deck. She knew she should let it go. Neave had found what she wanted and, should she wish to take it further, might eventually make contact with her Australian family.

Esme got up and leant on the ship's side, staring back towards Warren Quay and the cliffs beyond, aware that something troubled her. Neave hadn't made clear how the information explained Bella's visit to North Devon. When Neave first arrived, she'd been adamant that Giles Cooper tell her the reason for Bella's appointment, yet now, she seemed no longer interested.

Esme knew that if it had been her own mother who'd died in such circumstances, she couldn't rest until every single question had been answered.

But Bella wasn't her mother. It was Neave's choice, not hers. She must respect Neave's decision, let it go and carry on with what she was here to do.

But would she be able to shelve her misgivings so easily? And, more significantly, should she?

25

Esme was scribbling notes on a large sheet of paper on the kitchen table when Maddy appeared at the door of Breakers later that evening, breathless from her run along the cliff path.

'You run all the way from Warren Quay?' said Esme, looking up.

'Yeah.' Maddy wiped her face with the towel around her shoulders and headed to the sink. 'I like to have a good work out when it's been manic on the ship. And today was definitely one of those days.' She poured herself a glass of water and drank it down in one before filling a second glass.

'What're you doing?' she said, coming across to peer over Esme's shoulder.

In the centre of the paper Esme had written BELLA SHAW. Around the outside edges she'd written the pieces of information they'd gleaned with lines and arrows where she saw some sort of connection. 'Bella Shaw (suspicious death);' Maddy read out aloud. 'Linked to Sarah Baker (photo) and Nathan Shaw; linked to Kernworthy House and to William Ashgrove; linked to Australia via Declan Shaw, Bella's husband, born Australia, murdered North Devon.'

'I'm trying to get my head round all these tentative links back to Bella. See whether I can find a pattern.'

'So you're not letting it go, then?'

'Let's just say I'm curious.'

'Or suspicious.'

Esme peered at her over the top of her glasses. Maddy avoided her gaze and pointed to the name Nathan. 'This the guy Neave reckons Sarah married?'

'Yes. I'm just checking it out.'

'So you don't believe her.'

'I'm not sure it's that, exactly.' Esme rubbed her finger along her scar, trying to work out why she had her doubts. 'From the moment I first met her, I sensed Rohesia was lonely. Neave seems to have taken to her and it just seems so very convenient that Rohesia's uncovered all the answers so readily.'

Maddy sat down on the edge of the bench. 'You think she's made it up just to please Neave?'

Esme gave Maddy a weak smile. 'Sounds silly when you put it like that. Perhaps I'm just miffed for losing the job.'

Maddy took another draught of water and wiped her mouth with the corner of her towel. 'No, I hear what you're saying. Perhaps Neave's the daughter she never had. The Ashgroves don't have any children, I take it?'

'None that I know of.'

Esme glanced at her watch and pushed her chart to one side. 'Grace has found someone whose research covers the Shaws and has asked them to forward anything relevant. It should be through by now.' She pulled her laptop towards her and booted up the machine. 'I suppose it doesn't really matter if she's just being kind. If it comes to light later that it's all wrong, she can pretend her friend took a wrong turn in the research. It happens.'

'And if she's not just being kind? What other motives could she have?'

Esme recalled Miss Hodge's bewildered face as she appeared to recall something about the young Edward. 'Perhaps she's trying to protect her husband.'

'From what?'

'Well, if knew *that*...' The laptop sounded out its readiness and Esme slipped her reading glasses back on and scrolled down the list of e-mails, stopping at one with the subject heading *Your Shaw family enquiry.*

'Here we are.' She clicked on the e-mail and scanned the preamble. 'This guy Greg is a descendant of Connor Shaw, an ancestor of Declan's, Grace believes.' There was a family tree attached and she opened the file, filling the screen with a network of names and dates.

'Hey, this could be it,' said Maddy, moving round to sit next to Esme. 'Shove up.'

'We might find a Marsh. That could be handy.'

'Let's see if there's a Sarah Baker here, first.'

'OK.' Esme gave thanks for the technological genius of the search facility, typed in Sarah Baker and pressed ENTER. No matches. She took out the name Sarah and tried again with just Baker. Five matches. She clicked on the first. Albert Baker. The remaining four were obvious. Albert's sister and his own three daughters. No Sarah Baker.

Esme slumped back in her seat and let out an exasperated sigh. 'There must be something which ties up, surely?' She snatched up her piece of paper and stared at it. 'Perhaps I've been on the wrong track all along and Rohesia's friend's right after all.' She screwed up the paper and lobbed it at the wastepaper bin. It missed and rolled under the table.

'Oh, don't give up yet,' said Maddy. 'We know there's a link. Otherwise, why the photograph?'

'Yeah but we don't know how tentative the link is. Could be cousins, second cousins, third cousins once removed...' She shrugged. 'Think how many branches of a family tree there are. Even only back as far as your great-grandparents gives you eight different lines. With brothers, sisters, cousins, aunts, uncles going off in all directions...'

'OK, OK. I get it. So where do we start looking?'

Esme rubbed her hand over her face and took a deep breath. 'Right. Start again. OK. We need to be a bit more systematic. Let's start at the beginning and follow the trail through the direct line, looking at the details of each one. See if we can see any patterns, common names, that sort of thing. Sometimes middle names suggest connections with other parts of the family. A mother's maiden name, for instance.'

She started at the head of the tree, Connor Shaw, Declan's great-great-great-grandfather, and brought him and his family into the centre of the screen. Connor and his wife Ellen had three children, the eldest a son called Nathan.

'Look. Nathan. The name Neave gave me.' She frowned. 'Hang on. If he married Sarah Baker, why didn't her name come up on the search?' She clicked on his name. 'Born 1835 in New South Wales. Married in Sydney in 1865 to…God.' She put her hand to her mouth. 'Well, what about that for a connection.'

'Where?' said Maddy, grabbing the laptop and rotating it towards her.

'There,' said Esme, pointing. 'Nathan didn't marry Sarah Baker at all. Declan Shaw's great-great-grandmother was Clara Ashgrove.'

'Ashgrove?' said Maddy, staring at the screen. She sat back and folded her arms. 'You were right. Everything Rohesia's told Neave is completely false.'

26

The revelation debunked their theory that Rohesia was keen to get closer to Neave. Otherwise, why not celebrate their family connection? It was possible that Rohesia's friend had got the facts wrong. In genealogy it was all too easy to go off course and find yourself tracking the wrong bloodline. Perhaps they should verify everything before they jumped to conclusions.

The anomalies disturbed Esme's sleep and she woke before dawn, exhausted. She lay in the darkness, aware of her quickening heartbeat, frustrated at the loss of sleep and her over-active brain.

As she lay there, she sensed that something other than her frantic mind had disturbed her. Was someone prowling about outside? She listened, her ears straining for the sound of movement but all she could hear was the sigh of the sea.

But the suspicion wouldn't go away. She threw back the duvet and scrambled out of bed, fumbling around for the torch she kept in the drawer underneath. She didn't turn it on but gripped it like a weapon as she groped her way to the window and pulled back a corner of the curtain.

Outside the shadows played tricks on her vision. Was that someone on the veranda? Or were the still inanimate shapes of the deckchairs on the veranda mutating into stirring beings in front of her eyes?

She pulled back from the window and gave her head a shake. No need to feed her susceptible imagination. Her rational brain was already wary without being bombarded with fears of fancy.

She let go of the curtain and turned away as a light flickered into the room. She stopped and glanced down at her torch, confused. Then she spun round and stared at the curtain, still swaying slightly. But there was only darkness. She stood, glued to the floor, her stomach pitching inside, her rationale hunting for an explanation for the source of the light other than the obvious terrifying one. Someone was out there. And at this early hour in the morning, it was no social call.

So what did they want? Was it just to shake her up? Well, they'd succeeded there. Perhaps she might persuade them to leave if they knew the police had been called.

She slid a few steps along the side of the bed to the shelf where the phone sat. She dropped the torch on the bed and picked up the handset. As she focused on the screen, she hesitated, an image of Collins's sceptic expression projecting on to it. If there was no intruder she would only compound her already tarnished reputation for rational appraisal.

She put down the phone and grabbed a sweatshirt from off the end of the bed, pulling it on over her pyjamas. Then she picked up the phone again and pressed the number nine three times, connecting and then disconnecting. With the phone in her left hand and the torch in her right, she slipped her feet into her trainers and moved towards the door.

Still clutching the phone, and cradling the torch in the crook of her left arm, she turned the key with her free hand, the click of the lock setting her teeth on edge. She waited for a count of five, hardly daring to breathe, before slowly turning the door handle and pulling the door open just enough to slip her toe in the gap.

With her left thumb hovering over the phone's redial button and the torch grasped in her right, she switched on the torch and kicked open the door.

'What the hell d'you think you're playing at?' she shouted, arching the torch's penetrating beam around the veranda and out into the field.

Nothing.

She slid a few tentative steps in front of the cabin, her back to the wall. Another sweep of the torch revealed nothing but dewy grass. She shuffled a bit further along, casting a wary look towards the end. Was he hiding round the corner, waiting?

She stood up straight, taking deep controlled breaths, bracing herself to take one last stride to get to the corner. She counted to three and lunged, thrusting the beam up and out to where she imagined his face to be.

But the space was empty.

She withdrew back on to the veranda and leant against the timber wall of the cabin, her breaths short and rapid, her heart thumping inside her chest. What now? She shot a sharp glance back towards the door. Had he taken the chance to slip inside while she was checking out the other side of the cabin? Her thumb stroked the redial button again.

She kept flat against the wall, waiting while her breathing returned to normal. Far below, the waves hissed back and forth against the rocks. In the colourless half-light her eyes focused on the hazy outline of the cliff edge and she saw a light hurrying down the hill towards the coast path. She watched it bobbing up and down, moving in the direction of Warren Quay until it disappeared around the headland.

She waited for several minutes, she wasn't sure how many, until she was sure it wasn't about to return. Only then did she feel able to go back inside.

27

She was too tense to go back to sleep. She switched on every light in the cabin and turned on the radio. But when music failed to calm her nerves she turned it off and made herself a pot of tea. Cradling her mug to stop her hands from shaking she ventured back out on to the veranda, peering nervously out into the halo of muted light from the hurricane lantern hanging under the roof canopy for signs of unwelcome visitors.

She lowered herself on to the damp canvas of the deckchair and sipped her tea as dawn crept in through the sea mist, sensing a change in the air. Summer was on the wane.

As weak sunlight broke through she felt confident enough to leave her seat and wander out into the field. A man was walking his dog along the coast path below. She stood and watched the pair as they made their way towards Warren Quay. The masts of the *Mary Ann,* reaching up through the cloud, turned her thoughts to Sarah Baker. And to William. And to Clara Ashgrove.

Convict ships didn't only transport prisoners, Felix had told them. They carried free passengers, too. Military men and those seeking a life of opportunity in the new colony. Members of the convicts' families sometimes chose to accompany their loved ones into the unknown. Had William Ashgrove travelled to Australia with Sarah? Is that why he'd never returned home?

She hurried back to the cabin and dressed quickly before descending the hill to the coast path and on to Warren Quay, an idea brewing in her head. Maddy had mentioned that the *Mary Ann* held facsimiles of the logs of transport ships in its archives. She knew the name of the ship on which Sarah had sailed to Australia. If William had travelled too, his name might have been recorded on a passenger list.

When she reached the ship she saw Felix immediately. He was leaning against the ship's rail, an enamel mug in his hand, gazing out across the harbour. He turned sharply at his name and looked at her as though she'd appeared to him in a dream.

'Esme,' he said, recovering himself and walking towards her. 'To what do I owe such an early visit?'

She clambered aboard and told him about her theory.

'Be my guest,' he said, waving an arm in the direction of the cabin. 'If the logbook exists for real, there'll be a copy in there.' He emptied what was left in his mug over the side and wiped his mouth with the back of his hand. 'Here, I'll show you the system.'

Esme followed him into the cabin, greeted by the scent of beeswax. A faded watercolour print of a tall, bleak building, depressingly reminiscent of Dartmoor prison, hung on the wall. She wandered across to look.

'The Female Factory in Parramatta, circa 1819,' said Felix.

'Factory?' said Esme, grimacing. 'Sounds ominous.'

'Where the rejects went. The mad, the bad, the old and the ugly. Not a place your young lady would've ended up.'

Esme recalled Maddy's comments about Sarah being paraded on deck and picked out by militia men or free settlers. 'I didn't realise until Maddy told me that the convicts weren't simply imprisoned when they arrived.'

Felix shook his head. 'Only the real hard cases. The rest were a source of free labour, issued with a Ticket of Leave and released into the custody of whoever had use of their services.'

Esme pulled a face. 'And in the case of the women, "services" would have covered a multitude of sins, I don't doubt.'

'Giving rise to the misconception that Australia's founding mothers were all whores.' Felix pulled out a hardbacked notebook from one of the highly polished shelves. 'What was the name of the ship your girl was on?'

'The *Henry Wellesley*,' said Esme, turning away from the grim picture. 'Sailed in 1837. July, I think. She was convicted at the

142

midsummer assizes.'

Felix opened the book and ran his finger down the page. 'She was lucky, then. She didn't have to wait so long. Some poor buggers languished for months in rotting hulks at Woolwich before being sent on their way.' He tapped his finger on the page. 'Here it is. Departed London 29th July 1837.' He returned to the bookshelves and selected a slim leather-bound book. 'From 1815 every transport ship had a surgeon on board. He acted as supervisor to the prisoners, as well as a medical officer. He's the guy who might have noted what you're after. Some logs don't add up to much but others are pretty comprehensive.' He handed the book to Esme. 'Have a shifty in there.'

'Thanks, Felix. Appreciate it.'

'You're welcome. Let me know if there's anything else. I'll leave you to it.'

Esme sat down at the polished walnut table and opened up the book. Surgeon Superintendent William Leyson, it seemed, had kept a medical journal from 2nd June 1837 until 3rd January 1838. She scanned the entries, looking for a mention of passengers. The first prisoners, thirty-one women from Newgate Prison with seven of their children, were admitted on board at Woolwich on 26th June, with further prisoners received from various prisons across England and Wales. Leyson had recorded the general health of the prisoners, how several were afflicted by seasickness and of their daily duties on board ship. But he mentioned no passengers and certainly no William Ashgrove. She let out a long sigh of disappointment and slumped back in her seat. Just a silly romantic idea, then.

Felix put his head round the door of the cabin. 'Any luck?'

She shook her head. 'Either there were no passengers on board or he didn't bother to record their names.'

'Where d'you say this William ended up after he was turfed out?'

'Scotland somewhere. Don't know where, exactly.'

'He might not have found out what happened to her straight away, then. She could have been long gone. He could have gotten on a later ship.' He pointed to the thin volume on the sideboard behind her he'd consulted earlier. 'Take a look in there. The ships are listed by arrival chronologically and the log books arranged in alphabetical order of ship name.'

Esme jumped up with renewed hope. 'Right, thanks. I will.'

She found the entry for the *Henry Wellesley* noting that the *Sir Charles Forbes* had arrived in Australia only three days afterwards, on Christmas Day 1837. It had sailed from Liverpool on 27th July 1837 to Dublin, from where it departed on 11th August with 150 female prisoners. She found the corresponding logbook and scanned it hungrily, hoping that this surgeon was as diligent as William Leyson on the *Henry Wellesley* in recording the passengers' names. But although the incidence of scurvy was reported, along with damning remarks concerning the Irish convicts, '*desponding, indolent and disposed to dirt*', there was no mention of passengers.

The *Neptune* was next, followed by another ship of the same name which this time helpfully listed the passengers. But, sadly, no William.

Esme rubbed her eyes and reached for the next log, determined to check every ship before she'd reject her theory.

The *Waterloo* followed. 224 male prisoners, twenty-nine soldiers, two officers, seven women and fourteen children embarked at Woolwich and Sheerness in late September 1837. Surgeon James Ellis noted that the travellers came from different parts of England, Ireland and – Esme sat up with interest – Scotland.

The journey was long and tedious, according to Mr Ellis, and numbered a total of 127 days. The long voyage had resulted in prisoners and their guard suffering with dysentery, inflammatory fever and scurvy.

And he'd recorded the ship's passengers. Lieutenant Hare, 51st regiment, Mr Hill, 50th regiment, 29 rank and file of the 51st regiment, accompanied by their wives and children and…one Mr. W Ashgrove.

*

By the time Maddy arrived for her shift, Esme had established through a convicts' database recommended by Felix that Sarah Baker had applied for an 'application to marry' one William Ashgrove, a free settler. She was then able to locate the birth record of Sarah and William's children. Jane, born 1838 and Clara, born 1841, who married Nathan Shaw.

'So that confirms the connection,' said Maddy, leaning against the cabin doorpost. 'There *is* a direct link from Sarah Baker to Declan Shaw and Rohesia's information was flawed. Well done, you.'

'Sarah and William's elder daughter, Jane, married a Joseph Harding,' said Esme consulting her notes. 'They had a daughter, Emily, born in 1861 in Australia. I also found William Ashgrove's death in 1874 but nothing else after that date.'

Maddy stood upright. 'We've come full circle then. Back to that photograph. So which girl was torn off? And why?'

Esme took off her reading glasses. 'Can't answer that one yet.'

'So should we tell Neave?' said Maddy tugging her bonnet on to her head.

'Not until we understand why Rohesia told her the wrong information. We don't know for certain it wasn't a genuine mistake.' She returned the books to the shelves and they went out on deck. 'I thought perhaps I'd try and track down Ted Marsh,' she said, watching the museum team prepare for opening time. She'd better thank Felix for his help and get out of their way before the punters arrived.

'Are you sure that's a good idea?' said Maddy.

'Why not? If we can find him, he might fill in the blanks. Then we've got something to go to Neave with.'

'I've been thinking a lot about Bella recently,' said Maddy. She

145

smoothed down the front of her apron. 'And now with the photograph coming back to haunt us…'

'What are you saying?'

Maddy turned to Esme, her face pale, emphasised by the contrast between the pink patches on her nose and cheekbones where the sun had caught her skin and the white lace ruffle around her bonnet. 'What if Declan Shaw's death wasn't a random killing? Say it had something to do with that photograph?'

A knot in Esme's insides tightened. 'What sort of something?'

'I don't know exactly but it *was* found on his body, don't forget.' Maddy paused while one of the crew members walked past. 'Say, years later,' she continued in a hushed voice, 'Bella learns something about his murder and comes to North Devon to check it out. Maybe the photo is some sort of proof.'

'Are you saying she found out who killed him and came here to confront him? And he pushes her off a cliff to shut her up?'

'Bit stupid, I admit, meeting him on a cliff. But we know she'd been drinking. Perhaps it made her cocky.'

Esme digested Maddy's hypothesis for a moment. 'It's certainly a convincing theory.'

'Yeah, isn't it,' said Maddy. 'You know what it also means, don't you?'

Esme looked out across the deck of the ship, her gaze falling on the display of the convict mug shots on the board opposite. Hardened, filthy faces, scarred and frightening.

'Yes,' she said, lifting an involuntary hand to her own scar and fingering it. 'Declan Shaw's killer is still out there.'

28

As feared, Ted Marsh had long gone from the address Grace had given her but Esme was encouraged by the telephone message from the current owner who put her in touch with the couple next door, Jim and Ciss Thornton. They'd lived in the street for many years and Ted would have been their neighbour. Esme explained that her search was family history linked and although a little mystified that they could be of any help, the Thorntons agreed to meet her.

Jim answered the door, a bulky man with short greying hair, an exacting parting on one side. 'I don't know how much more we can tell you, though,' he said, repeating his response to Esme's telephone call.

He showed her through to a pristine conservatory furnished with two wicker chairs and a matching sofa. 'As I mentioned on the phone, we've not seen hide nor hair of him since he moved away all those years ago.'

He gestured for Esme to take a seat and slid open the patio door to call to his wife who was in the garden. She was unpegging washing from a rotary line in the middle of a tiny lawn edged with red begonias and blue lobelia. 'History lady's here, Ciss.'

He shuffled across the room and lowered his stout frame into the creaking wicker chair opposite Esme's. 'He talked of keeping in touch, of course. But you know how things are. Always the best intentions.'

His wife, elfin-like in comparison to her husband, arrived from outside with a washing basket on her hip. 'Easy for you to make excuses for him,' she grumbled.

'Now, Ciss, he was a good neighbour to us.'

She dumped the basket on the glass-topped table in the centre

147

of the room. 'We've never had so much as a Christmas card,' she told Esme, snatching up a tea towel from the basket. She gave it a sharp flick before folding it up and laying it down on the table.

'It was a long time ago now, love. No need to get upset all over again.'

'I'm not getting upset. I'm just telling it like it is.'

'Ciss used to mother him a bit,' explained Jim. 'Even with our own kids to deal with – and they were handful enough – Ciss always found time to help the little fella out with cleaning, cooking and such. You can understand why she was upset when he never kept in touch.'

'He lived alone, then?' asked Esme.

'That's right,' said Jim. 'Few years younger than us. Bit like having a younger brother living next door, wasn't it, Ciss?'

Ciss took a shirt from the pile and shook it. 'So what you want with him then?' she said, with a pointed look at Esme. 'Something to do with family history, Jim tells me. I thought that was all about dead folk.'

Esme tried to give her a reassuring smile. 'Sometimes people like to trace living relatives too.'

'Well I can't see what help we can be. We aren't family. Anyway, it's got to be getting on for thirty years since Ted left.'

'Do you know why he moved?' said Esme.

'Something about his job, weren't it Jim?'

'Promotion, I think,' said Jim. 'Talked about going up in the world. He was in sales, I believe, if memory serves. You have to move around a lot if you're in that game, don't you?'

'But he never said where he was going?'

Ciss pulled out a skirt from the basket and held it up to inspect. 'Jim reckoned he might have gone to Australia.'

'Really? Why was that?' Could it be this that had prompted Bella to engage Grace?

'On account of his Aussie cousin,' said Jim.

'Oh, so he had relatives in Australia?' This was looking promising.

148

'I reckon so. Anyhow, his cousin used to look him up now and again.'

'Now and again?' scoffed Ciss, dropping the skirt on to the pile. 'Round there night and day in the weeks before he moved. Dragging him off to the pub and coming home after closing time, drunk as skunks.'

'He was a grown man, Ciss. Up to him what company he kept. The man was family, remember.'

'Well, he should have known better. And that's a fact.' She plonked the pile of folded washing into the emptied basket.

'So, was this cousin just visiting?' said Esme.

Jim shrugged. 'Suppose so. Then when Ted left, I thought as maybe he'd gone with him, like. Emigrated. You know, after we never heard nothing. Made sense to me.'

'I don't suppose you remember his name, by any chance?' she said, glancing at each of them.

Ciss picked up the basket. 'No good asking me. I kept well out of it.' She left the room, basket back on her hip.

Jim scratched his head. 'Not sure I ever knew his name. Only really met him the once. Shifty customer, though. I do remember that. Bit of a chip on his shoulder, Ted used to say.'

'About what?'

Jim shrugged. 'No idea. Ted never said and I s'pose I never asked.' For a moment he looked distraught as though he'd let her down.

She smiled. 'Don't worry. It's probably not relevant anyway. Look, I won't take up any more of your time. It was very kind of you to agree to see me.'

'Not at all. Sorry we've not been more help.'

'Oh, one last thing, though,' she said, as the thought occurred to her. 'Has anyone else ever contacted you asking about Ted?'

'No,' said Jim. 'You're the first...' He stopped abruptly. 'Hang on, though. There was that woman.'

Ciss appeared on the threshold with a duster in her hand.

149

'What woman?' she said, stepping into the room, clutching her duster to her. 'You never told me about no woman.'

Jim swivelled round and looked at his wife over his shoulder. 'She stopped Nick while he was out front, mowing, that time. You remember.'

Ciss scowled. 'When? You never said.'

'Yes I did.'

'No you never.'

'Who's Nick?' said Esme.

Ciss jerked a nod towards the adjoining house. 'Nick and Gillian live next door where Ted used to.' She prodded Jim on the shoulder. 'I don't remember a woman asking after Ted. When was this?'

'Oh, long time ago.'

'How long?' asked Esme.

Jim turned back to Esme and leant back in his chair. He sucked in a long breath through his teeth and rubbed his chin. 'Let me see. Our youngest was still in nappies, I'm pretty sure.'

'Well, no wonder I don't remember if it was that long,' said Ciss. She looked across at Esme. 'Susan was thirty last birthday, so if she was still a baby, it must have been just after Nick and Gillian moved in."

Jim nodded. 'That'd be about right. 'Bout a year after Ted left.'

'So what did Nick tell this woman?' asked Esme. 'D'you know?'

'Nothing. Well, how could he? He knew nothing about Ted. He sold it to the Phillips, see, and Nick bought it off the Phillips. One more down the line.'

'The Phillips got divorced,' said Ciss, with a sage nod. 'Only been married five minutes.'

'So this woman spoke to Nick...' prompted Esme.

'That's right. And Nick calls over to me. Knowing that we'd known Ted, see.'

'So you spoke to her?'

150

Jim shook his head. 'No, nothing like that. Nick came and asked me over the hedge. She stayed on the pavement.'

'Can you remember anything about her? Was she young? Old?'

'Youngish, I'd say. Can't really say I took that much notice, if I'm honest.'

'And you told Nick then that you thought Ted might have gone to Australia.'

'I suppose I might've. To be honest, I can't really remember.'

'That's OK,' said Esme. 'It was only a thought.' She stood up. 'Well, I'll leave you in peace. Thanks so much for your time. You've been a great help.'

'Have we?' Jim got to his feet. 'We don't seem to have been able to tell you much. But you're very welcome, all the same.'

Ciss was staring at the floor and chewing her bottom lip, deliberating. She gripped the back of the chair and flicked Esme a sheepish glance. 'You'll let us know when you find Ted, won't you?' she said. 'I know I was a bit sharp earlier but it'd be nice to get in touch again, if he's of a mind.'

'I'll certainly pass on your message, if I trace him.' Esme smiled. 'At least he knows where to find you.'

'Scottish,' said Jim.

Ciss shot her husband a weary frown. 'What are you on about, Jim?'

'The cousin. He had a Scottish name, I'm sure of it.' He rubbed his chin. 'Or was it Welsh? Hang on, I'll think of it in a minute. Now what was it?'

Ciss shook her head and gave Esme a conspiratorial smile.

'Hang on,' said Jim. 'It's coming back to me now. Lochlan. That was it.'

Esme felt her stomach flip. 'Lochlan?'

Jim tugged at his earlobe. 'Something like that, anyway.'

'It wouldn't be Declan, would it?' she said, daring to hope.

A broad grin stretched across Jim's face. 'That's it!' He turned to his wife. 'She's right, isn't she, Ciss. Remember? He was called Declan.'

29

'Declan's cousin?' said Maddy.

'Not so loud,' said Esme, scanning the ship's deck, half expecting Rohesia to appear, demanding to know why they were still discussing Declan Shaw's ancestry.

'It's OK,' said Maddy, tying a white apron around her waist. 'No one else's arrived yet.'

It was early and the *Mary Ann* was not yet open for business. Esme had snatched the opportunity to catch Maddy before the visitors arrived. With the morning's heavy sea mist threatening to dampen the day, the museum was likely to be an attractive alternative to sitting on the beach or cliff walking.

'So did you find a connection?' added Maddy.

'Not so far and I can't see how Ted Marsh and Declan could be cousins. Declan's mother's maiden name was Brannon and she only had brothers, so all their offspring were Brannon. On the Shaw side, although his father had a sister, she married a Donnelly. So no cousins called Marsh that I could see.'

'Why would he lie about it?'

'Maybe he wasn't talking first cousins. Perhaps he simply meant it figuratively, suggesting they were related in some way. Assuming that's true, we can't know how far back the chain goes.'

'God, that's a whole new ball game,' groaned Maddy. 'It could take you forever.'

'And we've no idea if it's even relevant.' She glanced at the quayside. Two of the museum staff were coming across the gangway. Felix greeted them and directed them to different parts of the ship. 'I'd better get out of your hair,' said Esme, taking a step towards the exit.

'And I'd better go and find out what I'm doing today,' said

Maddy. She turned towards Felix, stopping and grabbing Esme's arm. 'That woman who Jim Thornton said asked his neighbour about Ted Marsh? It couldn't be Bella, could it?'

Esme shrugged. 'If it'd been a few weeks ago, then, pretty odds on. But this was only about a year or so after Ted moved out. About 1983.'

Maddy frowned. 'If it *was* Bella, and she learnt that he might have emigrated, why did it take her almost thirty years to step up the search?'

'Perhaps she did search but got nowhere and this time decided to employ Grace. What I want to know is what prompted her to go looking again, now?'

'And, critically,' said Maddy, her eyebrows raised, 'did she find him?'

*

By the time Esme arrived back at the cabin the mist had morphed into light drizzle. Strands of wet hair clung to her face. She retreated indoors to dry off and fix herself a belated breakfast.

She poured herself a bowl of cornflakes, wondering what direction to take next while reminding herself she should give some attention to *Safe*'s archive boxes or she wouldn't finish what she'd come here to do. But if time was running out for cataloguing *Safe*'s documents, it was also running out for digging up anything to link the Shaw and Ashgrove connection with Bella's death. She considered looking further into the cousin theory between Declan and Ted Marsh but she wasn't convinced it would lead her to anything useful. Though how could she judge, without knowing? It was frustrating and exhausting to gather bits of disconnected information without understanding how it all fitted together.

As she munched her cereal, the word 'cousin' resonated with something in her head. Miss Hodge said that Eleanor Ashgrove had fallen in love with a cousin on her mother's side, and it was to his great-grandchild that she'd left the estate. But a cousin of her mother's wouldn't be called Ashgrove.

She downed the last spoonful of breakfast and dumped the bowl in the sink, before picking up the phone and dialling Phyllis Hodge's number. She would know Ashgrove's former name, she'd known him as a child.

As the telephone rang out she recalled a police inspector once pointing out to her that anyone could call themselves whatever name they liked, unless it was with deliberate intent to defraud. But Eleanor's beneficiary might have chosen to adopt the name Ashgrove in gratitude for his good fortune or it might have been a condition of her will, to continue the family name.

When Miss Hodge's phone went unanswered, she dropped the receiver back in its cradle in frustration. She'd have to try again later. But if there had been such conditions in the will, any change of name would surely have to be official and declared. And published in the London Gazette which, helpfully, was available to view online. She opened up her laptop and turned it on.

Eleanor Ashgrove died in 1982. She may have required Edward to make the change before her death. Esme chose the period 1980 to 1985 to cover a few years after her death. She typed ASHGROVE and DEED POLL into the search engine and then hit the button.

Only one entry came up on the screen, but with no details. She clicked on 'view document' and an image of the full page appeared.

Notice is hereby given that by Deed Poll dated 19th October 1982 and enrolled in the Supreme Court of Judicature…EDWARD ASHGROVE of Kernworthy Manor, Warren, Bideford, Devon, single and a British subject abandoned the name of Edward Marsh and assumed the name of Edward Ashgrove.

Edward Marsh. Ted Marsh. The Thorntons neighbour.

So, Ted Marsh hadn't emigrated to Australia after all but had become Edward Ashgrove, inheriting Eleanor Ashgrove's estate and moving to Kernworthy Manor. Strange that he'd never kept in touch with his old friends and neighbours when he'd moved less than fifty miles away. But perhaps not so surprising. Maybe he'd made a conscious decision to break from the ties of his old life, uncomfortable or even embarrassed by his change in circumstances. Perhaps it explained why he appeared to prefer a reclusive existence.

She noted, with a little unease, that the acting solicitor recorded on the entry was Giles Cooper, though perhaps that was only to be expected, given what Dan had said about the Ashgroves having used Cooper's firm for generations.

What was most disturbing, though, was the implication that Bella had succeeded in tracking down Ted Marsh.

Was it Kernworthy Manor where she'd carried on drinking late into the night after leaving the Warren Quay Hotel? So why hadn't Edward Ashgrove come forward? He must have known of Bella, even if he'd never met her. She was Declan's widow. And, according to the Thorntons, he and Declan had spent many hours socialising.

Yet Rohesia had denied knowing the woman who'd fallen from the cliff. Had she been covering for her husband? Or was she unaware of his true past?

And if he'd kept it from her, what exactly was he hiding?

30

Esme added a completed archive box to the others in Maddy's stacked out hallway while Maddy digested the news of the discovery of Ted Marsh. She picked up another and took it into the living room and dumped it on the table.

Maddy dropped down on to a chair at the table and stared blankly out of the window. 'So she found him, then,' she said.

'That's certainly the way it looks,' said Esme. 'Though we still don't know why she was looking for him. It has to be about more than a cosy family reunion.'

'I still say she uncovered something about Declan's murder,' said Maddy.

Esme leant her arms on the edge of the box. 'Or, if she'd not uncovered anything herself, she thought Ashgrove – or Ted Marsh, if you prefer – knew something about it.'

'She might even have thought Ashgrove killed him.'

'Unless it wasn't Ashgrove at all and the real killer got to her before she got to Ashgrove. It would explain why Rohesia knew nothing.'

'That could be explained by her being out that night,' said Maddy. 'He could have seen Bella and disposed of her before Rohesia got home.'

Esme rubbed her hand across her face. 'This speculation isn't really getting us anywhere, though, is it?'

Maddy rested an elbow on the table, her chin cupped in her hand. 'Ashgrove must know Bella brought me the photo to restore. Neave would have mentioned it to Rohesia. If he's innocent, he'll assume it was for genealogy research but if his hands are dirty…' She sat back in her chair and looked at Esme, her face dark. 'What d'you think he'll do?'

Esme flinched at the memory of her early morning intruder. Ashgrove would be well aware of her involvement from what Neave would have said.

'What about Eleanor Ashgrove's will?' said Maddy. 'Could that be the 'legal query' Bella saw Cooper about?'

'What did you have in mind?'

'I don't know. I was just thinking how it all links up. Ted Marsh being the beneficiary. Bella looking for him. Her Ashgrove connection via Declan. Perhaps there was a discrepancy over the bequest.' She gave Esme an apologetic smile. 'Sorry, just clutching at straws, I guess.'

'No, I had a similar thought. I even thought of getting hold of a copy to take a look.'

'D'you think we should?'

Esme shook her head and lifted the lid of the archive box. 'Not really practical. It would take at least two weeks, for a start,' she said, picking out a bundle of papers from inside. 'And even if we did, I'm not sure how it would help. I mean, what *is* the legal position on raising any discrepancy once a will had been through probate and approved? Besides, Miss Hodge has already confirmed that Ashgrove was…'

'What?'

Esme dropped the bundle of papers back in the box. 'That day I first met Miss Hodge, we were talking about Ashgrove when he was a child. She suddenly went quiet. She said she'd recalled something but couldn't remember what.'

'Something about Ashgrove as a kid?'

'I think so. She dismissed it as unimportant but for a moment it really bothered her.'

'Not likely to be something connected with a murder though, is it? That's hardly going to slip your mind.'

'Maybe she saw something and didn't realise the significance until what I said triggered something.'

'What'd you been talking about?'

'I'm trying to think.' Esme stared out of Maddy's window on to the tiny front lawn, revisiting the garden scene in her head. A woman passed with a pushchair, a child skipping alongside her. The girl's laughter broke through her muddled thoughts. 'A poem,' she said. 'She quoted a poem that Edward had written as a boy.'

'What about?'

'Something about cries for help being drowned out by the sea. It set me thinking about Bella at the time.'

Maddy wrinkled her nose. 'Must have been pretty obscure. D'you really think it could be that important?'

'If she's remembered what it was, I might be able to answer the question. Perhaps I'll call in and ask her.'

'That photograph of Sarah Baker's still bugging me,' said Maddy. 'Yes, I know it all ties up family-wise and everything, but what's the significance?'

Esme frowned. 'Eleanor Ashgrove was researching Sarah Baker.'

'Yes, you said. Why? D'you know?'

'I assumed as part of the history of the house and its inhabitants.'

'Except we now know that Sarah Baker married William, her father's elder brother and so would have been Eleanor's aunt.'

Esme nodded. 'Exactly. So perhaps there was another reason she was so interested in her, something connected to what we're trying to find out now.'

'You need to talk to Miss Hodge, Esme. I don't like the way things are getting entangled. Be a good idea to find out straight away.'

31

Anxiety grew in Esme as she got into her car and set off for Miss Hodge's cottage. She didn't want to cause unnecessary panic by saying too much, though she sensed it would take a lot to unnerve the sensible and down-to-earth Miss Hodge. She decided to use the story of Sarah and William's reunion in Australia as the excuse for calling in unannounced.

Coastal mist seeped up the valley, chilling the air as Esme got out of the car. As she walked up the lane towards Miss Hodge's cottage, she could see lights on in the windows and smoke curling from the chimney. Good. She was at home.

Esme arrived at the garden gate and opened it, the hinge protesting as it swung across the path. Something stirred in the dimness up the lane and she turned her head towards the sound, blinking in the diminishing light. What was it? An animal? Someone snooping about?

She gave herself a mental kick and marched on through the gateway. Her mind was playing tricks, the spectre of the weekend's unwelcome visitor still haunting her. It was probably a fox or a badger.

She approached the front door, glancing in the sitting room window as she walked by. A table lamp was alight and the cottage looked cosy and inviting. She lifted the doorknocker and gave it a gentle tap-tap. The door opened instantly, taking Esme by surprise.

'Oh, it's you, Esme,' said Miss Hodge, slapping her chest with the flat of her hand, as though relieved. She laughed. 'How nice. Come on in.' She stood back and held open the door.

Esme looked over her shoulder into the gloom across the lawn. 'Did you see someone outside?' she said. Perhaps the

159

shadow she'd seen a moment earlier wasn't so innocent after all.

'No, nothing like that, I'm sure. It was probably you opening the gate. My hearing's not as sharp as it used to be. I can't always make things out, you know.'

She gestured for Esme to sit in the low armchair by the fireplace. A fire smouldered in the hearth and the room smelt of woodsmoke.

'Bit of a chill this evening,' said Miss Hodge. She put a log on the fire, sending a crackle of sparks up the chimney. 'Autumn's just round the corner. You can sense it in the air.' She settled herself in the winged seat opposite Esme.

'I was passing,' said Esme. 'And I couldn't resist calling in to update you on my latest finds.' She told Miss Hodge about Sarah and William.

'Oh, how delightful,' said Miss Hodge, pressing her palms together. 'A happy ending to a tragic tale. And how clever of you to find out.'

'Not really,' said Esme. 'There's so much out there on the internet if you know where to look, thanks to people taking the time to post their findings online.'

'What a pity such information wasn't so easily available when Eleanor was looking.'

'But she'd have grown up knowing all about her own family history without the need for the internet, surely?'

'Oh, she did. Diaries, estate books, photograph albums. Quite a treasure trove. There's a copy of her family tree hanging on the wall over there behind the settle. Would you like to see it?' She pushed herself to her feet on the arms of the chair and Esme followed her to the other side of the room. A muted pool of light glowed in the narrow passageway between the back of the settle and the bathroom wall.

'It's always been in the cottage,' said Miss Hodge, indicating a large plain black frame surrounding a faded and yellowing chart hanging from a nail. 'Eleanor's old nanny used to live here, many years ago. I believe it was given to her.'

Esme stepped nearer for a closer look, though in the poor light it was difficult to read. What she did notice, though, was that the family tree spanned little more than a hundred years, dating from 1798 and finishing at Eleanor Ashgrove's birth in 1885. 'I expected it to go back further than that,' she said.

'That's the year Thomas Ashgrove was born, Eleanor's grandfather. And when his father acquired the land, I believe, and built the manor.'

'So the Ashgroves aren't one of those families traceable back to Doomsday times, then?'

'Apparently not. There was a story that Kernworthy was won in a game of cards but I expect that's just a myth. You know how stories grow.'

Miss Hodge retreated into the sitting room and back to her chair. Esme cast one last glance at the family tree and joined her, certain she'd noticed something important but keen to ask a question which was bothering her.

'So when she was researching Sarah and William's story, that wasn't as part of her own family history?'

'No, of course not. Well, she wouldn't have known, would she?'

'So what prompted her to find out about Sarah?'

'I assume she'd heard something of their story. As I told you, the scandal was well known and she was very keen to hear what became of her. So she engaged a genealogist to undertake the necessary research.'

'A genealogist? She was quite serious about it, then?'

'Oh, certainly. It's a pity she never found out what you did, my dear, or she would have been quite buoyed by it. As it was, she seemed quite distressed. I imagine she was disappointed that the researcher had – what's the expression you family historians use – hit a brick wall.'

'Do you think the genealogist may have uncovered something

which might add to what I've found out?'

'I very much doubt it, my dear. It must be thirty years past since Eleanor employed him. Long before genealogy was the popular pastime it is today and long before the World Wide Web. As you said yourself, information is available to researchers these days that wasn't accessible back then.'

'Even so, it would be interesting to compare notes. I don't suppose you remember who he was, by any chance?'

'Actually, I do. In fact, I know him quite well.' Miss Hodge pointed towards a bureau in the corner of the room. 'Pass me that address book on the top there, would you, dear? And I'll give you his address.'

Esme fetched over the slim leather bound volume and dug out a notebook and pen from her bag.

'Even if he has nothing new to tell you,' Miss Hodge added, as Esme scribbled down the details, 'he'll be intrigued to hear what you've since discovered, I'm sure. He always said there were a few missing pieces in his research.'

*

It was dark by the time Esme left the cottage and Miss Hodge lent her a torch to find her way back to her car. She strode down the lane, sweeping the beam around in front of her, creating large looming shadows which shrank back into the undergrowth as she walked.

Frustratingly, Miss Hodge had remembered nothing of the fleeting thought she'd had that day about the young Edward. She wasn't even sure it had been about Edward and said it could have been something she needed to tell Walter about mending the handrail by the stream. Esme had hoped that by asking the question, it might have prompted the same thought but nothing came to mind before Esme left.

She climbed into her car and sat in the driver's seat for a few moments. Perhaps there *was* nothing to remember and in a way, that was a relief. Better that Miss Hodge knew nothing which put her in harm's way.

But without any new information they were no closer to prising open the casket of unanswered questions. Perhaps the genealogist had unearthed something which would give them another lead.

She started the car and pulled out of her parking space, turning back towards the cottage to drop off Miss Hodge's torch at the gate as agreed. As she swung round, in the instant before her headlights lit up the lane, she saw a pinprick of light moving in the road alongside the cottage. She stopped the car and peered out into the beam of the car's headlamps, catching sight of a fleeting shadow ahead. Someone was hurrying up the hill.

It couldn't be Miss Hodge, surely. Esme still had her torch.

She shoved the car into gear and raced up the lane, halting beside the garden gate. She scrambled out of the car and stared up the hill but whoever it was had disappeared. The front door to the cottage stood open, spilling light across the path, but there was no sign of Miss Hodge. Esme slammed the car door and ran down the path. 'Hello?' she called, pushing at the door to open it wider. 'Miss Hodge?' She stood on the threshold and held her breath, listening. No answer.

She stepped inside the cottage. A languid wisp of smoke from the dying fire, subdued and silent in the grate, was the only sign of life. Crossing the room, her pulse pounding in her ears, she lifted the latch of the kitchen door and peered inside. The room was in darkness. She fumbled for the light switch, blinking as the harsh fluorescent strip flickered and clicked into life. The kitchen was empty.

She withdrew and tried the bathroom and the small ante-room beyond. No sign of Miss Hodge. She stood at the bottom of the stairs and stared up towards the only room left in the house she hadn't checked. It seemed inconceivable that Miss Hodge would go up to her bedroom, leaving the front door open and the fire unguarded, but she'd better check. She grabbed the banister rail and ran up the stairs, calling Miss Hodge's name as she unlatched the short oak door and looked in. A lamp burned on the bedside table, and the bedclothes had been pulled back as though Miss Hodge had been about to go to bed. But the old lady herself was not in the room.

Esme clattered back down the stairs. If Miss Hodge wasn't in the cottage, she had to be outside somewhere. She ran to fetch the torch from her car, turning it on and doing a sweep of the lane before hurrying back through the gate and into the garden. She stood on the edge of the path and waved the beam of light in an arc across the lawn, straining her ears against the gushing of the stream. Again, nothing.

She turned back to where Walter had been working the day they'd sat in the garden. Training the torch beam ahead of her, she followed the path down the side of the cottage, calling as she went, until she came to a flight of shallow steps cut into the bank. She stood on the first step and, lifting up the torch, aimed it at the rushing water.

And there in the stream, half submerged and motionless, lay Miss Hodge.

32

Esme rushed down the steps and waded into the water, discarding the torch on the bank. By the time she'd reached Miss Hodge, her eyes had adjusted to the dark. She tugged at the old lady's arm and managed to heave her upper body on to the lower step. To her relief, Miss Hodge groaned and retched. Esme put her arm around her shoulders and held her, until she'd recovered.

'Come on,' she said, helping Miss Hodge to her feet. 'Let's get you inside.'

*

Esme sat Miss Hodge beside the warm comfort of the Rayburn and fetched a blanket from the airing cupboard in the bathroom to wrap around her. She wanted to call an ambulance but Miss Hodge was adamant she didn't want a fuss.

'But you ought to be checked over,' argued Esme, drying herself off as best she could with the towel she'd plucked from the range's rail. 'You've had a shock.'

'My own silly fault. I knew that handrail was unsafe.'

Esme stopped towelling. 'There's nothing wrong with the handrail. Walter mended it, remember? He was working on it when I came that afternoon we sat in the garden.'

Miss Hodge looked confused. Esme pulled up a chair beside her and sat down. 'Tell me what happened?'

Miss Hodge pulled the blanket tighter around herself. 'I heard a noise. Like an animal in distress. I went out to see what it was. It seemed to be coming from the stream and I went down the steps for a closer look. The next thing I remember...' She looked at Esme with rheumy eyes. 'Well, the next thing I remember is you pulling me out of the water. Thank goodness you came back,

Esme, or I could have lain there all night. Did you forget something?'

Should she mention the person she saw running away? Should she let Miss Hodge think it was an accident? 'I came to drop off the torch, don't you remember? And I saw your front door was open.' She began to peel off her socks to dry her feet. Her trainers would have to stay wet.

'What is it, Esme?' said Miss Hodge. 'Something's bothering you.'

'You are, for a start,' said Esme, deflecting her question. 'I'm still not sure I shouldn't veto you and phone for an ambulance.'

'What you asked me earlier, about me recalling something about young Edward. It's bothering you, isn't it? You think it's important.'

Esme jumped up. 'What am I thinking of? I ought to be making you a cup of something hot to warm you up.' She turned round and snatched up the kettle from the hob. As she took it over to the sink Miss Hodge stood up.

'Where are you going?' said Esme, spinning round.

'To get into some dry clothes,' said Miss Hodge. 'And I'll see what I can find for you, too. Or you'll catch your death, wandering around in bare feet and wet jeans.' She shuffled out of the kitchen.

As the kettle boiled, Esme stood by the sink and stared out of the window into the blackness. She shivered, partly from the clammy dampness of her clothes, but mainly from the realisation that if she'd not seen that pinprick of light, she might have left the torch by the gate as they'd agreed and gone on her way. Thank God she'd sat in her car, contemplating matters. Whoever it was must have assumed she'd driven off.

The kettle boiled and she made tea, searching around for a tray which she found beside the fridge. She put it on the kitchen table, pushing aside some opened post. Something on the letter heading caught her eye – the name Bradford, Harper & Co.

She stared down at the name, telling herself there was no

166

reason why Miss Hodge shouldn't have a letter from Bradford, Harper & Co. But Giles Cooper and his firm were cropping up far too regularly for comfort. Bella and her mysterious legal consultation. To Ted Marsh and his name change. To Ashgrove and the antagonism with Dan Ryder and his rent. And here he was again. What had Miss Hodge done to deserve his attention?

Before she could talk herself out of it she snatched up the letter and scanned the page. It was dated a week ago. It began in an ambiguous tone but by the time Esme had read it through, she was in no doubt. Miss Hodge was about to be evicted from her cottage.

Miss Hodge appeared at the kitchen doorway, a bundle of clothes in her hand. She glanced at the letter and at Esme.

'Sorry,' said Esme, dropping the letter back on the table. 'I didn't mean to pry. I saw who it was from. I've come across him a few times since I've been here and he strikes me as someone to avoid at all costs.'

'He's a bully,' said Miss Hodge, in a matter-of-fact way. 'But I've met bullies before. I know how to deal with them.'

'This isn't an eight year old kid being horrible to a classmate,' said Esme, failing to keep the alarm from her voice.

Miss Hodge sat down next to the Rayburn. 'You can't really think he's got something to do with what's happened tonight?'

'It's possible.' Miss Hodge pressed her lips together and stared at the floor, her brow drawn together. 'Cooper is Edward Ashgrove's solicitor,' added Esme. 'If you know something from Edward's past which he thinks could cause him a problem...'

'Esme,' said Miss Hodge, an impatient tone creeping into her voice. 'What could I possibly know to make someone take such a risk? Tell me that.'

'If I knew, I would.' Esme stabbed her finger up and down on the letter. 'But I don't like this. And I'm worried your little episode out there was no coincidence. Someone was poking about earlier. I saw them. So what did they want?'

Miss Hodge shook her head. 'Come on. Get out of those wet things.' She thrust the clothes at Esme. 'Not the most flattering, but they'll do well enough until you get home.'

'Thank you,' said Esme. She took the clothes, a floral skirt and something reminiscent of navy-blue PE knickers from her school days, and appraised the elderly teacher. Miss Hodge might well be a strong-minded woman with many years experience of dealing with life's problems, but it didn't make her any less vulnerable. 'What if he tries again?' she said. 'Have you got somewhere you could go for a while?'

'I'm not running away, my dear. Fear is what a bully thrives on.'

'Not running. Just moving out of harm's way.'

Miss Hodge said nothing. Esme waited for her answer, rubbing the tip of her index finger along her scar until she realised what she was doing. She flushed and shoved her hand in her pocket.

'I sense you have some insight into a situation like this, Esme,' said Miss Hodge.

Esme glanced away. Admitting that her slashed cheek was the price of knowing more than was good for her would certainly endorse her argument. But she had no intention of referring to the episode. She'd survived. Tim hadn't. It wasn't a subject she was prepared to discuss.

She pushed the memories from her mind and cleared her throat. 'All I'm saying is, it could be more serious than you appreciate.' She looked up. 'Is it worth the risk?'

Miss Hodge inclined her head and nodded. 'All right,' she said, sighing. 'If you think it wise. I could perhaps visit my sister for a week or so.'

Esme smiled. 'Good. Thank you.'

'Now,' said Miss Hodge, nodding towards the clothes in Esme's hand. 'Your turn to take some advice from me. Get out of those wet things.'

33

Esme woke the following morning to another e-mail from Greg, the enthusiastic family historian who'd researched the Shaw family. He'd attached a copy of Nathan Shaw and Clara Ashgrove's wedding certificate, along with a grainy wedding photograph.

She pounced on the documents with an enlivened sense of hope. Did they hold some relevant and vital information? She opened the files and studied the screen images. The date of the wedding was 1865 and later, therefore, than the family scene Maddy had restored for Bella. In a time before white weddings, bridesmaids or group photographs were commonplace, the photograph depicted a typical mid-Victorian wedding portrait of the couple only; bride seated, groom standing beside his wife, both dressed in their best attire. According to the address on the mount, the photographer was located in the same vicinity as the church recorded on the marriage certificate, suggesting the newly weds had hurried round to the studio to mark the occasion a short time after the ceremony.

The certificate revealed little more than to confirm the merger of the Shaw and Ashgrove families, though she did notice that the fathers of neither bride nor groom had been witnesses. In fact, no Ashgrove was represented on the document and neither had a member of the Shaw family witnessed the union. Had they even attended the wedding?

Perhaps Clara's parents didn't approve of their future son-in-law. Given the dubious reputation of the Shaws, William and Sarah's concern at their daughter marrying into such a family was understandable. She pictured the scene, Nathan asking William for Clara's hand, William refusing, Clara accusing her parents of hypocrisy, given their own circumstances. And then the final rebellion. Clara abandoning her family for love. History repeating itself.

It would explain the defaced photograph, implying the missing daughter sliced from the image was Clara. So who had made the cut? Had the Ashgroves removed Clara from the family portrait? Or had it been Clara, severing herself from the Ashgroves? Given that the piece had been kept by the Shaw family, it suggested the latter. So why keep the part depicting the Ashgroves? Perhaps if it had been Nathan's doing, Clara may have retained the piece afterwards, secretly maybe, as one lasting connection with her family. And what of the missing piece? Had she kept that too? What had happened to it?

She wandered over to the window of the cabin and stared out. The mist from earlier in the week was back and hid the cliff edge precipice to the churning sea. Greg's information added an intriguing element to the nineteenth century part of the story but how could it possibly have any relevance to the tragic events of the twenty-first?

*

Esme showed Maddy the document and photograph over lunch at Warren Quay as they retreated from the damp of the picnic tables to the corner of the pub. She also told her about Miss Hodge's misadventure.

'Is she going to report it?' said Maddy.

'I might have persuaded her, had I got a decent look at the person I saw poking about but without anything more credible, she says they'll only put it down to an old lady taking a fall in the dark.' She rubbed her eyes and yawned. The late night was taking its toll.

'We could tackle Cooper,' said Maddy.

Esme shot her a look, her tired eyes opening wide suddenly. 'Tackle? What exactly are you suggesting?'

'Challenge him. Accuse him of bullying Miss Hodge. He won't expect us to know anything about it. It might freak him out enough for him to let slip something about the Ashgrove situation.'

'We don't know threatening Miss Hodge is connected to the Ashgrove situation.'

'How can you say that? He's their solicitor. *And* he lied to Neave about Bella's appointment.'

'I accept the logic,' said Esme, aware she'd used the same argument to persuade Miss Hodge to visit her sister. 'But if he can trot out a feasible explanation, we'll just look like idiots.'

A scowl crossed Maddy's face. She snatched up her sandwich and took a bite.

'I'm just being realistic, Maddy,' said Esme. 'And I certainly don't need to give him another excuse to come prowling around my place in the small hours, thank you very much.'

Maddy put her sandwich back on the plate and frowned at Esme. 'Your place? I thought it was Miss Hodge's we were talking about?'

'Yes, we were,' Esme stammered, censuring herself for letting the comment slip out and racking her brain for something feasible to deflect the conversation.

'But?' Maddy narrowed her eyes. 'There's something else.'

Esme shook her head. 'I woke early the other day and got a bit spooked, that's all,' she finished lamely. She picked up her drink and gazed out of the window. A toddler was sitting in a pushchair licking an ice cream, most of which was around his mouth and down the front of his T-shirt.

'So are you going to tell me?' said Maddy.

Esme replaced her glass on the table, lining it up on the beer mat. 'I woke up convinced someone was poking about outside the cabin. But I was just feeling jumpy after a lousy night. You know how it is. Half asleep. Think you hear sounds than you really didn't.'

'So what happened exactly?'

Esme shook her head. 'Forget it, Madds. If I tell you, it'll sound like more than it really was, honestly.'

'Tell me anyway.'

Esme sighed and gave her a summary of events.

'You should have phoned the police,' said Maddy, when she'd finished.

'And tell them what? That someone dared to go for a pre-dawn walk on the cliffs with a torch? They'd think I'm even battier than they do already. Besides, what evidence have I got that he had his sights on me? Night walks aren't exactly unheard of, you know. He could be a genuine rambler.'

'D'you believe that? Especially now, after what's happened to Miss Hodge.'

Esme shrugged. 'I don't know. Anyway, it's over with now. And he hasn't been back so more than likely, it was my overactive brain.' She recalled the light directed in through the window and shivered.

'Well, if it happens again, now we're getting closer...' began Maddy.

'If it happens again, I'll take it more seriously, won't I?'

She looked up as she heard Maddy's name called from the other side of the pub. Ruth was on the phone, gesturing at them to come over.

Maddy got up and hurried to the bar. Esme followed on behind.

'Yes, she's just here,' Ruth was saying into the telephone. 'I'll put her on.'

She handed the receiver to Maddy.

'What's going on?' Esme asked Ruth, as Maddy took the phone.

'It's her next door neighbour,' said Ruth. 'There's been a break-in at Maddy's house.'

34

They clambered aboard Maddy's camper and pulled out of the car park, passing a family walking down to the quay from the upper park, children with buckets and spades in hand. They flattened themselves against the grassy bank as the camper shot past.

'I hope this is just a coincidence,' Esme said, grabbing hold of the facia to steady herself as Maddy swung round the corner and on up the hill.

Maddy threw her a wary glance. 'Of course it is,' she said. 'There's been a spate of them lately. Bored kids during the school holidays, probably.'

Esme sensed Maddy was trying to convince herself as much as Esme.

*

Maddy's neighbour, Mrs Bristow, a round elderly woman wearing a quilt gilet and huge tartan slippers, stood outside Maddy's house talking to a uniformed police officer. Maddy ran on ahead and was in deep conversation with the constable by the time Esme caught up.

Mrs Bristow scooped up the ginger tom which was rubbing up against the officer's legs and accosted Esme as she reached the garden path.

'It was him what gave it away,' she said, stroking Ginger. 'He was peering at me from out the window of the front room. Well, I knew something was up. Maddy don't let them in there, see, when she's not there and I knew she was out.' She turned and nodded towards the front door. 'So I went and looked, and the door wasn't latched. Just pushed right open, didn't it.'

'Perhaps she just forgot to close it properly?' said Esme.

'No, dear. The sitting room door was open, too. And the curtains were closed. We've had one or two round here.'

'Yes, so Maddy said.'

With details taken and notes made, the police constable left. Esme stood in the hallway looking into the sitting room. There wasn't much to indicate an intruder, other than an upturned archive box on the floor, its contents spewed on to the carpet, the box on top, suggesting it had been knocked off the table rather than tipped out and rifled through.

'So what do the police reckon?' Esme asked as Maddy closed the front door.

Maddy shrugged. '£20 gone from the kitchen worktop and nothing else obvious disturbed apart from what you see. What do *you* think?'

'They obviously didn't think the computer worth nicking.' A sudden thought. 'What about your photographic gear?'

'With me, fortunately. Anyway, according to the copper, if it was kids, as seems likely, they're only interested in cash and small stuff they can slip in their pocket.'

'Does that mean they're not taking it any further?'

Maddy shook her head. 'No point. It's only cash that's missing. What are they gonna do?'

Esme looked down at the upended box spewed across the carpet. 'So we can clear this up, then?'

'I guess so.'

Esme knelt down and turned the box the right way up. 'Well, at least they haven't trashed your whole house,' she said, piling the papers back inside. 'That's something to be grateful for.' She picked up a long thick envelope with a partly torn flap hanging loose and vulnerable and put the envelope up to her nose, indulging in the musty scent of old paper. 'I just love the smell of these things. Is it addictive, d'you think?'

Maddy laughed. 'Oh, Esme. You've solved it. An old document junkie did it. Broke in, after a fix.'

'I confess, m'lord,' said Esme, grinning. 'It was me all along.' She glanced down at the envelope. 'So had you catalogued this box already?'

'Some of it's done. We'd better check it off as we go.' She grabbed a notepad and pen off the table and consulted a list. 'What have you got there?'

'*Notices of a public meeting,* according to what's scribbled on the front. Ring any bells?'

'Let's see.'

While Maddy scanned her notes, Esme studied the envelope, which was stuffed full, round and bulging and the end flap didn't close properly. She tipped it up and teased out the bundle of papers within, carefully opening them out and laying them flat. She read the notice out loud. '*The public is invited to a meeting, where our founder, Miss E Harding, will address the audience on...*' Esme turned to Maddy. 'Harding? Where have I seen that name before?'

'Dan would've mentioned it,' said Maddy. 'It was his great-great-grandmother Emily Harding who set up the charity.'

'No, I've read it recently somewhere else. Harding. Where did I see it?' An image flashed into her head and she turned to Maddy in excitement. 'It was on William and Sarah's family tree.'

'Was it?'

'Yes,' said Esme, going over to her bag and pulling out her laptop. She opened up the machine and switched it on. 'William and Sarah's daughter Jane married a Joseph Harding and had a daughter, Emily. Emily Harding. Remember?'

'In Australia?'

'Yes.'

Maddy stopped what she was doing and frowned at Esme. 'You think Dan's Emily Harding could be William and Sarah's granddaughter? Meaning Dan's related to the Ashgroves?'

'It's possible.' She examined the idea, her brain grasping at the potential implications.

Maddy pulled at a strand of hair. 'That would mean that the

family – or one of them at least – came back to England. How likely's that?'

'A pretty rare event, I grant you. But not impossible.' She knew that few convicts returned home after being issued their Freedom Certificate, the document officially declaring completion of their sentence. The unaffordable cost of the return voyage was one reason. But many prisoners had made a new life for themselves in the colony by the end of their sentence, particularly if they had a trade to offer the number of growing free settlers. Painful memories of the poverty which may have played a part in driving them to the crime for which they'd been transported would have tempered their desire to return to their homeland. Why return to such unfavourable conditions when the colony offered those prepared to work hard an opportunity to make something of themselves?

Maddy came over and balanced on the arm of the sofa. 'But even less likely in Emily's case, surely? It's not as though she'd have a yearning to come home. You said she was born in Australia.'

'Yes she was.' Emily was born a 'currency' child, one of the new generation of Australians in their emerging country. For her, returning to the United Kingdom wouldn't feel like a homecoming. So why had she come to Devon?

'Let's establish whether the Hardings did actually come here, first,' said Esme as the laptop rang out its signature tune of readiness. She peered at the screen and found the online census records for England and Wales.

The first true census of 1841 listed a name, place of residence, approximate age, occupation and a simple yes or no as to whether the person listed was born in the county of current residence. Every decade since, barring wartime, the census had collated additional information – the resident's relationship to the head of the household, place of birth, and whether married, unmarried or widowed. By 1901, religion, number of rooms and windows in the residence, even whether an individual was deaf, dumb, blind, imbecile, idiot or lunatic was noted.

'The photograph puts the family in Sydney in the late 1860s,' Esme said. 'So let's try 1871.' She typed both Harding and Ashgrove names into the search boxes, limiting the scope of possibilities by restricting residency to Devon. But the database revealed nothing which fitted either family.

'Try 81,' said Maddy.

Esme repeated the search, this time for 1881. The screen flickered and reset itself, showing a list of possible matches.

'Looks promising,' said Esme, pointing to the screen. 'Joseph Harding, head of household, wife Jane.' She clicked on the option to see an image of the original document, the page on which the enumerator, the official collecting the information, had painstakingly recorded the details of the family. 'There!' said Esme, turning to look at Maddy. 'Emily Harding, daughter, aged 16, a seamstress, born Australia. And look. On the line below. Sarah Ashgrove, aged 61, widow, mother-in-law, born Hartland, Devon.'

'Well that's it, then,' said Maddy. 'There's the proof. Dan's family and the Ashgroves are related.' She folded her arms. 'Do you think Dan knows?'

Esme shook her head. 'No reason why he should. Unless you catch the family history bug, most people's knowledge of their genealogy – assuming they know anything at all – only goes back as far as their great-grandparents at best. Emily Harding goes back four generations and she started the charity. As far as Dan's family are concerned, their history begins there. They could easily not know anything about what happened before.'

'Maybe Dan can chalk this up to his advantage,' laughed Maddy, standing up and stretching, 'and get his rent reduced. Especially as his side of the family were dealt such a poor hand compared with the Ashgroves left behind at the manor.'

Esme stared at the screen without focusing. 'So how the hell does this tie up with Bella's death and Declan's murder?'

Maddy dropped back down on to her chair, a dark shadow passing across her face.

'What's the matter?' said Esme.

'Something I just said. That William would have inherited the manor, if he hadn't been kicked out to end up in Australia.' Maddy hugged herself. 'You don't think this is about revenge, do you?'

35

Their trawl through the remaining *Safe* archive boxes took on a new significance, as they convinced themselves the answers to questions behind Declan's murder and Bella's tragedy must lie amongst the historical documents of the charity.

But despite a thorough search, they came up with nothing suggesting a toxic link between Dan's family and nineteenth-century events.

'Perhaps it doesn't go back that far,' said Maddy. 'Maybe this is about something more recent.'

'Then why the photograph?' said Esme, scouring her brain for a scenario which might fit the facts. 'That photograph links everyone. It shows Sarah Baker's connection with the Ashgroves, on account of her marrying William Ashgrove, and also with the Shaws, because their daughter married Nathan Shaw. Sarah's own granddaughter set up the charity, the charity rents Ashgrove land and Bella – a Shaw – was on her way to visit the Ashgroves. Full circle. It's just that I can't think what it could be about this story which would lead to Bella's death?'

'Esme,' said Maddy, resting on the box edge and looking at her. 'You do realise that this could all be explained away as a drunken accident, don't you? That she never made it to the Ashgroves, and that Ashgrove wasn't aware she was on her way.'

'So where does Declan Shaw's murder fit in then?'

'Don't know.'

'And what did she mean by I lied?'

'Don't know.'

'And what had she been to see Cooper about?'

'Don't know.'

Esme folded her arms and glowered down at the disobliging

179

documents. 'I'm not good with questions I can't answer.'

'You might have to get used to it,' said Maddy, dropping everything back in the box. 'Looks like we've drawn a blank.' She pulled Esme's laptop towards her and again studied the census page which Esme had found earlier.

'*Living on own means,*' Maddy read. 'Either William left Sarah well provided for or she came home to tap into the Ashgrove pot after he died. She might have done that.'

'It's possible, I suppose, though they're living in a fairly modest cottage.'

'Well, she's hardly likely to be invited to take up residence in the manor.'

'Maybe Sarah just wanted to see her own family again having lost William.'

Maddy picked up the lid from off the table and plonked it back on the box. 'Well, I guess there's nothing else we're likely to find now.'

Esme chewed the ball of her thumb. 'Is this everything *Safe* has, as far as records go?' she said, recalling something Maddy had said when she'd first arrived.

'Far as I know. No, hang on. Dan's mum said she'd catalogued some of the early stuff years ago, when they first took over from Dan's gran.'

'So where's that?'

'Not at Kernworthy Farm, that's for sure,' said Maddy. 'You could check if the county holds anything.'

Esme turned back to her laptop and accessed The National Archives website which held an index listing all depositories across the country along with their contents. 'Yes, you're right,' she said, as a list of reference numbers appeared on the screen. 'There's a small collection in Barnstaple.' She grabbed her phone and stabbed in the number for the records office. 'I'll get Jack to dig it out. I can go and take a look this afternoon.

*

Jack was talking to a colleague when she arrived but he excused himself and led her across the room to a battered box file on one of the reading tables.

'Looking for anything particular?' he said.

'Won't know until I find it,' Esme told him, taking off her jacket and laying it across the back of the chair.

'Sounds intriguing.'

'Could be. On the other hand, could be wasting my time. We'll see.' She hesitated, the image of the upturned box in Maddy's front room suddenly coming to mind. 'Has anyone accessed these files recently?'

'Not that I know of. I can double check, though, if you like.'

'OK, thanks. I'd be interested to know.'

But Jack remained where he was, taking his glasses off and polishing them with the corner of his shirt.

She laid her hand on the box and gave him a quizzical look. 'Anything wrong?'

Jack slid his glasses back on his nose, glancing around before perching on the edge of the table. 'Have you spoken to Neave, recently?' he said in a low voice.

'Not for a while. Why?'

'You know I mentioned about...well, about her dad in the newspaper and everything.' He coloured.

'Yes, she told me.' Esme removed the dilapidated lid and peered inside. The box was about two-thirds full. A fair bit to get through before closing time. 'Don't worry. I'm sure she realised that you weren't being deliberately insensitive.' She took out the first item and peered at it. A newspaper cutting showing a grainy photograph of Dan's grandmother, according to the caption, at a local fund raising event.

'Are you? I hope so. I felt a right bloody idiot. I should never

181

have mentioned Vince.'

Esme looked up from the clipping. 'Is Vince the mortuary attendant? Neave said something about him having suspicions about her father's murder.'

He grimaced and closed his eyes. 'Oh don't go there, Esme. You don't need to know about Vince's ridiculous theories.'

'What sort of theories?' Jack looked wary. 'Go on. Humour me.'

He sighed and shook his head. 'Look, it's really nothing you could hang your hat on. He's always maintained that nothing fitted in the case, that's all. Take no notice. He's just a wannabe, Esme. His fifteen minutes of fame. I should have kept my mouth shut. Anyway, what I wanted to ask was, would you grovel for me, when you next see Neave?'

'I doubt I'll see her again, now. She's gone back home.'

'So this isn't connected then?' he said, glancing at the box.

'Just something I'm helping Maddy with,' she said. She nodded at the clock. 'And I'm a bit up against it.'

'Hey, sorry,' he said, bouncing up. 'I'll get out of your hair. Hope you find what you're looking for.'

'Yeah, me too.'

A summary sift through the items told her that the most recent item was 1958, the date of the newspaper cutting, which fitted with what they knew. 1958 was the year Dan's grandmother had taken over the running of the charity. Had there been any controversy about her taking the reins? Was there evidence of some sort of financial scandal amongst the files?

She dipped into the box again, slowly emptying it, scanning each bundle in turn and piling them on the table beside her. Accounts of monies raised in neatly typed lists, letters from supporters, copies of letters of thanks from the charity to said supporters for their patronage, letters of correspondence on organisational matters. But there was no mention of disagreements between sponsors, no slanderous comments,

182

nothing out of the ordinary at all. It was the same with all the newspaper reports. All very routine and predictable.

She let out a long sigh and took off her reading glasses to rub her eyes. Perhaps Jack was wrong. Maybe someone had been there before her and anything which raised dubious questions had already been removed.

She began returning the bundles to the box. As she lifted the first pile back in, she noticed the corner of a tiny envelope caught between one wall and the base. She pulled it free. With a flicker of excitement she saw it was addressed, in sloping looped handwriting, to Miss Emily Harding. She glanced at the clock. Just enough time for a quick peek.

Eagerly she slipped out the flimsy sheet of paper and read it.

Dear Miss Harding,

I write to express my gratitude for your understanding in the matter we discussed Wednesday last regarding your charitable institution.

I have today commissioned that the appropriate legal minutiae be put in place to ensure my continued pecuniary support so long as our agreement of confidentiality stands.

I remain, yours,
James Ashgrove Esquire

The cursive script blurred in front of her eyes. James Ashgrove. William Ashgrove's brother and Eleanor's father, was a sponsor to Emily's charity? But why did he want the fact to remain secret? Modesty?

She hastily piled the bundles back in the box. It was time she tracked down the genealogist that Eleanor Ashgrove had employed. There must be some light he could throw on the story.

36

Morris Beveridge lived in a row of Edwardian villas in a quiet part of Bideford. Esme found a parking space a few yards away and walked back along the street, turning into the long path to his front door. The lawn was neatly clipped and ended in a bustle of hydrangeas, now a fusion of mauve and pink blooms, enlivening what, for most of the year, would be a featureless green space.

A round white bell-push, helpfully embossed with the word 'press' in its centre, adorned the door frame. She duly obliged and heard its tones echo inside. But no one came to answer the door.

She lifted the letterbox and peered inside. Tessellated tiles of green-blue and terracotta stretched out down the hallway, bordered by closed panelled doors. She could see the corner of a buff envelope and a coloured circular lying on the mat. Did that mean he was away from home? She let the flap drop and stepped back, starting as she noticed a red-faced woman with a broom in her hand gaping at her from the path next door.

Esme forced a smile. 'Doesn't look like Morris is in,' she said, hoping the suggestion that she and Beveridge were on first name terms might yield some information. 'Any idea when he'll be back?'

The neighbour rubbed her nose on the back of her hand. 'It's Friday, dear. Clovelly day.'

'Clovelly day?'

'That's right. Does them…what d'you call it? Talks for the visitors. Takes them all round the village telling them the history and wotnot.'

'A tour guide, you mean?'

'You got it, dear.' She started sweeping again. ''E won't be home fur a while yet. Not on Clovelly days. Busy time of the year.'

'Not to worry, I'll phone him later,' said Esme, heading back down the path. 'Thanks for your help.'

She hurried back to her car. It should be easy enough to track Beveridge down. Clovelly was a small village, after all. She started the car and turned it towards the unique tourist honey-pot.

*

Crowds were already building on Clovelly's main street. Esme hurried along the cobbles, darting between women teetering on inappropriate heels on their way down and those flushed and breathless on their way up.

At The New Inn, where the street narrowed, she stopped and peered down the hill. But she could see no tour group huddled together along the main route. Everyone was either coming or going. She turned right and took a side route around the back of the pub and down the narrow path which ran parallel with the main street. She emerged at the tiny chapel and looked around. A small queue of people stood waiting to enter the Fisherman's Cottage, set up to reflect a typical family home in the village in the 1930s, but no sign of Beveridge and his entourage. She continued along the alleyway past the museum and back on to the main street, turning right down the hill.

At The Look Out she paused and gazed down at the dramatic view of the harbour and the bay beyond. Immediately below where the cobbles circled underneath Temple Bar Cottage, the tail end of a crocodile of people told her she'd found him.

She zigzagged around the bend and tagged on the end, keeping to the back as the visitors slowed to a halt and shuffled up to hear Beveridge, flamboyantly dressed in a snugly fitting red waistcoat and matching bowtie, as he told the tragic tale of Kate Lyall, the eighteenth-century fisherman's wife sent mad with grief after witnessing her husband drown in the bay. Her cottage, reputed to be the oldest in Clovelly, had since been known as Crazy Kate's.

Beveridge completed the story and everyone moved down the

hill to reassemble in the harbour, massing beneath the lime kiln above the water where thick chains for securing boats to the shore lay across the tiny beach. When he'd completed his spiel and dismissed the group, Esme pushed through the crowd to introduce herself. Beveridge peered back at her coolly through thick, rimless lenses and she wondered if Miss Hodge's confidence in his potential collaboration had been misplaced.

But when she mention Miss Hodge's name, Beveridge's hard expression softened and she was able to explain fully her reasons for searching him out.

'I certainly remember the lady,' he said, wagging a fat finger at her. 'Though it was some considerable time ago now.'

'Of course I do realise that, but Miss Hodge said you'd said there'd been some missing pieces to your research and thought you'd welcome the opportunity to fill in a few gaps. For your own curiosity, if nothing else.'

He flushed and Esme suspected he was flattered by Miss Hodge's recommendation. 'Well, if Phyllis thinks I can help,' he said, tugging his waistcoat straight. 'I'll certainly do my best.'

They adjourned to the harbour and found a stone plinth at the base of the giant boulder wall where they could sit down. Esme gazed back towards the village at the slow mosaic of people spilling down the hill.

'What prompted Eleanor Ashgrove to search for Sarah Baker in the first place?' she said. That simple fact might explain so much.

Beveridge sat focused on the lifeboat house, broad hands gripping his knees. 'I wasn't made party to her personal reasons for the research. I'm not sure it would have been my place to ask.'

'Obviously you discovered that Sarah had married Eleanor's uncle, William Ashgrove, rightful heir to the Ashgrove estate before he disgraced himself.'

Beveridge turned his head and studied her. 'If you've established all that, then I'm not sure what else I can tell you, Mrs

Quentin.'

'You must have also found out that Eleanor's father, James, was *Safe*'s initial sponsor from the letter in the charity's archives. Do you know why he wanted his support to be a secret?'

Beveridge turned his gaze towards the lime kiln. 'Confidentiality is not uncommon in such matters.'

'There was more to it than that, though, wasn't there?'

He inclined his head. 'I suspect you may be right. And it may well have been to make amends for what had been done, without disgracing the family name.'

'Oh?' said Esme, catching her breath. 'Make amends for what?'

'It was when the family were desperate to rid themselves of Sarah and remove her from William's temptation.' Beveridge brushed away a fleck from his trousers.

'Go on.'

He turned to look at her, his eyes oversized through the lenses of his spectacles. 'Sarah Baker never took the watch she was accused of stealing. William's father perjured himself to secure a conviction, confident that Sarah would be transported for the crime.'

Maddy's words echoed in her head. You don't think this is about revenge, do you?

37

'*Behold, the daughter of innocence,*' said Esme, almost to herself.

'Pardon?'

She told Beveridge about the words on the embroidery sampler.

He pressed his palms together. 'Most prophetic,' he said, resting his fingers against his chin.

She thought again of the terrifying ordeal Sarah would have experienced after her conviction, exacerbated by the anger at being so accused. And such was her station in life; she would have no recourse against the destiny wrongfully inflicted upon her. Many would have felt a similar outrage at the punishment meted out for their minor crimes. Crimes often provoked by hunger and destitution at a time when half of England's population lived at subsistence level or below.

'How did you find out the truth?' she asked.

'From Sarah's great-great-granddaughter, Agnes.'

'This would be the granddaughter of Emily Harding, the woman who set up *Safe*?'

'Quite so. Word reached her that I was researching Sarah's story and she invited me to visit her. According to Agnes, Emily discovered her grandmother's pitiful story after Sarah's death and decided to set up the charity.'

'Did Emily know the part the Ashgrove family played in her grandmother's fate?'

Beveridge nodded. 'Emily went to see James and confronted him. At first he dismissed her accusations but it seems he subsequently discovered the truth because, as you have learnt, he became the foundation's foremost sponsor. His father was dead by then but his mother would have still been alive. Agnes assumed it was she who confirmed what Emily alleged.'

'Perhaps it was precisely because of his mother still being alive that James didn't wish his involvement to be known,' suggested Esme. 'It must have raised a few eyebrows when Sarah came back to Devon as an Ashgrove.'

'I'm sure it did, which was perhaps another reason why James didn't wish to declare publicly any association with Sarah's family. Emily, I understand, wanted to call the charity the Sarah Ashgrove Foundation but James wouldn't hear of it. Given the nature of the charity's aims, Emily added the word Enterprise to the name and agreed to it being known by its acronym, SAFE. Thereafter, the identity of both Sarah and James remained secret.'

Beveridge stood up. 'I'm afraid I'm due at the visitor's centre shortly.' He checked his watch. 'And your intervention has made me miss my lift. I must get away or I shall be late.' He held out his hand. 'Good to have met you, Mrs Quentin. Do remember me to Phyllis.'

Esme thanked him and watched him walk away along the edge of the harbour. But as she reflected on what she'd learnt, she realised there was something she'd forgotten to ask. She jumped up and climbed back up the cobbled street after him, weaving between the tourists streaming down the hill.

'One other thing,' she said, as she caught him up.

He turned round, startled, as a young lad in a baseball cap swerved between them, his mother calling after him not to run. Beveridge steadied himself against the wall alongside the path. 'I can't imagine what else I can tell you,' he told Esme.

She stepped out of the way of the throng piling down and joined him by the wall. 'What do you know about Clara?'

'Very little,' he said, when he'd recovered himself. 'My brief concerned the family who settled back in Devon, not those who'd stayed behind.'

'You must have learnt something about them?' said Esme, as they renewed their climb.

'There was some mention of an estrangement, but other than that…'

'That's right. There were no Ashgroves at Clara's wedding. I'm guessing William and Sarah didn't approve of Clara's choice of husband.'

They stood aside to allow a jumble of children to clatter past.

'I assume their objection was because of the Shaw's ruthless reputation,' said Esme, as they continued. 'Nathan's father, Connor Shaw, had been transported from Ireland for dissent and was involved in the 1804 uprising.'

'Oh, the families' dislike of one other would have been mutual.'

'Why?'

'As you'll know, many Irish families were evicted from their homes by English landlords. At that time the Ashgrove family owned a considerable amount of land in Ireland.'

Esme stopped. 'The Shaws lived on Ashgrove land?' she said, catching Beveridge's sleeve.

'And were driven out, yes.'

'*Liberty or death.*'

'I'm sorry?'

She explained about the photograph. 'To the Shaws, Nathan's marrying into the family of a hated absentee landlord was betraying his Irish roots. Perhaps Nathan wrote it to demonstrate his continued loyalty despite…' She realised Beveridge was frowning at her. 'What?'

'I don't recall seeing those words. Do you mean the photograph of Sarah, William and the two girls, taken around 1850?'

'You've seen it?'

'Yes. In Agnes's house, when I went to talk to her about Sarah and Emily.' He shook his head. 'But it was neatly framed on her sideboard.'

'And both girls were in the picture?'

'Yes. I know nothing of Clara being cut out.'

Beveridge pulled a large white handkerchief from his pocket and dabbed his forehead. 'Shall we take a breather for a moment? I forget how steep this hill is.'

'Yes, of course,' said Esme.

There was a bench a short way ahead and they sank down on it, grateful at the opportunity to rest. Beveridge leaned forward, resting his elbows on his knees. 'Interestingly, though,' he said. 'You've reminded me of something.'

'Have I?'

'This does throw some light on something Agnes once said which I didn't grasp at the time.'

'What did she say?' said Esme, trying not to sound over eager.

He scratched his head. 'I can't recall her exact words but it was something about a threat, that I do remember. I believe it was why the family returned to England.'

'A threat of what?' said Esme, shifting to the edge of the bench and swivelling round to face Beveridge.

'Oh, I got the distinct impression they'd been in fear of their lives. William was supposed to have said, *discretion is the better part of valour,* which I assume to mean they left Australia.'

Esme shook her head. 'They didn't come back to England until after William died.'

'Well then, perhaps I jumped to conclusions. I did ask for clarification but she wouldn't be drawn further. I think she was concerned she'd already said too much.'

Beveridge bundled his handkerchief back in his pocket and stood up. 'And now I really must go. I hope the information has been of some use to you, Mrs Quentin.'

Esme thanked him again and they parted. Beveridge hurried on ahead, leaving Esme on the bench, turning over everything in her mind.

And suddenly the meaning behind the message *Liberty or Death* made perfect sense. It wasn't, on this occasion, for its 'Irish against English' connotation, though that perhaps was the additional irony. It was a personal warning. *Liberty* was Nathan Shaw's demand for William to liberate Clara and allow her to marry him, and death was what would happen if he dared to stand in his way. *Discretion is the better part of valour.* William had no choice but to consent or risk harm to his family.

But while one chink of light appeared, the rest remained in darkness. What was its relevance to Bella's death and Declan's murder? Perhaps the complete photograph would explain. If it had been on Agnes's sideboard, maybe it had been passed down to Dan's family. Did they still have it?

She got to her feet and pulled out her phone from her bag, climbing up the path to get a signal. But there was no reply at Kernworthy Farm. She left a message for Dan and disconnected. She'd try again later.

She rejoined the path to the car park, looking up as she sensed someone watching her, expecting to see Beveridge at the top of the path, having remembered something else to tell her.

But it wasn't Beveridge. Hurrying up the lane was the retreating figure of Ashgrove's over zealous employee, Sergei.

38

Esme stood on the pub terrace at Warren Quay, scanning the pub's picnic tables for Maddy. A man in a Panama hat engrossed in a newspaper crossword seemed to be the only customer but the rush to lunch hadn't started yet. She spotted Maddy at the end of the path gazing out to sea, wisps of copper hair waving in the breeze, and hurried over.

'I was just thinking of poor Bella,' said Maddy, turning round as Esme reached her. She leant back against the wall. 'We haven't made much progress, have we?'

'I've learnt a bit more, though,' said Esme. 'I managed to pin down the genealogist Miss Hodges mentioned. Morris Beveridge.'

Maddy stood upright. 'And? What d'he say?'

'Let's sit down and I'll fill you in.'

They took the path on to the adjoining promontory of land and sat down on a bench overlooking the harbour. 'I almost bumped into someone else, too.' She told Maddy about seeing Sergei in the crowd.

'Do you think he was following you?'

Esme shrugged. 'Can't see what good that would do him. It could be coincidence?'

Maddy put her heels on the edge of the seat and hugged her knees. 'He could be your dawn visitor. Have you thought of that? Perhaps it means we're getting close.'

Esme wasn't sure if that was good or bad and decided not to dwell on it. Instead she relayed what she'd learnt from Beveridge.

Maddy pushed the strands of hair off her face and shook her head. 'So Sarah was set up? Poor kid. God, they must have been well desperate to get rid of her. Now, if it was Bella who'd stitched her up, the "I lied" confession would fit. But we can't pin that on her. There's a two hundred year gap.'

'I'd like to have a look at the photograph,' said Esme. 'The complete one that Agnes had. If it still exists. I'm hoping Dan's family might have inherited it. I've left a message to ask him.'

'But what could that possibly tell us that we don't already know from the one Bella gave me?'

'Not sure until we see it.'

'It's not likely to give us anything on the legal issue that Bella saw Cooper about.'

'Now we know there's a connection with Dan's family, I wonder whether it's got anything to do with this ongoing rent dispute. We know James Ashgrove was a principal sponsor of *Safe*, so maybe he set up some sort of legal agreement which isn't being honoured by Edward Ashgrove and he's trying to wriggle out of it?'

'Like a covenant?'

'Something like that. Though someone once told me covenants aren't as chipped in stone as I'd always understood.'

'In that case, it's hardly a motive for murder.'

'No, true. So perhaps I'm way off the mark, then.'

'You need to pick the brains of a good solicitor.' Maddy laughed. 'Like Giles Cooper, perhaps?'

Esme recalled Cooper's condescending expression as he swept past her on the ship the previous week and grimaced. 'I'll skip on that one, if you don't mind.'

Maddy checked her watch. 'Sorry, Esme but I'm gonna have to go. I'm due on the *Mary Ann*.' She stood up and tightened her hair in its knot. 'It's hopeless, this, isn't it? We're getting nowhere.'

'Well, we can't approach the police until we've got something concrete to tell them.' The image of Sergei's glare the split second before he hurried away loomed up in her psyche. 'And I suspect we're already treading on toes.'

'Are you saying you want out?'

Esme blinked. 'No, of course not. I'm just saying we don't

194

need to attract unnecessary attention, that's all.'

'Isn't it a bit late for that?' said Maddy, tying her sweatshirt around her waist. 'You can't make an omelette without breaking eggs.'

*

Esme wandered back towards the hotel, thinking over what Maddy had said. She was right. It might already be too late to keep a low profile. So what did that mean? Back off? Finish the cataloguing and scurry back home without getting to the truth? No one was pressuring them. Even Neave seemed content to believe her mother had let her drinking determine her fate. So who cared one way or the other?

Gulls screeched above her head. She stopped to watch as they circled the cliffs above. Impossible not to think of Bella. Impossible to block the distressing image of her lying injured and dying on those rocks. Impossible to escape the unanswered questions.

She turned round and gazed down to the harbour at the ship, its deck milling with visitors, reminding her that its stay would soon be over. Surely there was still time to get to the truth? There was Dan's family photograph to study and, despite Jack's attitude, she didn't think his brother-in-law's suspicions about Declan Shaw's murder should be dismissed so lightly.

She passed a family sitting on the grass tucking into a picnic and realised she was hungry. She called in at the bar for a cheese sandwich and took it outside.

Mr Panama hat was still absorbed in his crossword and although she slowed to pass the time of day he didn't look up. She carried on past and sat down at the furthest picnic table, her back to the pub and a view out to sea.

As she ate her lunch she mulled over everything they'd uncovered. They'd always imagined that by discovering the link they'd understand more but in the end, it had told them nothing.

There had to be something else.

The clattering of plates behind her broke her musings and she heard the barmaid's voice talking to a customer as she cleared the tables. Esme swallowed the last piece of sandwich and picked up her own plate to return it to the bar. As she stood up she heard the barmaid say, 'Thanks, Mr Ashgrove.'

She spun round. Panama man was Edward Ashgrove? She plonked down the plate and hurried over.

'Mr Ashgrove?' she said, halting on the other side of the table.

He looked up from his crossword and scowled at her with dark eyes, deeply set under a heavy brow. The downturn of his mouth suggested that smiling wasn't something with which his facial muscles were over familiar. Rohesia hadn't exaggerated when she explained how he craved solitude. His message couldn't be clearer if it had been tattooed on his forehead.

She refused to be intimidated and held out her hand. 'Pleased to meet you, Mr Ashgrove. My name's Esme Quentin. I'm a friend of Neave's. I met your wife the other day as I was walking the cliff path.'

'Indeed,' he grunted. He didn't take her hand and seemed taken aback by her bold approach, if not alarmed by it. Doubtless the locals gave him a wide berth.

He stood up and slipped his pen inside his jacket. He was well over six feet tall and Esme struggled to maintain eye contact as he loomed above her.

'As I told your wife, I'm interested in family history,' Esme pressed on. 'Did Neave tell you about her ancestor who worked at Kernworthy Manor in the nineteenth century? No doubt you're familiar with your house's history.'

'Kernworthy Manor is a private home,' he said, slipping his folded newspaper under his arm. 'Not a tourist curiosity.' And with a final glare of disdain, he turned and strode away.

Esme turned and walked back to collect her plate, swallowing her discomfort at so blatant a rebuff. Obnoxious individual. There

196

seemed little left of the small boy whom Miss Hodge so fondly remembered. If he did still write poetry, it was probably dark and melancholy, expressing repugnance towards his fellow man. Little Leonardo had clearly transformed into…

She stopped in mid-stride. Leonardo. Miss Hodge said they'd given him the nickname on account of his mirror writing. *Not uncommon in left handed people,* she'd said.

But Esme had just watched Ashgrove filling in his crossword. He was most definitely right handed. He couldn't be Miss Hodge's Little Leonardo. Which meant he wasn't Ted Marsh.

39

Maddy stood on her front garden path hugging a padded mailbag to her, brought to a halt by Esme's pronouncement. Esme waited, watching Maddy's face as the truth seeped into Maddy's consciousness.

'Edward Ashgrove isn't Ted Marsh?' said Maddy, her brow puckered.

'No. He can't be.' She nodded at the package in Maddy's hands. 'You're on your way somewhere. Shall we talk as we go?'

'What?' Maddy glanced down at the parcel as though she'd not noticed it before. 'Oh, yeah. I was off to the post.'

They tramped down the hill past the church and turned out into the street.

'God, just when we think we've got a handle on this…' Maddy shook her head. 'So if Ashgrove isn't Ted Marsh…' They stood on the edge of the pavement waiting to cross the road.

'He's someone claiming to be him, to inherit the Ashgrove Estate in his stead. '

'But…?' said Maddy. She threw Esme a sceptical look. 'Oh come on. There'd be checks. The executors of the will would…' Esme watched as realisation lit up on Maddy's face. 'Oh, I get it. Eleanor Ashgrove's executor was her solicitor.'

'Exactly. Giles Cooper.'

*

They wandered down to the post office in subdued silence. Esme left Maddy to her transaction and continued along the quay parallel to the park. She leant on the railings and looked out across the River Torridge to the Tarka trail cycle path on the opposite bank.

If Cooper was at the heart of the deception, and it seemed likely, given he had links with all the people involved, it would explain his intimidation of Miss Hodge. He must have come to realise she knew enough to expose both him and Ashgrove. But where did Bella fit in? What had she known, and how had she come by the information?

'So who is he, and why's he pretending to be Edward Ashgrove?' asked Maddy, when she arrived.

'Well, the second part's obvious, isn't it? Who wouldn't fancy coming into a legacy like that?'

'He had to have known before hand. You don't just walk in off the street one day on the off-chance that some old lady had popped her clogs that week and you're in with a chance of claiming to be her long lost whoever.'

'No, I agree. And Giles Cooper's got to have been a key player. The two of them must have cooked it up between them.'

Maddy hugged herself. 'And Cooper tried to dispose of poor old Phyllis Hodge because she knows Ashgrove's not who he is. But why now? He's been playing this part for years.'

'She'd only bumped into him recently. The real Ted Marsh would remember his childhood jaunts to the coast but his impostor wouldn't know anything about them, until Miss Hodge stopped for a chat and reminded him.'

'Blissfully unaware she'd made herself a target.'

'It must have dawned on her later that he didn't fit the profile,' said Esme, as she pictured Miss Hodge's face when she'd realised something was wrong but couldn't put her finger on what. 'Maybe she saw him swing a golf club.' She put her hand to her mouth. 'Your point about the timing is significant, though, Madds. She wasn't the only one who could have blown his cover. And maybe threatened to do so thirty years ago.'

'Declan,' said Maddy, catching on.

Esme nodded. 'Declan and Ted Marsh knew one another. Declan would know straight away he wasn't the real Ted.'

'So he had to go. And when Bella finds out years later, he has to silence her too.'

Esme realised she was shaking. She peered down at the rusty trawler moored close to the quay wall. The sound of grinding metal deep down in the boat's bowels set her teeth on edge.

'Why didn't she go to the police?' said Maddy. 'Wouldn't you, if you'd worked out who killed your husband?'

'Perhaps she did and they didn't believe her. Perhaps she turned up drunk and they put her accusations down to the ranting of a disturbed alcoholic.' She considered for a moment. 'Though if she had, you'd have thought they'd have taken more interest in her death.'

'It was thirty years ago,' said Maddy. 'Anyone involved in the case is probably retired by now. There'd be no one to put two and two together to go and check the files.' Esme felt a twinge of irritation that Neave hadn't done as she'd suggested and told the police about the photograph coincidence. It could have been enough to trigger a search.

'I wonder how she found out in the first place?' said Esme.

'She was Declan's wife. Perhaps he confided in her.'

'So why leave it so long to do anything about it?' Esme shook her head. 'No. Whatever she found out, she must have discovered long after his death.'

They resumed their walk towards the new road bridge which crossed the river Torridge a mile down river. 'Well, we'd better make sure we don't make the same mistake as Bella,' said Maddy after a while.

'What mistake?'

'Not going to the police.'

'And just what do you suggest we tell them?'

'What we've worked out.'

'But aren't we in the same situation as we ever were? We've no evidence to back up our theory.'

'Phyllis Hodge? She can say he's not Ted Marsh on account of

200

his not being left handed.'

'I'm not sure it's going to be as simple as that. Ashgrove will just say she's muddled him up with another child. It'll be her word against his.'

'But there'll be records, school stuff.'

'Not locally. He didn't attend the school, he only visited it. The point is, even if there were school records, what we've got so far isn't necessarily enough to convince the police to go looking. It's a vicious circle.'

They arrived at the end of the path. Shouts were coming from the skateboard park beyond the car park. 'And Ashgrove's had years to establish his credentials, don't forget,' Esme added, watching the skateboarders' antics. 'Any question to his legitimacy is going to need serious backup. Giles Cooper would have made sure all legalities will be cast-iron. He can't afford to expose his own position.'

'What about the Thorntons?' said Maddy, energised. 'They knew him. You could get them to intervene.'

Esme shook her head and sighed. 'I don't know. It's all too flimsy. I'm scared Ashgrove will just talk his way out of it, Maddy. We need more. I just wish I could think of what might do it.'

'What about the real Ted Marsh? He could point the finger. Didn't the Thorntons think he'd gone to Australia? He probably doesn't even know he's come into money.'

'But Grace has already tried to find him and failed. We don't need to go down another blind alley. We haven't got time.' They turned back the way they'd come, standing back to allow a mother and a twin buggy down the slope.

'Look, let's think this through,' said Esme, as they carried on walking. 'OK, so it looks like Ashgrove is not kosher and probably killed Declan who found him out and could have exposed him. Ditto Bella. But none of that tells us anything about the significance of the Sarah Baker and William Ashgrove connection, or the photograph that both Bella and Declan had on them when

201

they died.'

'Why does that matter? That'll come out once the police get involved.'

'It matters because it suggests there are still pieces missing from this puzzle. Pieces we need to blow the whole thing open. Without that, Ashgrove will just sweet talk his way out of it.' Half way along the quay her mobile rang out. 'Oh, I don't know,' she said, pulling her phone out of her bag with an exasperated sigh. 'It's hopeless. Hello?'

'Esme. Got your message,' said Dan.

'Dan! Hi.' She glanced at Maddy. Perhaps there was still a chance, after all. 'Do you know anything about the photograph I was talking about?' she said.

'Sure. But how come you know about it?'

'Look, can we come and see you? Now? There's something you need to know.'

40

'So what's all this about?' said Dan, as he showed them into the office. He followed them in and picked up a framed photograph from off the desk. 'I've got the photo you wanted to see. Looks pretty ordinary to me.'

'First thing's first,' said Maddy, plonking herself down on a stool beside the desk. 'Esme's got something to tell you.'

Dan gave Esme a bemused smile and dropped the picture back on the desk. 'Sounds ominous,' he said, folding his arms and propping himself against the edge of the office table.

Esme slipped her bag off her shoulder. 'You could say that,' she said, pulling up a chair. 'You might need to sit down.'

*

Dan's mouth dropped to a perfect O and stayed like it as she told him what they'd uncovered about his family history. At the end of her account he sat for a moment, his eyes fixed on her notes on the table.

'I knew about Emily Harding setting up the charity on account of her grandmother, of course,' he said eventually. 'But the rest...' He rubbed his chin. 'So the gran who inspired Emily was this Sarah Baker? And she was that girl you were looking into, who worked at the manor?'

'Yes. Convicted of theft in 1837 and transported to Australia.'

'Except that she didn't disappear without a trace,' said Maddy. 'Because William Ashgrove, heir to the estate and who has the hots for her, follows her to Aussie, marries her and they have a couple of little Ashgrove girls, Jane and Clara. Jane marries Joseph Harding and they have a daughter, Emily. Voila!'

'Awesome,' said Dan, shaking his head. 'Mum'll be blown away.'

Esme sat back in her chair. 'There's something else you should know, though.'

'Yeah?'

She tapped the end of her pen on the table top, unsure how to continue. Such devastating information wasn't easy to convey in a few short sentences. 'There's another link.' She glanced at Maddy for support. 'With Bella Shaw.'

Dan frowned. 'The woman who fell off the cliff? Neave's mother?'

Esme nodded.

'Whoa!' he said, peering at her. 'From the look on your face, I'm guessing I'm not gonna like the sound of this.'

'No,' said Maddy. 'You won't.'

Esme cleared her throat. 'Bella's late husband, Neave's father, was also related to Sarah Baker. His ancestor married Sarah Baker's other daughter. Which means, of course, that he was also a descendent of the Ashgroves.'

Dan continued to stare at her. 'Right.' Then he shook his head. 'No, sorry. I'm not really joining up the dots here.'

'It might help to look at the photo,' suggested Maddy.

Dan reached behind him for the photograph. Maddy got up and stood beside him, to name the people in the picture.

'So this isn't Emily Harding, then?' Dan said, pointing to Sarah. 'I've always assumed it was.'

'Two generations earlier, actually,' said Maddy. 'That's Sarah Baker.'

Dan scratched his head. 'One sepia photograph looks the same as another to me.'

'It's an easy mistake to make,' said Maddy. 'The changes in fashion are pretty subtle unless you know what you're looking for.' She pointed to the photo. 'That's William Ashgrove. And that's Jane and Clara. Clara's the daughter who married a Shaw.'

'Can I see?' said Esme. Dan handed her the photograph and she took it eagerly, hoping to see something important. But it remained the familiar scene as before, albeit with Clara back where she belonged, beside her parents and sister, Jane. She passed it to Maddy.

'So where does Neave's mother fit in?' said Dan.

'She had a piece of this photograph with her when she fell,' said Maddy.

'This one?'

'As did her husband, Declan Shaw, when he was murdered…'

'Murdered?'

'…in Barnstaple thirty odd years ago. We think there's a connection.'

Esme watched Dan's puzzled face as he struggled to assimilate the information. She guessed he'd never had such a confusing history lesson before.

'Can't say anything's leaping out at me,' said Maddy, handing the photograph back to Esme.

Esme shook her head. 'Me neither.' She looked at it again. 'Although…'

'Although?'

'I've seen her before somewhere,' said Esme, tapping her finger on Clara.

Maddy bent over for closer inspection. 'She does look a lot like her mother. Perhaps it's that.'

Esme studied the picture. 'Could be. Or that it's too familiar. I've looked at it often enough, even with Clara missing.'

'So, run this past me again,' said Dan. 'Neave's dad's done in, and years later Neave's mother turns up with this photo. Then what?'

Maddy slid on to the desk and swung her legs over the side. 'To cut a very long story short,' she said, 'we don't think Edward Ashgrove's who he says he is. We also suspect he's Declan Shaw's killer.'

Dan stood, blinking, his face blank. 'Christ.' He ran his hand across his face. 'So who's the guy up at the manor?'

'Oh God!' said Esme, her hand to her mouth. 'You've just triggered something.'

'You've seen it somewhere else?'

Esme shook her head. 'No, not *it*. I've seen *her*. I've seen Clara.'

'Where?'

'At Kernworthy Manor. On the desk in the study. Definitely. I saw it just before Sergei grabbed me.'

*

'Why would a picture of Clara Ashgrove be in Kernworthy Manor?' said Maddy, as she drove Esme back to Warren Quay. 'It makes no sense.'

'We haven't got this wrong, have we?' said Esme, her face burning. 'Tell me a good scenario of why Clara's photo is there, please.'

'It could have been there from before, when Eleanor Ashgrove was alive.'

'So why would she have a picture of Clara? The family were estranged.'

'But she got to the truth, didn't she? Agnes filled her in, remember?'

'So why not have a photo of the whole family group?' said Esme, the pitch of her voice indicating her increasing exasperation. 'Why only Clara? We're missing something.'

They fell silent. Esme needed a walk to clear her head. She must be able to come up with some sort of theory but her mind felt like a tangle of seaweed, coarse and knotted from being churned about in the surf.

Maddy stopped the camper in the upper car park. In the harbour below, the *Mary Ann* towered majestically into the late summer sky, its rigging swaying in the onshore breeze. 'You're brewing something,' she said, cutting the engine. 'What is it?'

'I keep thinking about something Jack said about his brother-in-law.'

206

'The mortuary attendant? I thought Jack reckoned he was a time waster.'

'Yes, but what if there really *was* something that didn't add up about Declan Shaw's murder? What if he really does know something important but no one's ever taken him seriously?'

Maddy rested her arms on the steering wheel. 'OK. Let's get him over and see what he's got to say.'

41

Jack stood on Maddy's doorstep, crane flies dive-bombing the porch light above. A podgy man with wispy hair and freckles skulked beside him.

'My brother-in-law, Vince Proctor,' said Jack, pushing his glasses on to the bridge of his nose with one finger.

Maddy stood back, inviting them into the hall.

'Thanks for coming,' said Esme, from the living room doorway.

Jack looked at her as though he thought she'd lost her mind. He'd taken some persuading when she'd phoned to ask to be put in touch with Vince. Jack had agreed on condition he tagged along. 'You'll need a crap-o-meter, Esme, believe me,' he'd told her.

Maddy gestured them into the living room. 'Take a seat,' she said, dropping on to the sofa. 'And let's get on with it. It's already late.'

'Yes, sorry about that,' said Vince, fiddling with the hem of his jacket. 'Jack said it was urgent but I had to be somewhere else earlier. I'm in Am-dram, you see, and we had an important rehearsal tonight...'

'They don't need your bloody life history,' said Jack, shoving his hands in his pockets. Vince flushed and Esme felt sorry for him. At the same time, his involvement in amateur dramatics should sound a warning bell. Perhaps the Declan Shaw story was all in his imagination after all, and their questions were about to expose him as the fantasist he was.

'How about you sit down, Vince,' she said, taking a seat next to Maddy. 'And then tell us your thoughts. Jack says there was something about Declan Shaw's murder that bothered you.'

'Jack doesn't believe me,' said Vince, casting a disparaging glance at his brother-in-law. 'But I know what I saw.'

Jack muttered something under his breath. He pulled out a chair from under the table and sat down.

'Now then, Vince,' said Esme, with an encouraging smile. 'You were the mortuary attendant, I understand.'

Vince nodded. He lowered himself on to the armchair, balancing awkwardly on the edge of the seat, and cleared his throat. 'People don't really understand our role,' he said, putting his palms together between his knees. 'Respect, that's what it's about. Respecting who the person once was. They were someone's loved one. Even the tramp off the street was once someone's son. Or daughter. Cos it's not just old men with a bottle in their hands, these days, is it? Young girls, old women. People don't stop to think.'

Esme could almost hear Maddy groaning inwardly. 'No, I'm sure they don't,' she said. 'Go on.'

He nodded. 'We have to do our best for them. And especially in those circumstances, when something dreadful's happened and their next of kin have to identify their body. They want to remember them fondly, don't they? Not dressed in any old ill-fitting garb. Smart, presentable.'

Jack got up from his chair with a sigh. Everyone looked up as he wandered over to the window and peered out of the uncurtained windows into the dimly lit street.

Esme turned back to Vince. 'Yes, I can understand that. So was there something about Declan Shaw...?'

'Well, it was all wrong, wasn't it? I could see that, straight away. It just didn't fit. Well, I just felt I'd let him down and that's a fact. But what could I do? You can only work with what you've got, can't you?'

He paused, looking at Esme intently. She sensed he was waiting for her to acknowledge what he'd said, show surprise, even shock. But she couldn't grasp his meaning. It was obvious why he'd found it hard convincing anyone to take him seriously.

'Is that it?' said Maddy. 'Is that the sum total of what you've been harbouring all these years?'

'Hang on,' said Esme, laying a hand on Maddy's arm as something began to register. 'What did you mean when you said you'd let him down. That you could only work with what you'd got?'

'Well, it's true, isn't it? Can't make a silk purse out of a sow's ear, can you? Stands to reason. But at the end of the day, what could I do? He was just a skinny little chap.'

'Skinny?' The significance of what he was saying oozed like sweet syrup through her brain. 'Are you saying his clothes didn't fit him?'

'Way, way too big,' said Vince, his excitement palpable now his audience had finally got the message. He wagged his finger. 'That leather jacket…'

'Leather jacket?' said Esme, jerking forward. 'What sort of leather jacket?'

'With tassels on. You know, cowboy style.' Vince shook his head. 'But it was never his. Never in a million years.'

'So whose jacket was it then?' asked Jack, in a bored voice from across the room.

'Oh, it was Declan Shaw's jacket, all right,' said Esme, recalling the photograph of Neave's parents on their wedding day. 'But it wasn't Declan Shaw wearing it.'

Jack's head shot round suddenly interested. 'So who was the poor bugger on the slab, then?'

42

Esme let Jack's words hang in the air, as though he'd asked a rhetorical question, even though Jim Thornton's words echoed in her head; *Ciss always found time to help the little fella out with cleaning, cooking and such.* Ted Marsh hadn't murdered Declan Shaw. It was the other way around.

They agreed that Vince should take his information to the police and Maddy ushered the two men out, Vince twittering on about his relief at being vindicated at last.

Jack grimaced at Esme. 'He'll be even more unbearable now,' he complained, under his breath. She smiled and gave him a sympathetic pat on the shoulder, recommending that he accompany Vince to act as translator, or the message might fail to reach its target once again.

Maddy closed the front door behind them, leaning back against it, anxiety clear in her eyes.

'It's Declan Shaw up at the manor, isn't it?' she said.

Esme nodded. 'It has to be.' She told Maddy about Jim Thornton's remarks about Ted Marsh being a small man. She shook her head. 'Stupid not to have thought of it before.'

'You were half way there, realising Ashgrove wasn't the real Ted Marsh.'

'Jack had told me before that Vince maintained something didn't fit. Jack had assumed, as anyone might, he meant that something didn't add up, not *literally* that something didn't fit.'

They wandered back into the sitting room. Esme rubbed her eyes, trying to ward off a headache which was rapidly building in the front of her head. 'I'd never have made the connection,' she said, 'if I hadn't known about him being left-handed and realising that Ashgrove wasn't.'

Maddy picked up the tabby kitten which had sneaked back into the sitting room now that the scary visitors had left. She buried her face in its fur. 'Thank God we didn't go to the police half-cocked, suggesting Declan had sussed a fraudulent Ted Marsh and been silenced for it. Sorry, Esme. You were right to hang fire.' She sat down on the floor in front of the fireplace. The kitten wriggled off her lap to find other games to play. 'That explains why you saw a picture of Clara at the manor. She's his direct ancestor. The Ashgrove who became a Shaw.'

'That photograph of the Shaws on their wedding day,' said Esme. 'You'll have a scan of it, won't you, from when you restored it for Neave?'

'Sure,' said Maddy, getting up and going over to the filing cabinet.

'Add a beard, a Panama hat and thirty years, and with luck, it'll confirm what we've worked out. And we'll need a copy to show the police.'

'What I don't get,' said Maddy, pulling open the drawer, 'is how Bella could make such a mistake. Even if he was wearing the same leather jacket as in that photo, surely she'd know the body wasn't Declan's...' Her jaw dropped and she stared at Esme.

Esme nodded. '*I lied.* Exactly.'

'But why would she?'

'Maybe she was in on the scam to start with but he ran out on her. Gwen told Neave that Bella was angry after he'd died. I didn't read anything into it because it's not an uncommon emotion after losing someone.'

'And she was stuck with it, then, wasn't she? It would look weird to suddenly change her mind and say it wasn't him after all. She could've put it down to stress, though, that she'd made a mistake?'

'How could she? She'd have to keep to her story, all the time waiting for him to get in touch. How long, I wonder, did it take for her to realise he'd double-crossed her?'

'God, what a mess.' Maddy turned back to the cabinet and began flicking through the files. 'Oh, what the hell have I done with that? I'll have to get it off the PC.' She banged the drawer closed. 'How did she find him, d'you think?' she said, switching on the computer.

Esme shrugged. 'I don't know. Perhaps she was looking for Ted Marsh because she assumed he'd be using that name.'

'Which suggests she knew about how Ted Marsh fitted in.'

Maddy turned her attention to the screen as Esme's thoughts drifted, summarising what they must tell the police and praying their story wouldn't be dismissed out of hand. At least with Vince's testimony to back it up, there was more chance of convincing Sergeant Collins there was something worth investigating. They must make sure that the two statements didn't end up in two different in-trays, never to be merged.

'Esme?'

She looked round. 'Mmm?'

Maddy's face was pinched, her eyes wide. 'I can't find it.'

'Find what?'

'Declan Shaw's photograph. It's not in the filing cabinet or on the computer.'

Esme stood up. 'It has to be.'

Maddy shook her head. 'It's gone. Someone's deleted the file.'

They both stared at one another as the truth hit them. The break-in. It hadn't been kids on a holiday jolly at all.

Esme swallowed. 'But you've got a backup, right? On the Cloud, or a memory stick or something?'

Maddy stared back, wide eyed. 'You're missing the point, Esme,' she said, her face flushed. 'They know we're on to them.'

43

'It's usually me pacing up and down,' said Esme, as Maddy completed the fourth circuit of her living room. 'And I'm just realising what a headache it is for those watching. Sit down, can't you? We can't do anything about it now. It's after midnight. And if you're thinking they might come back, forget it. They've got what they wanted. They'll think they're safe.'

'Even so, best you stay here tonight.'

Esme thought of her dawn prowler. 'Yes, good idea. Thanks.'

'And we'll see the police tomorrow, won't we?' said Maddy, dropping down on to the arm of the chair. 'You're not going to come up with another reason for delay?'

'Good God, no. There's enough there for them to get their teeth into. Let them stir up a few things. We've done our bit.'

Maddy rubbed her face. 'I'm knackered but I doubt I'll sleep.' She got up and began pacing again.

'Got any milk?' said Esme, standing up. 'I know it's a cliché but a hot drink might help.'

'No, we had the last of it earlier.' She sat on the arm of the sofa, jiggling her knee up and down. Esme sat down again and closed her eyes, uncertain if Maddy's pacing wasn't preferable to her vibrating her knee.

'Why do you think Bella had the photograph of Sarah Baker?' said Maddy.

'Proof that she'd made the connection with his past, I assume.'

'And Declan, when he died? I mean when Ted Marsh died.'

'To show to Ted to prove his family connection, I suppose. Jim said something about him having a chip on his shoulder. Perhaps he thought he had a legitimate claim on the Ashgrove estate and it should be his, not Ted's. Perhaps murder only came on to the agenda once it was obvious Ted wasn't about to relinquish his own claim.'

'Well he was hardly likely to do that, was he?' scoffed Maddy.

They fell silent. Esme felt her mind drifting. They ought to try and get in some sleep before the morning but she didn't have the will power to get up off the chair in search of a bed.

'So do you think Bella knew any of this?' said Maddy, after a while.

Esme yawned and forced open her eyes. Maddy obviously needed to talk things through. And perhaps they should get everything clear in their minds. Perhaps they'd sleep better without it going round and round in their heads. She stretched out her arms above her head. 'I doubt she knew the details or she'd have known where to find him long before now, wouldn't she?'

'God!' said Maddy. 'She must have been so angry when she finally tracked him down. There he is; new wife, big house, wealthy as hell. And all thanks to her falsely identifying Ted Marsh's body as his.'

'Was it a shock when she turned up on his doorstep, I wonder, or did he already know she was on to him?'

Maddy leant forward. 'He might have planned it, d'you mean?'

'She was about to wreck his life unless he stopped her.'

'But he could afford to pay her off, surely? He didn't need to kill her.'

'Yes, but like you said, she'd be angry. Maybe he did offer to pay her off…'

'Perhaps that was Cooper's role, why he contacted her. He discovered she'd found him out – by whatever means – and they decided to make her an offer for keeping quiet.'

Esme nodded. 'Maybe she thought by agreeing, she was letting him off the hook too easily and wanted to vent her anger directly to his face.'

'In the end it was Bella who paid.'

Esme squeezed the bridge of her nose. She saw Bella

remonstrating with Declan, her face burning with thirty years of repressed rage. Declan shouting, grabbing her arm and shaking her. Bella running off, screaming that he wasn't going to get away with it. Him running after her, driving her towards the cliff edge…

'Oh no, poor Neave,' she said, as the consequences of their findings penetrated her tired brain. 'What effect will that have on her, learning her dad's still alive after all she's been told?'

'Not to mention that he's a murderer,' added Maddy grimly. She bit her bottom lip. 'You don't think Ashgrove has told her that he's her father, do you?'

Esme pulled a face. 'No. Telling her would open a huge can of worms. And Rohesia might not even know. He was single when he changed his name. It could have been long before she came on the scene. I reckon he'd stay quiet.' She recalled the conversation she'd had with Rohesia that day as they stood on the cliff path, marvelling at the view. *I can't imagine living anywhere else,* she'd said. What would happen to her when it was revealed that her world was a sham? It would destroy her.

Esme leant back into the padding of the sofa and chewed at her bottom lip. 'I ought to be the one to tell Neave. I started it, in a way.'

'Better coming from you than some anonymous official.'

'I'll give her a call in the morning,' said Esme, her eyelids heavy. 'If you've got a blanket, I'll kip on here.'

'Pity she's gone home, though, or you could've told her face to face.'

'On the contrary,' said Esme, flinching as the implications shot through her like an electrical charge. 'It's as well she's safely out of the way. She's the one person who can prove that Ashgrove is a fraud. Through her DNA.'

44

Maddy upgraded Esme from the sofa to the spare room. But the evening's events were not conducive to rest. Despite her weariness, Esme woke often, her mind dwelling on the ordeal Neave had to come and agonising over the realisation that Ashgrove might have guessed they were on to him.

It was still early when she dragged herself out of bed but to stay was pointless. She'd only waste her time fretting about meeting Collins and convincing him that their suspicions concerning Ashgrove were real. Her greatest fear was that Ashgrove would find a way of deflecting their accusations and that by the time the police realised the truth, something terrible would happen. Her angst over Neave's well-being was upper most in her mind.

She ventured downstairs looking for Maddy, encountering only a line of cats in the kitchen waiting for breakfast. They peered up at her expectantly. Maddy must still be asleep.

'Not before I get my tea,' she told them, filling a kettle and flicking the switch. She was hunting around for cat food when the front door burst open and Maddy sprinted down the hall dressed in running gear. She clutched a carton of milk in one hand and held her phone against her ear with the other.

'Right. Thanks.'

'Who was that?' said Esme, as Maddy ended the call and dumped the milk on the worktop.

'Felix. Told him I wouldn't be in. It was too complicated to explain why. I just said it was an emergency.' She lifted the lid of a large enamel container labelled 'Flour' and pulled out a box of cat food. 'Collins's on duty later this afternoon so I've arranged for us to see him. Give us time to gather up everything we've got to show him.'

'And get hold of Neave,' said Esme. 'Put her in the picture before the balloon goes up.'

'Good idea.' Maddy poured out the cats' biscuits into bowls and put them on the floor. 'We can get her to e-mail us a copy of the photo of her father, too. Show the police.'

Esme wasn't sure how such traumatic news and a request for the damning photograph could be so easily merged into the same conversation.

'And when we've offloaded everything,' Maddy added, standing up and giving Esme a smile of satisfaction, 'we can cry halleluiah and let rip at the ship's leaving party.'

Esme nodded. But she wasn't convinced she'd be in the right frame of mind. She was too uncomfortably aware of what both Neave and Rohesia had yet to face.

*

They sat opposite Sergeant Collins, Esme trying not to shake while he absorbed everything they'd told him, willing him not to slide the photographs, notes and family tree she'd drawn up back across the table with some withering remark.

With Vince Proctor's evidence, he must surely now accept that she'd been justified in her concerns over Bella's death.

'As you can see,' she said, leaning over and pointing to the family tree. 'Declan Shaw has a direct bloodline back to the Ashgroves because his ancestor, Nathan Shaw, married Clara Ashgrove, the daughter of William Ashgrove and Sarah Baker.'

The sergeant nodded, still studying the diagram.

'Whereas Ted Marsh, on the other hand,' she continued, sliding her finger across to the other side of the page, 'was only related by marriage.'

'Yet he was the late Miss Ashgrove's beneficiary?'

Esme nodded. 'Yes. Ted was a descendent of Eleanor Ashgrove's favourite cousin, Henry Lambert, on her mother's side

218

of the family.'

'We reckon that was his motive,' said Maddy. 'Declan Shaw thought he had a greater claim on the Ashgrove estate than Ted Marsh. He probably thought that killing him and taking on Marsh's identity had a greater chance at success than a protracted legal challenge.'

Collins sat back in his chair, chewing his lip. 'And you're saying that Bella Shaw knew this?'

'Enough to do her bit by misidentifying Ted Marsh's body as her husband's,' said Esme. 'Though why she didn't end up at Kernworthy Manor with him, I've no idea. But she found out eventually and it cost her her life.'

'But for him to carry it off for so long?' Collins sounded doubtful.

Maddy stabbed a finger on the sheets of notes. 'Thanks to Giles Cooper. His grubby fingers are all over this too, don't forget.'

'We're guessing he supplied any necessary documentation to cover the legal angle,' added Esme.

'You need to talk to him,' said Maddy.

'Ah. That might present a slight problem at the moment.'

'Why?' said Esme, her innards taking a backwards flip.

Collins hesitated, as though assessing whether it was within his remit to say more. 'He's just been reported missing.'

'Oh that's just great,' said Maddy, slumping back in her seat. 'I just knew the bugger would get away with it.' She turned to Esme. 'I told you we should have tackled him.'

'I wouldn't have recommended it, Miss Henderson,' said Collins.

'Oh?' said Esme, throwing Maddy a told-you-so look. 'That sounds as if you know something about this already.'

'We have our own reasons for wishing to talk to Mr Cooper.'

Maddy folded her arms. 'Cleared off with the petty cash, did he?' she said.

'You do appreciate Neave's vulnerability, don't you?' Esme said. The frustration of not being able to contact Neave was growing like a heavy weight on her chest, restricting her breathing. She'd rehearsed the conversation over and over in her head that morning but so far had only managed to reach Neave's voicemail. It wasn't something you could sum up in a phone message. 'Bella never got the chance to tell her,' she told the sergeant now. 'And I'd like to be the one to explain it all because it was me she asked to search for her father in the first place.'

The sergeant inclined his head. 'I understand. Though I can't make any promises.'

'Hell, what about Cooper?' said Maddy, grabbing Esme's arm. 'He might have gone after her already. Perhaps that's why he's bolted?'

'Doubtful,' said Collins. 'If he'd Miss Shaw in his sights, I think we'd have heard about it by now. More likely he's gone into hiding.' There was a tap on the door. They all turned to look as Collins's colleague peered in and cocked his head over his shoulder before disappearing. Collins stood up. 'Excuse me a moment, ladies.'

'What's Gwen's reaction going to be, d'you think?' said Esme, as Collins left the room. 'Her opinion of her son-in-law was always pretty low. Now not only is she about to discover he's alive but that he was responsible for Bella's death. I can't even begin to imagine the effect on her.'

Maddy folded her arms and sat back in her chair. 'It's a bloody mess, isn't it?'

'Murder usually is,' said Esme. She recalled once discussing the subject with her niece. Crime victims weren't only those in the direct line of fire. Like a pebble thrown in a pool, the ripples spread to the very edges.

Collins returned, closing the door behind him.

'Well, I can set your mind at rest on one point,' he said, resuming his seat. 'Neave Shaw isn't under any threat from

Cooper. He's just been picked up boarding a plane to Australia.'

'Australia?' said Esme, latching on to the connection. 'Has he got links over there?'

'Family, I understand,' admitted Collins after a moment's hesitation.

Esme leant across the table. 'If you discover they live on the Gold Coast, it could explain a lot. Declan Shaw's family come from there. It could be where he and Cooper first met and hatched this whole scheme.'

'Cooper's father represented the Ashgroves for years,' Maddy told Collins. 'Giles took on the business in his twenties, when his old man died unexpectedly. You might just find the timing's significant.'

Collins gathered up the documents and papers from the table. 'Well, thank you for this,' he said standing up and sliding back his chair. 'We'll take it from here.'

'So, what happens now?' said Esme. 'You will go after him, won't you?'

'And for God's sake, don't let him blag his way out of it,' added Maddy.

'Don't worry,' said the sergeant, with a reassuring smile. 'You can leave it with us now.'

*

As they came out of the police station, Esme checked her phone again. Still no response from Neave. Maddy said she'd dig out Gwen Preston's number and give her a call. Neave might be with her. They parted company, agreeing to meet up at the party later. Esme headed back to Breakers in a sombre mood.

*

Music vibrated inside Esme's head and she sat upright on her bed, blinking. The last thing she remembered was flopping back against the pillow and closing her tired eyes. She must have dozed

221

off. How long had she been asleep? Had Neave tried to reach her? She swung her legs over the edge and reached for her phone. No messages showed on the screen.

She got up and went out on to the veranda. The party must have started. The music she'd heard was the sound of the band penetrating the mist which was curling up over the cliffs. She supposed she ought to change into her glad-rags and get down there.

As she searched through the wardrobe for something suitable to wear, she wondered what the police were doing. Had they arrested Ashgrove yet? She hoped they hadn't been hampered by paperwork, arrest warrants and procedures. Or any other bureaucratic hoops Collins was required to jump. The ship was leaving tomorrow morning and Ashgrove would be on it, if they didn't act quickly. She should have mentioned that. Perhaps she and Maddy had presumed too much. But Collins had reassured them, hadn't he?

What had been Rohesia's response to the police arriving on Kernworthy Manor's doorstep? She tried to picture Rohesia's reaction, imaging her own if the police had turned up saying that her husband wasn't Tim Quentin but an impostor. She'd have dismissed the idea as ludicrous, of course, as Rohesia would surely do, at first. But she and Tim lived in a shabby flat in London, just about making ends meet, not savouring the delights of an eighteenth-century manor house, with more than ample income for any eventuality. And that was the nub of her concern. Ashgrove had the resources to hire the best legal advice available.

She pulled out a long cotton print skirt from the wardrobe and sat down on the bed, trying to summon up the energy for a badly timed social event. She looked around. The simple accommodation which had served her so well as a temporary home now seemed bland and merely functional. She should be looking forward to going home to the comfortable reassurance of personal and familiar possessions. But until things were settled, she wasn't ready to let go and leave.

She stood up and clicked her tongue. Turning herself into a melee of knots wasn't going to help anyone. She snatched up her skirt as her phone rang.

She leapt on it. Perhaps it was Neave phoning at last. But it was Maddy's name which appeared on the screen.

'Did you get hold of Gwen?' she said, before Maddy had a chance to speak.

'Eventually, yes.'

'And? Was Neave there? Does she know anything, yet?'

'Gwen knows but Neave doesn't. She wasn't there. She's still on holiday.'

'Oh holiday?' Esme's fingers tightened around the handset. 'Please tell me she's gone away to Lanzarote or something.'

'Wish I could. But Gwen said she extended her leave and came back to North Devon.'

'Oh God.' Esme closed her eyes, images chasing around her head of Neave's shocked and horrified face at Ashgrove's arrest. 'What must she think of me, letting her find out the truth like that?'

'Sod that,' said Maddy, her voice urgent. 'We don't know if the police have got to him. We need to find Neave before Ashgrove twigs what's happening.'

45

The party was well under way as Esme arrived. She could feel the rhythmic base notes vibrating the ground under her feet as she arrived in Warren Quay from the coast path and headed for the hotel. Maddy was to join her once she'd alerted Sergeant Collins.

She squeezed her way through the crowd spilling out of the pub and through to the bar, exchanging a few words on the way and scanning the crush of bodies for any sign of Neave.

Someone touched her elbow and she looked round to see Felix. He bent down and yelled in her ear. 'What's this about the police?'

She shook her head. The situation was too complicated to explain in a few words barked against the noise. 'Have you seen Neave?' she shouted, instead.

'No. Why?' He glanced up as something caught his eye and cocked his head across the room. 'You're wanted,' he said.

Esme looked round to see Ruth gesturing at her from behind the bar. She manoeuvred her way through the packed room to see what she wanted. Perhaps there was news from the manor. Had the arrest made the local news?

Ruth was serving a heavyset man with a dimpled chin, sporting a sugar-pink carnation in his buttonhole. Ruth acknowledged her with a nod and when she had dealt with her customer, she hurried over.

'Maddy phoned,' she said, her face hot and flushed. 'Said you were looking for Neave.'

Esme nodded and leaned across the bar. 'You haven't seen her today, by any chance? She's not staying here?' It was a slim hope. Neave had stayed at the manor since being taken under Rohesia's wing.

Ruth pointed towards the harbour but her words were drowned out by a loud guffaw by Mr Pink Carnation. She said something which could have been 'five' or 'tired', Esme wasn't sure.

Esme leaned closer. 'Sorry? Didn't catch it.'

Ruth beckoned for Esme to go to the end of the bar. Esme fought her way through and met her at the hatch.

'God, it's going to be a long night,' said Ruth, wiping her forehead with the back of her hand.

'What were you saying about Neave?'

'I saw her heading down to the ship. I thought it was closed up now, ready for the off?'

'It is. So when was this?'

'Just as it started to get busy. I'd just nipped out to empty the bins. I thought she'd gone home.'

Esme nodded. 'So did we. Look, I can't explain now. I'd better see if I can find her. Thanks, Ruth.' She turned to make her way through the partygoers. 'Oh,' she added, turning back. 'Can you let Maddy know where I've gone?' But Ruth was already serving drinks again. No matter. With any luck, she'd be back in the pub with Neave by the time Maddy arrived.

The cool sea air was welcome relief from the claustrophobia of the crowded bar. She headed down the path towards the harbour, breathing in the fresh salty smell hanging on the onshore breeze. Pools of light from the lampposts reflected in the water as it swayed up and down with the swell.

At the head of the slope, she stopped at the last lamp, narrowing her eyes to peer into the dark of the lower harbour, where the *Mary Ann* was moored. The water lapped gently against the sea wall and what little moon there was bathed the ship's three masts in a soft eerie blush of silver.

All was still and there was no sign of life. Neave could have visited the ship, found no one there and left again. Though if she was still on board, the peaceful atmosphere of the deserted ship might provide the ideal location for Esme to break the shocking news.

As she stood deliberating, a light flickered in the distance. She strained her eyes to see through the mist. Perhaps she'd imagined it. But no. Just as she'd convinced herself her eyes were playing tricks, she saw it again. And it was on the ship.

She glanced back towards the hotel. Should she double back and borrow a torch? It wasn't completely dark yet but the mist had robbed the cove of the last residues of dying daylight. A torch might help her see her way more easily along the quayside. But the thought of having to wade through the hoards of partygoers to fetch one dissuaded her. Besides, her eyes would adjust soon enough.

She blinked into the shadows before setting off down the slope and along the stone walkway, using the wall on her left as a guide and reassuring handhold. As she got further along, it became easier to see and she realised that there were several lights on board, regular halos along the sides of the ship, defining its outline. She speeded up, more confident now, as the towering silhouette of the ship emerged in front of her.

When she was level with the stern she let go of the wall and took a few tentative steps towards the giant structure, pausing at the quayside edge to listen to the dark water below, slapping between ship and shore, in rhythm with the creak of the ship's timbers.

'Neave?' she called out. No response. 'Neave, is that you?'

There was definitely someone on board. She could hear faint sounds from deep in the bowels of the ship. She took a step closer, nervous of the gangway in the semi-darkness, though the rope strapped to the rail at the opposite end assured her that the walkway was secure. Besides, she couldn't go back without checking whether or not it was Neave on board. Not having got this far.

As she reached out and grabbed the gang-plank rail, the

upsetting scenario formed in her head of Neave being at the manor when the police came for Ashgrove. Perhaps Neave had come down to the deserted ship to seek sanctuary while she came to terms with what she'd learnt. And having discovered the truth, she might need a sympathetic ear and someone to talk to. Esme took a deep breath and walked aboard.

The lights she'd seen were the bulbous lamps shining low down at intervals along the sides of the ship, bringing the coiled ropes which hung below them into sharp contrast. She strode across to the middle of the deck where the hatch door to the lower levels stood open. Perhaps members of the crew were doing something in readiness for tomorrow's sailing? They may have seen Neave or knew where she'd gone.

She bent over and called into the void. 'Hello? Anyone down there?'

No reply.

She lowered herself on to the ladder and made her way down backwards, gripping the smooth polished handrail. At the lower deck she glanced around, blinking in the weak lamplight chosen to replicate the minimal glow of an oil lamp familiar to the prisoners. But there was no one there. The clattering noises were coming from the orlop deck, another level below, which explained why no one had heard her calling.

She descended to the next level, this time with a twisted rope to guide her down the narrow treads. At the bottom of the ladder, she swivelled round.

But it wasn't Neave who stepped out of the shadows. Neither was it a member of the crew. It was Rohesia Ashgrove.

And as they focused on one another, Esme saw the hatred in Rohesia's eyes.

46

Esme swallowed and tightened her grip on the rope. 'Rohesia,' she said, seized by an inexplicable urge to flee. Though perhaps not so inexplicable. Rohesia's life was on the verge of disintegration and from her expression, she clearly held Esme responsible.

'I was looking for Neave,' Esme managed, eventually. 'I'm sorry if I disturbed you. I didn't realise you were here.'

Rohesia's lack of response and her sour expression did nothing to alleviate Esme's disquiet. Bizarrely, she thought of William's words, which Agnes had repeated to Morris Beveridge. *Discretion is the better part of valour.*

'Well, if Neave's not here,' she began. 'I'll leave you in…'

'The police came today,' said Rohesia. 'But I expect you already know that.'

Esme stopped and closed her eyes, giving silent thanks that Neave was safe. She turned back, overcome with sympathy. 'I'm so sorry, Rohesia. I don't know what to say. The shock of finding out how…' She faltered over his name. '…how Edward deceived you, must have been devastating.' She thought of Rohesia alone in the empty manor and wondered if she had family she could turn to. She'd spoken of her family once, when they'd talked about her name.

'You're right,' said Rohesia. 'It was a shock.' Her tone was cold. 'I hadn't realised how much you knew.'

For a moment Esme was confused. 'You think I should have warned you?'

Rohesia snorted and turned away.

'How could I?' said Esme. 'I've only just found out everything myself. That's why I was looking for Neave. To explain.'

228

Rohesia sat down on a wooden trunk and dragged a set of shackles from off the floor. The chain grated against the side of the trunk, setting Esme's teeth on edge. 'I have dreamed of this project for as long as I can remember,' she said in a dull voice. 'And now, having finally achieved my aim…the whole project is threatened just when it was becoming a success.'

'Not necessarily.' Though even as Esme spoke she knew her words were hollow. How could the Ashgrove wealth, so cruelly taken, remain in Rohesia's charge? It no more belonged to Rohesia than it did her husband. She supposed Rohesia would seek legal advice and immediately thought of Cooper. Had he made provision for Rohesia, should the fraud be exposed? She doubted it. Any protection Cooper would have arranged would have been for himself, in the form of his Australian bolt-hole. She wondered if Rohesia knew that by now.

'I suppose you see him the same way as the Georgians and Victorians would have done,' said Rohesia. 'Someone to be got rid of. To be erased from the social map.' Rohesia rested the irons in her lap. 'Those poor unfortunates were *forced* into criminality.'

Esme sat down on the bottom step and eyed Rohesia, warily. 'Surely you're not trying to put your husband in the same category as a starving convict?'

Rohesia stared into the middle distance and fingered the irons. 'Con-vict,' she said, emphasising the word, separating it into two distinct syllables. 'The very word conjures up fear and distaste, doesn't it? A pitiful creature, emerging from a boggy landscape like a character from a Dickensian novel, desperate and violent, an escapee from the hulk ships in the Thames. Not unlike the lepers of old. And similarly treated. Banished and left to rot in some remote place, forgotten, dispensed with like rancid waste so as not to pollute gentile society.'

Esme wasn't sure how she was expected to respond, so said nothing. She watched as Rohesia slipped her wrist through the iron ankle ring, the taut pull of anxiety stirring inside as she recalled Rohesia's reference to the manacles when they'd toured the ship. *It was impossible for them to move but at the risk of both their legs being broken.*

'They virtually starved the prisoners, you know,' said Rohesia. She sat fixated, her face ashen and her mouth turned down in disgust, as though she could see the misery in front of her. 'If a prisoner died, the poor wretches who were chained to him would stay quiet, telling no one so they could eat his rations.'

'Rohesia…' It was as though she was deliberately distressing herself. To mask the pain of what she'd discovered, perhaps? A mental form of self-harm?

'They'd tolerate the increasing stench of the decomposing body, until they could stand it no longer. Can you begin to imagine what that was like?'

'I'm sure I can't,' said Esme, moving towards her. 'Look, I really don't think you should…'

Rohesia shot her head round and locked her eyes on Esme. 'You've got it all wrong, you know.'

Esme shook her head. 'No, Rohesia. I'm sorry but I haven't.'

'You have. Edward is entitled to everything. It was bequeathed to him.'

Esme crouched down in front of her. 'Edward isn't who he says he is, Rohesia, whatever he's told you.'

'It's not true.'

It could be that the police hadn't been completely candid about the reason for Ashgrove's arrest. She took hold of Rohesia's hands and squeezed them. 'Edward doesn't own the estate, Rohesia. And Edward's not his real name. It's Declan. Declan Shaw.' She was tempted to say more but it was clear that Rohesia was struggling to absorb what she'd already been told.

'Is there anything I can do?' Esme asked. 'Is there someone I can contact to…?'

'No.'

'Someone in your family, perhaps?'

230

'No.'

Rohesia stared ahead, her breathing fast and shallow, as Esme continued to hold her hands, the intense smell of her perfume becoming nauseating in the enclosed space.

'Rohesia, I know how much you love Kernworthy,' she said. 'But…' She hesitated. Would the bold truth shake Rohesia out of her state of denial? She cleared her throat. 'I know it's hard, Rohesia, but you have to understand. Edward killed to get the Ashgrove estate and he killed Bella to keep her quiet.'

Rohesia pulled away from Esme's grasp, dropping her head into her hands, her body shuddering. Esme withdrew, wondering if she should go for help. But Rohesia's sobs grew quieter and eventually ceased. Esme dared to hope she'd finally convinced Rohesia of the truth, however unpalatable.

She laid her hand on Rohesia's shoulder. 'Where's Neave, Rohesia?' she said.

'What?' Rohesia sniffed and pulled a tissue from her pocket. 'Why are you looking for Neave?' she said, wiping her face. 'I don't see…' Her voice faltered.

'You know Neave's his daughter, don't you?' said Esme.

Rohesia closed her eyes and gave a slight nod.

'So you must realise that her DNA can prove Edward's true identity.' Esme waited for Rohesia's reaction, wondering how likely it was she'd cooperate. Would protecting her husband take a greater priority?

'Where is she, Rohesia?' Esme prompted, gently. 'Do you know?'

Rohesia let out a jerky sigh. 'She's up at the manor.' She looked up, her red-rimmed eyes wide with alarm, and grasped Esme's arm.

'Oh God,' she said, scrambling to her feet and pushing past Esme to the ladder. 'Edward's there.'

47

Rohesia had reached the top of the ladder before Esme had made sense of Rohesia's words. Why the hell hadn't they arrested Ashgrove? What had gone wrong?

She chased after her, catching her up half way across the top deck. 'I don't understand,' she panted. 'Why is Edward still at the manor? I thought you said the police came.'

'They wanted to talk to him,' said Rohesia, over her shoulder. 'But he wasn't at home and they went away.' Esme cursed under her breath. Surely he couldn't slip the net that easily? She rushed after Rohesia, fear and fury driving her on, relieved that at least Rohesia understood the danger facing Neave and the urgency of finding her.

The music from the party echoed around the harbour as they hurried towards the hotel. Guests congregated along the terrace, almost as far as the ramp to the beach, drinking and laughing, like an inappropriate video playing on a giant screen.

'We'll use my car,' said Rohesia, pulling a set of keys from her pocket. Esme had little choice but to agree as her own car was still parked beside the cabin. She fell into step with Rohesia, her thoughts a muddled mess in her head, imagining what was happening at the manor and wondering how much Neave already knew. Rohesia's actions had been swift, for which Esme was grateful. But was there a specific reason for her haste, which went further than a sudden realisation of the danger Neave was in? She was afraid to ask.

As they passed the heaving bar, Esme scanned the faces of the people who'd spilled outside, looking for Ruth. Someone needed to update the police. Maddy was the only person aware of all the facts and able to convey the necessary urgency to an anonymous control centre. But had she arrived?

She slowed. 'Perhaps I'd better let someone know…'

'No time,' said Rohesia, pulling at her arm. 'Come on. We have to get back to the manor.'

'Yes, you're right,' said Esme, envisaging the futility of trying to make herself heard above the din, let alone understood. 'We'll phone from the manor.' Maddy would have already left a message with Collins about Neave's whereabouts. The police might not be far away.

Rohesia hurried across the car park to a dark blue Mercedes parked beside the sea wall. The lights flashed like a warning beacon in the darkness as the locking device de-activated and they scrambled inside. Rohesia started the engine, thrust the car into gear and they roared out of the car park up the steep hill, almost careering into a pedestrian on the roadside.

Esme looked across at Rohesia in the gloom of the car interior. 'Does Neave know Edward's her father?' she asked. The glow of the instrument panel cast an odd light across Rohesia's face, making it impossible to read her expression.

'Well, I haven't told her,' said Rohesia, her clipped tones betraying how close her emotions were to the surface.

Esme wondered if Rohesia was jealous of her husband, as well as angry with him. She turned away and focused on the road ahead. Perhaps it was better not to talk. Rohesia's state of mind was already fragile. One ill-judged word and she might drive them off the road. Esme wasn't keen to end up in a ditch.

The car headlights lit up the cottages as they weaved through the upper village. Rohesia turned the car sharp left on to the narrow lane leading to Kernworthy Manor. They were travelling at speed, now. Esme gripped the side of her seat, praying that they didn't meet another vehicle. She tried closing her eyes so she couldn't see the darkened hedges rushing by but instead her brain conjured up images of wrecked and twisted metal. She opened them again, only to see two headlights coming straight towards them.

She gasped as Rohesia hit the brakes and they skewed to a shuddering halt as the approaching car nipped into a gateway. Rohesia rammed the Mercedes into gear and sped off again, presumably leaving the occupants of the other car to wonder at the sanity of the driver. Esme pressed herself back against the car seat, thankful that it was only a few hundred yards to Kernworthy Manor.

They slewed off the metalled lane and bumped along the final approach to the manor. Rohesia expertly flicked the Mercedes into the courtyard, juddered to a halt and killed the engine. Esme uttered a silent prayer to the travel gods and climbed out, her knees shaking. She scanned around, recalling her last visit and expecting Sergei to appear from one of the outbuildings. But all seemed quiet.

'Where will they be?' she asked Rohesia across the roof of the car.

'Let's find out.' Rohesia slammed the driver's door and marched across the courtyard towards the house, Esme following as Rohesia headed for a door which opened into the kitchen. They stepped inside and stood in silence, listening. Muted lights glowed from underneath a row of wall cupboards. The hum of the fridge was the only sound.

Rohesia turned towards Esme and held a finger across her lips. Esme nodded, though having arrived in the courtyard in a blaze of Mercedes power, Rohesia's belated caution seemed misplaced.

Rohesia led the way slowly across the tiled floor, ushering Esme behind her. They emerged into an ornate dining room, its walls painted in pale ochre and decked with heavy framed oil paintings. The centre of the room was dominated by an elegant Queen Anne table, its graceful legs and oval top highly polished.

Rohesia headed towards the panelled door on the other side of the room, Esme in her wake, their footsteps silent on the plush plain carpet. Half way across, the door opened. Rohesia stepped backwards, knocking into Esme.

Into the room, carrying a large leather holdall, walked Edward Ashgrove.

48

Neave lay still, her eyes closed, trying to remember where she was. She turned her head to the side, wincing at the jarring pain in her temple and the nausea washing over her. She laid a hand on her forehead. Good God, how much had she drunk? She couldn't recall having more than one glass but perhaps that's what champagne did to you. And it was easy to lose track if it had been topped up without her noticing.

She propped herself up on her elbow and risked opening an eye. The dim cabin swayed in front of her, compounded by the ship's gentle rocking motion on the water. She hoped this wasn't a sign of her inadequate sea legs. The trip to Ireland wasn't going to be much fun if she felt like this all the way.

She swung her feet off the bunk and sat hunched on the edge. She could do with a drink of water. The cabin had a small wash-hand basin in the corner but Rohesia said it came from a tank and wasn't fit for drinking. Sod it. A mouthful wouldn't kill her. She could always go in search of more when she'd wet her palette.

She pulled herself to her feet and took several wobbly steps across to the sink, slurping a few mouthfuls of water from the tap before rubbing a wet hand over her face. She stretched, pausing to listen when she heard footsteps running across the deck. Stumbling to the door, she turned the handle and pulled. Nothing happened. She laughed at her stupidity and reached for the key. Only to find there wasn't one. She crouched down and peered through the keyhole. The key was on the other side of the door. She stood up again and banged on the panelling, shouting for someone to come.

But no one came and the actions did nothing for her throbbing head. She sat back down on the bunk, trying to recall what had happened. The last thing she could remember was raising a toast to tomorrow's Ireland trip. Rohesia had said they were entitled to celebrate early, ahead of the party. Rohesia was so excited, like a child anticipating a birthday treat. Odd that Edward wasn't there. But there was something going on between Rohesia and Edward, Neave realised. Perhaps her presence was causing tension between them, yet both had insisted she was welcome on the voyage.

She heard a sound from above and lifted her head to listen. Footsteps again, on the deck above. She leapt to the door and beat her fists against the wood. 'In here,' she shouted. 'I'm locked in.'

The footsteps quickened and she paused to press her ear to the door. A voice called out.

'Esme? That you?'

Neave hammered on the door. 'It's me,' she yelled. 'Neave.'

The footsteps hastened, the key clicked and the door swung open. And in the corridor stood Maddy.

*

Neave sat at a picnic table on Warren Quay opposite Maddy. The noise from the bar made her headache worse and she'd asked to stay outside.

'This is so embarrassing,' she told Maddy. 'I don't usually drink.'

'That probably explains it then,' said Maddy. 'If you're not used to it, champagne can do that to you. They say it's the bubbles.'

Ruth emerged from the kitchen door and hurried over to the table. 'There you go,' she said, plonking down a mug in front of Neave. 'Sweet tea. Just the thing.'

Neave pulled a face. 'I don't take sugar.'

'Strong coffee might be more appropriate, Ruth,' said Maddy. 'Neave's blaming the champagne.' She leant across the table. 'I don't get why you were locked in?'

Neave shrugged. 'Perhaps Rohesia thought I might wander off and fall in or something. I must have been well out of it.'

'Rohesia Ashgrove was with you?' said Ruth, frowning.

Neave nodded. 'We were toasting the success of the ship project. We're sailing to Ireland in the morning.' She looked up at the two women and gave them a tired smile. 'Rohesia's invited me along.'

'Did Esme speak to you?' said Maddy. She reached over and laid her hand on Neave's.

Neave pulled it away. 'I haven't seen Esme,' she said. She didn't like the way Maddy and Ruth kept looking at one another. 'I've already told you.'

'You'd better tell her,' said Ruth, her hands clasped tightly against her.

'Tell me what?' said Neave. 'What's going on?'

Maddy wriggled in her seat. 'The thing is, Neave, Esme and I have uncovered something rather disturbing. She was trying to find you to warn you.'

'Warn me? About what?'

Maddy bit her lip and glanced at Ruth, before saying, 'I think you're going to need Ruth's sweet tea, Neave. This is going to be one hell of a shock.'

*

I don't understand. I don't understand. The words kept circling in her head but she didn't seem to be able to say them out loud. Her father was alive? And he was Edward Ashgrove? How could he be? Had Bella known? Was that what she'd meant in the letter? Neave closed her eyes, squeezing the tears back. If only she'd responded straight away instead of ignoring her. They could have gone to see him together, but instead Bella had resorted to the Dutch courage she'd always mistakenly assumed would help her through a crisis, and somehow plunged to her death off the coastal path.

Her eyes drifted up at Maddy who was studying her, as though braced for...what? A reaction? Questions?

And she did have questions. 'Does he know about me?' she managed, after a while. 'Has anyone told him who I am?'

Maddy chewed her bottom lip. 'We're not sure...' she said, throwing another glance at Ruth.

'I want to know where Esme is,' said Ruth, pacing up and down. 'I knew something like this would happen.' She laid her palms on the table and leaned towards Neave. 'Esme was looking for you and I told her I'd seen you down by the ship. And that's where she went, as far as I know. So why didn't she find you?'

'I don't know, do I?' said Neave, staring back. The lines on Ruth's soft face seemed deeper than she'd noticed before, pulling Ruth's mouth downwards in a taut arc. 'Maybe she came down while I was asleep.'

Ruth gave an irritated sigh and stood up straight. 'Someone must have seen her,' she said. 'I'm going to ask around.'

Neave watched her hurry back to the pub, sensing Ruth held her responsible for whatever crisis this was but with no idea why.

'Drink your tea,' said Maddy, giving Neave a sympathetic smile. 'It might help.'

Neave stared down at the insipid liquid cooling in the mug but didn't seem capable of lifting it to her lips. 'I don't understand,' she said eventually. It seemed such an inadequate statement to express the turmoil of confusion going round in her head.

'Hardly surprising,' said Maddy. 'It can't be easy, finding out about your dad like that.'

An image of Edward Ashgrove's face floated into Neave's mind. It seemed absurd that he could be her father. 'He's always been so nice to me,' she said, as much to herself as to Maddy. 'Different from the way he is with other people.'

Maddy pressed her lips together, as though she wanted to say something but didn't know how to phrase it. She sighed, looking at Neave with troubled eyes.

'Maddy!'

They both turned to see Ruth running towards them. 'Dan's seen her,' she said as she reached the table, her voice urgent. 'He's seen Esme.'

'Thank God for that,' said Maddy, letting out a long breath. She looked over her shoulder towards the hotel.

'No, she's not here. He saw her getting in a car.'

'Her car?' Maddy frowned.

'Not hers. Something flashy.' She rubbed her forehead. 'A Merk I think he said. Would that be it?'

'What colour?' said Maddy. 'Was it blue?'

'I don't know,' said Ruth, puzzled. 'Dark, he said. Why?'

Maddy gave her head a toss backwards. 'One nearly mowed me down on my way here, earlier.'

'Rohesia's got a dark blue Mercedes,' said Neave. They both turned towards her. She recoiled at the alarm in their faces. 'We came down in it earlier on?' she finished. 'I suppose it could be hers?'

Maddy stood up. 'They'll have gone up to the manor, I bet.' She reached across to snatch up her bag from the end of the bench.

'You're not going up there?' said Ruth, her face ashen.

'Why not?'

'You know why not.' Ruth cast a wary glance at Neave before answering. 'He might be there. You said the police didn't…'

'Police?' said Neave, getting to her feet. She glared at Maddy. 'There's something you're not telling me, isn't there?'

'I'm not completely stupid, Ruth,' said Maddy, ignoring Neave.

'Then call the police. Let them deal with him.'

Neave scrambled off the bench, panic building inside her, as though she was part of a dream she knew was going to end badly and unable to escape. 'For God's sake, will someone tell me what the hell's going on?'

Maddy pulled a set of car keys out of her bag. 'Good idea,

Ruth. You call the police and explain everything to Neave. I'll go and find Esme.'

Ruth grabbed Maddy's arm. 'Maddy, no. You must wait for the police to get here.'

'Are you kidding? It'll take them at least half an hour. And that's assuming they're not dealing with town centre revellers.' She threw the bag over her shoulder and ran.

Ruth, having failed to stop Maddy, turned her attention to Neave. 'Let me make that call,' she said, patting Neave's arm. 'Then you can…'

Neave pulled away. 'No, I'm going with her.' She ran after Maddy. 'Wait!'

Maddy stopped, throwing back her head and sighing, as though she was dealing with a difficult child. 'I really don't think that's a good idea,' she said, as Neave came alongside.

'Neither do I,' said Ruth, coming up behind them. She took Neave's arm. 'Come and wait in the pub.'

'No.' Neave yanked herself free. She stood in front of Maddy, blocking her way. 'You might as well take me. I'll only go on my own anyway.'

Maddy paused for a moment, chewing at her bottom lip. 'OK, but on one condition.'

'Which is?'

Maddy thrust her face at Neave and gave her a stern look. 'That if I decide it's too dangerous, we walk away.'

'Dangerous?'

'Yes, dangerous.' Neave saw Maddy's eyes flicker to Ruth's anxious face. 'There's something you haven't yet grasped about your dad, Neave. You need to know exactly what you're walking into.'

49

What's she doing here?' said Ashgrove, dropping the holdall to the floor.

Esme glared back. 'What have you done with Neave?' She tried to superimpose the photograph of him laughing with Bella in Brighton in an effort to re-brand him as Declan Shaw but her brain wouldn't cooperate. He remained the fictitious Edward Ashgrove.

'Neave?' said Ashgrove, frowning at Rohesia. 'What's she talking about?'

'Esme's looking for Neave,' said Rohesia, her voice low. Esme watched her, sensing her apprehension. This was one encounter Rohesia must have hoped to avoid.

Esme turned back to Ashgrove. 'So where is she?'

He turned his gaze on his wife. 'I thought you said…'

'Perhaps she's upstairs in her room, Edward?' said Rohesia.

The silence hung in the air as they waited for his response. Ashgrove looked first at his wife and then at Esme. He shrugged. 'I suppose she could be.'

'I'll go,' said Esme. She ran out into the hall beyond, leaving Rohesia and Ashgrove locked in visual combat.

A wide sweeping staircase graced the elegant entrance hall at the front of the house. She darted across and ran up the stairs. At the top, an ornate oriole window lit a landing which disappeared into the distance in both directions. She turned right and sprinted along its length, calling Neave's name and throwing open doors.

The bedrooms varied in style but all were richly decorated with heavy furniture pieces and flocked wallpaper, two with four poster beds draped with elaborate hangings. All faced the sea and none looked lived in.

If Neave was here, unaware of the threat Ashgrove posed, she would have responded to Esme calling her name by now. Did that mean she was wasting her time? Or that Neave was locked in somewhere, frightened and desperate.

She ran back along the passageway and checked the rooms on the other side of the stairs. Themed rooms with décor of Chinese or chintz. Dark and austere rooms with oak carved furniture, staged and impersonal.

Esme paused on the landing. Not only was there no sign of Neave, but none of the rooms showed any evidence of twenty-first century inhabitants. No alarm clock or radio beside the bed, no books on the bedside table, no toiletries on the dressing tables. Like a stately home being mothballed and made ready for the winter period when it would be closed to the public.

She closed the final door. Neave wasn't up here. But it was a big house. There were rooms downstairs to search, even a cellar. And there was still time to find Neave safe and well. Ashgrove would be more agitated by their arrival if…She didn't allow herself to complete the thought.

She could hear the murmur of voices from below. Perhaps Rohesia had persuaded her husband to confess as to Neave's whereabouts. She glanced out of the landing window and across the garden. She could see the archway in the wall where she'd walked with Rohesia that day. On the other side lay the courtyard flanked with a range of outbuildings. Was Neave out there somewhere? Yes, of course. Much more likely than in the house. While Rohesia kept Ashgrove busy she must keep searching.

But as she turned away, someone came out of a barn and across the courtyard. She stepped back away from the window, her heart pounding. Sergei. Was Ashgrove so calm because it wasn't he who'd got his hands dirty? Why hadn't Rohesia mentioned him? Why wasn't she concerned that he might turn up at any moment? Perhaps she wasn't expecting him to be here.

Esme headed to the top of the stairs, passing a huge frame

hanging on the wall. She gave it a cursory glance as she went by. The Ashgrove family tree, beautifully hand written in neat italic script. She glanced at it as she ran past, reminded of something she'd seen on the version on Miss Hodge's wall which hadn't made sense. She clicked her tongue and headed down the stairs. This wasn't the time to dwell on such matters. She had to find Neave.

She hurried across the hall to the dining room, slowing at the sound of raised voices.

'So what are you going to do?' she heard Ashgrove say. Despite being muffled by the closed door, his sarcasm was clear. 'Ply her with drink and send her over the edge? They won't fall for that a second time.'

She stumbled backwards, a blood-rush of terror setting her heart racing as the words told the dreadful truth. Rohesia's compliance had been a sham. She had every intention of shielding her husband. And whose impending disposal were they discussing? Neave's? Or hers?

She didn't plan to stay long enough to find out. She'd slip out through the grandiose front door and make her escape along the coast path to raise the alarm. She reeled round. And smacked straight into the solid mass of Sergei.

She yelped as his merciless grip clamped round her upper arm. He pushed open the dining room door and thrust her inside.

'Look who listen at key hole,' he grunted.

50

Neave blinked out into the dimness ahead as Maddy's camper bumped along the lane, droplets of water from the sea mist playing in the headlight beam.

'You've no proof it was him,' she said. Her protest sounded pathetic, like a child complaining life was unfair.

'He's been sitting pretty for thirty years with a wad of cash and the type of house most of us only visit on a bank holiday weekend. He's not going to let that go lightly, is he? Think about it, Neave. I know it's tough but he had too much to lose to let your mum blow it all away.'

'How d'you know he didn't pay her off?' said Neave. 'She could have got pissed celebrating. It'd be just the sort of thing she'd do.'

Maddy didn't say anything and Neave turned away, smothering a sudden urge to cry.

'Anyway,' she added, forcing down the sob rising in her throat. 'The police didn't arrest him. Ruth said as much. That must say something.'

'Only because they couldn't find him.'

'You don't know that was the reason.'

Maddy swore under her breath.

'What's that?' said Neave.

Maddy shook her head. 'Forget it.'

Neave squeezed her eyes shut and opened them again. This wasn't really happening. There was some mistake. There had to be. Maddy and Esme weren't detectives. They'd got it all wrong. Her father had not killed someone and taken his place. He hadn't killed her mother. Even her gran said her father had loved her mother. He wouldn't kill her. It didn't make sense.

Maddy stopped the camper and peered out of the nearside window. 'Is it up here?' she asked. Neave nodded.

The camper turned and crawled along the track, rocking from side to side.

'What's at the end?' said Maddy, slowing slightly. 'Is there somewhere to turn?'

'There's a courtyard at the back. The lane peters out just past that, as you reach the coast path.'

They trundled along a little further, brambles arching over the roof of the camper, their thorns scraping the paintwork, like fingernails down a blackboard. Up ahead, the manor loomed out of the shadows, smudges of light visible at the windows.

Maddy slowed and pulled the camper in against the hedge. She ratcheted on the hand brake and cut the engine. Silence.

Neave unbuckled her seat belt and grabbed the door handle.

'No, wait,' said Maddy.

'What's the point in coming if we're just going to wait?' said Neave, shocked at the tetchiness in her voice.

Maddy sighed. 'All right, we'll take a look around. But quietly, OK? We don't want anyone to know we're here.'

Neave said nothing. She opened the door and squeezed out of the camper, remembering just in time not to slam the door. They began walking up the track towards the lights. The gate to the courtyard stood open and Rohesia's Mercedes sat on the gravel, bathed in the brightness of a security light.

Maddy stopped and grabbed Neave's arm. 'Where does the heavy hang out?' she whispered, dragging Neave into the shadows along the edge of the lane.

'You mean Sergei?'

'That's him.'

Neave hesitated. For the first time, wariness found a weak spot in her stomach and settled there. 'He's OK. He knows who I am.'

'That's what I mean,' said Maddy. Her voice softened. 'Neave, have you taken on board anything I've told you? You're

246

Ashgrove's nemesis. You and your DNA can blow his whole world apart.' She swore under her breath. 'I was stupid to bring you here. What the bloody hell was I thinking of?'

Neave turned on her. 'I'm not here because of you,' she hissed. 'I would have come anyway. I don't need you.'

She pulled out of Maddy's grasp and ran up the lane towards the house, shutting out Maddy's warning voice behind her. She crunched across the gravel and up the path to the back door. As she pushed it open and stepped inside, she heard voices coming from the room beyond. She ran forward, yanked open the door and burst into the dining room.

'Neave, darling,' said Rohesia. 'How timely. We were just talking about you.'

51

All eyes focused on Neave. In the stillness which followed all Esme could think about was whether Neave knew the truth about Ashgrove. The bewilderment on Neave's face told her nothing. Seeing Esme locked in Sergei's grip with Rohesia and Ashgrove looking on, apparently untroubled, would have resulted in the same expression of incredulity.

The momentary stillness grew into seconds of empty space as everyone appeared to wait for someone else to break the spell.

Esme yanked her arm free from Sergei's grasp. 'Neave,' she said, moving towards her. 'Thank God, you're OK. I've been looking for you all over the place.'

Neave blinked at Esme, her eyes dark and heavy, the corners of her mouth turned down. 'Maddy's told me,' she said, her voice unsteady. Her eyes flitted to Ashgrove. 'She said you killed my mother.'

'No, Neave, I would never...'

'Aren't we all getting rather over-wrought?' said Rohesia. She pointed to the holdall Ashgrove had dumped on the floor earlier. 'Put that in the car, Sergei,' she said. 'And then come back here.' The jangle of her bracelets jarred in the tense atmosphere, reminding Esme of the clang of the shackles on the ship which had set her teeth on edge.

Sergei did as he was bid, pushing past Neave into the centre of the room. Esme made a move towards the door, seeing a chance to escape the toxic scene before Sergei reappeared. She put her arm around Neave's shoulders and tried to steer her away. 'Come on, Neave. Let's go.'

'No,' said Neave, her fists clenched. 'I want someone to tell me the truth about what happened to my mother.'

'Neave, my dear,' said Rohesia, with a laugh. 'I don't know what ridiculous lies you've been told but you really need to get ready for the morning. We sail on the early tide, remember.'

'Rohesia,' said Esme. 'Pretending this isn't happening is *not* going to make it go away. You owe Neave an explanation. You told me you didn't know who Bella was but you do. She came to challenge your husband. You saw her that night, didn't you?'

'Rohesia,' said Neave, near to tears. 'I need to know what happened.'

Rohesia snorted, sitting down on one of the dining chairs. 'I'm not sure you do, my dear. Your mother was not quite the innocent victim you'd like to believe.' Her mouth formed a hard line. 'The truth is she was a parasite who threatened to destroy everything we'd achieved with her little blackmailing scheme.'

Neave gave out a pained cry and slumped against the sideboard.

Rohesia leant over and tapped the polished table with a manicured finger. 'She thought she could just walk in with her demands. As though he owed her something.'

'He did owe her something,' said Esme. 'She was his wife. He betrayed her and then he killed her for daring to find him out.'

'She had a choice,' said Rohesia, cocking her chin. 'She could have freed him from that obligation and gone on her way. But she didn't. She made the wrong decision.'

Esme recoiled at the chilling echo of history they'd recently uncovered. 'Liberty or death?' She turned on Ashgrove. 'Is that the choice you gave her? Let you off the hook or die?'

'No, you don't understand...' he began.

'It hardly matters whether she understands or not,' said Rohesia getting to her feet and walking over to the window. She folded her arms and gazed out into the blackness beyond. 'They can prove nothing.'

'*I* can, though.' Neave's voice sounded fragile compared to the harshness of Rohesia's arrogant tone. She glared at Ashgrove. 'But not to claim any link to you. Only to expose you as my mother's killer.'

'I've told you, Neave,' said Ashgrove, staring back, his head shaking. 'It's not like you think. I loved Bella.'

'Then why did you abandon her?' Neave stabbed her forefinger against her chest. 'And *me*.'

Ashgrove glowered at Rohesia. 'It was never meant to be like that. '

Rohesia groaned. 'Oh, for God's sake. My soul weeps.'

Esme watched her, confused at the change. From anxious and watchful, Rohesia seemed suddenly to be in control.

The back door clattered, announcing Sergei's return. Esme pulled Neave close to her, cursing for allowing Neave's need for answers to distort her judgment. She should have insisted they left while they had the chance.

Ashgrove stood up straight. 'This has gone far enough,' he said, eyeing Sergei.

'Keep out of this,' said Rohesia, her back to the room. 'I know what I'm doing.'

Ashgrove marched round the table and grabbed her arm, forcing her to look at him. 'No, I won't keep out of it. Not this time.' He jabbed a finger towards Sergei. 'You call him off. Now.'

'Oh for pity's sake.' She yanked her arm out of his grasp and folded her arms, sneering at him. 'Do you really think we can play happy families? She's your Achilles heel. Don't you realise that? Shut up and let me deal with it.'

'No. Not this time. It's over. I've danced to your tune long enough.'

'Don't be ridiculous. You need me. You always have. You'd be eking out a living doing some sordid low-life job with a brood of mouths to feed and still married to that jumped up, drunken bitch of a wife, if it wasn't for me.'

'She wasn't a drunken bitch when I married her. That was your doing. You turned her into that.'

'Me? Don't be ridiculous.'

'I wanted her in on it, but you didn't, did you? All that crap about only telling her so much for her own safety, until the time was right? She was just a means to an end, for you, wasn't she? *Find an English girl to marry you*, you said, *legitimise yourself.* You never had any intention of including her.'

Rohesia glared. 'You know why, you stupid man. It was too risky. She had family. One word in the wrong place...' She closed her eyes. 'Sweet Jesus, how many times do I have to spell it out?'

Ashgrove pointed a finger at her, his face dark and his voice sour. 'That wasn't the reason. You were terrified what it'd mean for you, whether you'd be able to get me to do what you wanted, if Bella was part of it. You wanted complete control and I was green enough to go along with it. But not any longer. You've controlled my life since I was a dumb kid, old enough to understand your instructions. I didn't know any better then, did I? I did exactly what you told me, whatever trouble it got me into.' He banged his fist on the table. 'Well, I've had enough, you embittered old spinster, d'you hear? It's over.'

'How dare you.'

Esme baulked. Embittered old spinster? She watched the two of them snarling at one another, their blue eyes defiant. And the truth hit her. Pale skin, dark hair, crystal blue eyes.

Rohesia was not Declan Shaw's wife. She was his sister.

52

Esme stared at the sparring siblings, recalling the information on the Shaw family which Greg had sent her. And something else, too. Something she'd seen which had troubled her. A name she'd registered but not realised.

'You're Colleen Shaw,' said Esme.

Rohesia stiffened. 'I don't recognise that name any more. Colleen Shaw no longer exists. I'm an Ashgrove now.'

'You took the name Rohesia from the Ashgrove family tree,' Esme continued. 'You stole it, along with everything else.'

'I stole nothing that wasn't already mine. We are direct descendents. If the Ashgroves hadn't despised the Shaw family…'

'Except it wasn't only about the Ashgroves hating the Shaws, was it? The Shaws didn't want their son to marry into a hated English family who'd evicted them from their Irish home.'

A cold smile played on Rohesia's lips. 'Then what better way to take back what was stolen.'

'The Ashgrove estate no longer owns Irish land, Rohesia. You're two centuries too late.'

Sergei moved and Esme recoiled, grabbing Neave and pulling her away from him. But Sergei made no move towards them. Instead he retreated into the kitchen and ran out of the back door, leaving it swinging open. As Esme struggled to comprehend his actions, a distant sound explained everything. The wail of sirens.

Rohesia had heard them too. She pushed past Esme and Neave, out into the hall. Ashgrove slumped down on to a chair, staring at the floor as the sirens reached a climax.

As they ceased, Esme heard footsteps and Maddy appeared through the kitchen door. She saw Esme and hurried over.

'You guys all right?'

Esme nodded. 'Go with Maddy,' she said, guiding Neave towards her. 'She'll look after you.'

And before Maddy had time to ask the question, Esme headed off after Rohesia.

*

On the front terrace the moonlight pooled on the flagstones allowing Esme enough light to orientate herself. Where would Rohesia go? But even as she formed the question, she knew.

She waited for a few moments to allow her eyes to adjust to the dark, before stepping on to the gravel drive and walking to where the shrubs hid the short cut to the cliff path. At the gap in the shrubbery she stopped and listened to the breathing of the sea in the distance. The sweet smell of night-scented stock growing along the grass edge bordering the drive seemed incompatible against the unfolding drama.

She parted the laurels and made her way through the narrow gap, fending off the branches as they whipped her face. The dark foliage blocked out the moonlight and she had to rely on instinct to guide her. She pushed on into the unknown, concerned she'd taken a wrong turn until the greenery opened out and she found herself in the lane which adjoined the coast path. She turned towards the sea and hurried on to where the broken tarmac merged with the grass of the cliff top.

A warm onshore breeze greeted her as she stepped out of the shelter of the hedge-bank. She tucked a strand of hair behind her ear and gazed about. Out at sea, a path of silver glinted on the surface of the water, its eerie light unnerving her. Where was Rohesia?

A movement caught in her peripheral vision and she saw Rohesia, silhouetted against the sky. She was standing on the mound where they'd marvelled at the beauty of the seascape, the day Esme had come looking for Neave.

Esme walked towards her, the sound of breaking waves against the rocks below mounting as she approached. At the foot of the mound she stopped. Rohesia was standing right on the very edge of the grass, her chin up and her back stiff. The wind played with her hair, flicking it on and off her face.

'I was wrong about you, Esme,' said Rohesia. She stared ahead into the dark nothingness, her back to Esme, her voice flat and sullen. 'I expected you to understand. You're an historian. You know what those women suffered under The System.'

'Many of our ancestors suffered, Rohesia. And not just under transportation. Poverty, wars, social injustice…'

Rohesia's head shot round. 'Those women were exploited. Maligned as whores and degenerates, used and abused. And by the very men who should have protected them. My great-great-grandmother was one of those women, Esme, but she had the spirit to stand up to them. And they categorized her as a criminal and shaved her head as a mark of disgrace.'

'She was sent to the Female Factory, I assume?'

Rohesia spat into the air. 'The very name is an outrage.'

Esme heard the sound of tyres creeping along gravel. She kept her eyes focused on Rohesia as the car halted at the end of the lane, its pulsating light bathing the scene, and Rohesia, in a sickly blue.

'The factory must have been a terrifying place,' said Esme. 'I saw the picture on the *Mary Ann*.'

'That?' scoffed Rohesia. 'That came years after. When she was incarcerated, it was nothing but a loft above a gaol, with rotting timber floors and stinking privies.'

'I know how appalling conditions were, Rohesia, and I do understand.'

'Of course you don't, Esme. How could you? You don't understand that when I lie on my bed, it's atonement for the infested pallet on which she lay. Or that when I cover myself with soft, clean bedding it's reparation for the feeble sacking which covered her.' She looked up towards the manor. 'And the roof

254

over my head, the antithesis to her roof, decrepit and leaking, which failed to protect her from the driving rain. You understand nothing.'

'But it was two hundred years ago.'

'What relevance is time? Governments across the world are only now apologising for atrocities they committed centuries ago.' Rohesia returned her gaze to the sea. 'When I first realised Giles Cooper's father was the Ashgrove's solicitor, I knew then. It was meant to be. So I began to plan. It was easy, of course, to find out what I wanted to know. Cooper was utterly obsessed with me. He'd agree to anything so long as I allowed him a sweaty grope once in a while.' She snorted. 'He never did get over the fact that I wouldn't be his wife when I stepped on to UK soil. And by then, there was no turning back. He was too heavily in debt to walk away. Though why he imagined I would swap my beautiful ancestral home, having worked so hard to reclaim it, for some vulgar new box-like monstrosity, I've no idea. However much it cost him.'

'And Declan's role in this plan?'

'Ah. Poor pathetic Declan. My biddable shadow since he drew his very first breath. I am his entire world, Esme. Always have been. Always will be. What you saw back there was merely an act. He can't even sneeze without my say-so. And whatever he *thinks* he felt for *her*...Well, it's simply not true. I'm the one he truly loves. But he'll learn. He'll learn the hard way.'

Esme sensed someone behind her. She flicked a wary glance over her shoulder. Sergeant Collins was a few feet away. She lifted her hand and he responded by staying back at the edge of the path.

Esme turned back to Rohesia. 'And Bella?' She had to ask. Neave would want to know.

'It was so refreshingly simple. What other outcome could there be for someone so very, very drunk? So easy while she stumbled in the dark to steer her over the edge.'

'Rohesia...' Esme stepped forward.

'Stay where you are!'

'Then come away from the edge.'

'And do what? Give myself up to a life of incarceration?' She turned towards Esme, her features blackened shadows but her voice clear. 'Never. It would be a betrayal.'

'You don't have to do this.'

'My choice is made, Esme.'

'What choice?' But as she asked, she already knew. *Liberty or death.*

Rohesia lunged forward.

'No!' Esme reached out but someone held her back and Rohesia's shadowy profile was gone.

Esme dropped to her knees, closing her eyes tight against the image of Rohesia's final impact on the unforgiving rocks below. A bitter echo of Bella's pitiful fate.

53

Esme loaded the last bag into the boot of her Peugeot and slammed the lid. The childhood memory of her mother's voice calling her and her sister to get in the car echoed in her head. She walked to the front of the car and leant against the bonnet, gazing seaward. Don't fret, her father would say, attempting to reinstate smiles on their despondent faces, we'll be back next year. She and Elizabeth would trudge back up the hill, arguing. A prelude to the long and tedious journey home.

A voice calling her name cut through her reminiscences and she turned to see Ruth coming across the field from the farm, Neave alongside her. She waved and went over to meet them. Neave was sporting a floppy brimmed sunhat, a floral sash around its crown which matched her skirt. The outfit was softer and more relaxed in style than clothes she'd worn before. She hoped it was a good sign.

Neave pulled off her sunhat and threw her head back, filling her lungs with sea air. 'I do love this place!'

'Neave's meeting Dan on the quay,' said Ruth, with a wink.

'Hello, Neave,' said Esme. 'Have you come to see the *Mary Ann* go, too?'

Neave nodded and gave Esme an awkward smile. 'I thought it might be cathartic, seeing it sail away into the distance.'

'It would be nice to think so, wouldn't it?' said Esme, flushing. She looked away, conscious of her own part in what Neave must now learn to cope with.

'Well, I for one will be glad to see it go,' said Ruth, propping herself against the bonnet of Esme's car. 'I was worried it was going to sit there for weeks as a sinister reminder of what happened.'

'It would have done, if it still belonged to the Ashgroves,' said Esme. 'For which, though it pains me to say it, we've Giles Cooper to thank.' Somehow Cooper had managed to engineer the sale of the ship right under Rohesia's nose and squirrel away the proceeds to fund his escape plan. Even as Rohesia was proudly declaring ownership to Esme, Cooper was concluding negotiations; aware that time was running out. And he should know. It had been Cooper who'd notified Bella of her husband's location, in a fit of pique after a dispute with Rohesia. The argument which Esme overheard from the cabin of the *Mary Ann* was Rohesia expressing her frustration that Cooper had, predictably, failed to discover the identity of Bella's informant.

Ruth folded her arms. 'Fancy them living up there all that time and no one knew their secret. And as for that woman...' She looked at Neave from under her brow. 'Sorry, Neave. I know she was your aunt but...'

Neave looked taken aback, as though the familial title hadn't occurred to her before. She shook her head and looked away. 'Don't worry, Ruth. She's not exactly earned any loyalty from me.'

'No, of course not. And it must be so difficult, trying to understand it all.' Ruth appealed to Esme. 'I mean, goodness knows, we're all pretty familiar with the horrors of transportation now, thanks to the *Mary Ann* but to end up so...destructive.'

'She seemed to be obsessed with what her ancestor, Ellen Murphy, suffered in the Female Factory,' said Esme. 'I suppose if she was force-fed such stories from an early age and they were couched in a particular way, who knows what affect it had on her.' She shuddered, recalling Rohesia's assumption that Esme should show some kind of allegiance for her cause. 'The irony, though, which occurred to me the other day, is that Sarah Baker also would have ended up in the Female Factory.'

'Really?' said Neave. 'Why?'

'She was pregnant. Her daughter Jane was born in February 1838. Pregnant women and those with babies were generally sent to the factory on their arrival. Which is where William found her when he reached Australia a few months later.'

'And he was able to get her out of there?'

'Yes. The Female Factory was regarded as a sort of marriage bureau. Men looking for a wife would visit and appraise what was on offer. For the women who'd ended up there, it was their ticket out.'

Ruth clicked her tongue. 'Those poor women. It's all very well labelling them as morally unsound. Sounds to me as though they didn't have much say in it.'

'That was more or less Rohesia's point of view, Ruth,' said Esme, suppressing a smile at the look of horror on Ruth's face. She glanced at her watch. 'Hey, we'd better get a move on or that ship will have sailed off before we get there.'

'Goodness, yes,' said Ruth, taking hold of Neave's arm. 'And Dan will be waiting, wondering where you've got to.'

They started down the hill where small groups of walkers were stretched out along the coast path heading for Warren Quay. A flotilla of boats bobbed up and down out on the bay, waiting to accompany the departing ship.

'Interesting about Ellen and Sarah both ending up in the same appalling conditions,' said Neave, as they walked. 'Yet, one of them inspired the foundation of a charity and the other used the experience as an excuse to peddle ill-will and resentment.'

Esme recalled Rohesia's cold sneer as she defended her crimes. 'It certainly wouldn't be the first family to breed hatred and bitterness across the generations.' The spectre of a convict ancestor perched on a family tree would, until more enlightened times, be a stigma to keep hidden, regarded as a genetic stain passed down the so-called Criminal Class. Now it was seen as intriguing or amusing, even. A 'character', an eccentric with a story to tell to enhance the family legend. Not so, though, for Neave.

Neave fiddled with the sash on her hat. 'She was planning to get rid of me overboard on the way to Ireland, wasn't she?'

Ruth gasped.

'You can't be sure of that,' said Esme, her eyes pleading with Ruth not to worsen matters with histrionics. She'd hoped that Neave had been unaware of that possibility.

Neave shook her head. 'You don't need to protect me, Esme. She pushed Mum off that cliff. She'd have no hesitation in pushing me off a moving boat.' She turned to Esme, her face troubled. 'Remember that woman they thought might have witnessed Ted Marsh's murder? They reckon it was her. She was no witness, though. She killed him.'

Esme pictured Ashgrove being bundled into the car at the manor after his arrest, pleading his innocence. 'So your father was telling the truth.'

'I don't see what difference it makes. He may not be technically guilty, but he was complicit.'

They arrived on the edge of the coast path and Neave stopped, a shadow falling across her face. 'He keeps asking to see me.'

Esme wasn't surprised, remembering Ashgrove's defiance against Rohesia, prompted by concern for the fate of his daughter. 'What will you do?'

Neave shook her head. 'I don't know. If I agree, it feels like I'm condoning what he did. If I refuse…well, I'm as bad as her, aren't I? Denying him contact with his family.'

Esme nodded, uncertain what to say which might help ease her dilemma.

'There's time enough to decide,' said Ruth, squeezing Neave's arm. 'He's not going anywhere, is he? You go off and find Dan. We'll watch from the cliff top. No need for us to get caught up with the crowds. I'll see you later.'

'Thanks for everything,' said Neave, glancing at them both. 'Dan's asked me to help with the kids' holidays next year,' she added, her face softening a little.

Esme smiled. 'You'll like that.'

She nodded. 'I think I will.'

They watched as Neave hurried along the coast path, the sash on her hat fluttering out behind her.

'I sense a romance blossoming,' said Ruth, with a chuckle.

Esme laughed. 'You always were a hopeless romantic.'

'Yes, but nice to think the Shaws and the Ashgroves might be reunited at last, though, don't you think?'

They found a place to sit on a tuft of grass over-looking the bay and sat in silence, listening to the gulls calling overhead and allowing the warm sun to bathe their faces. Below them, a family picked their way over the rocks which ran across the beach, their frequent shouts of discovery buffeted on the wind. Down in Warren Quay people milled around the quay like foam along the waterline and shimmering car roofs and windscreens discharged flares of sunlight across the cove.

'You're still feeling guilty about Neave, aren't you?' said Ruth, turning towards her, shading her eyes from the sun with her palm.

Esme looked away, taken aback at Ruth's blunt question. '"Evil happens when good men do nothing" was one of Tim's favourite quotes,' she said, gazing out to sea. 'But I'm not sure it's as simple as that. How do you expose the bad deeds of others without causing pain to the innocent?'

'But what else could you have done?' said Ruth.

Ruth's words echoed something she'd said to Ruth when she arrived. They'd been talking about Elizabeth. *She's my sister. What else could I have done?*

'Remember that time we got caught by the tide?' said Ruth.

Esme frowned. 'Vaguely. Why?'

Ruth plucked a stalk of grass and chewed it. 'I'd completely forgotten why we went to those caves without checking the tides,' she said. 'Until the day you found Bella Shaw. It brought it all back. I recognised the same mood. There was an energy about you. You knew something was wrong.' She turned to Esme. 'Do you remember? We'd seen those children go down to the caves. You were convinced they'd get trapped.'

'Was I?' Esme scratched around in her memory. 'I do recall something, now you say.'

'And you were right to worry. They hadn't a clue.' She grabbed Esme's hand. 'If you'd not insisted on going after them, they'd have been cut off. They could have drowned.'

Esme gave a half laugh and shook her head. 'Oh come on, Ruth. I'm sure it wasn't as heroic as you make out.'

Ruth patted Esme's hand and smiled. 'Have it your own way. I'm just saying. I know what you're like.'

She turned away to look back across the bay as Esme tried to recall the incident. She remembered getting their feet wet and Ruth crying, certain she'd get into trouble for ruining her new sandals.

'There it is,' said Ruth, thrusting out her arm and pointing. 'It's off.'

The shouts of the crew echoed off the rocks as the order was given to raise the sails. They watched, mesmerised at its splendour, as the tall ship slipped into the bay and out to open sea. What cruel irony that such beauty and magnificence represented so brutal an era in history.

They watched until the *Mary Ann* was a distant icon on the horizon before climbing back up the hill to Ravens Farm.

'I hope what's happened hasn't spoilt the place for you,' said Ruth, as they reached the cabin.

Esme shook her head. 'No, of course not.'

'So you'll come again?'

'Yes, I'm sure I will.'

Ruth stopped and turned towards her. 'Don't leave it so long next time, eh?'

'No I won't.'

'Promise?'

Esme smiled. 'Promise.'

Historical note

Inspiration for *The Indelible Stain* began with an article on researching convict ancestry but was fuelled by my reading of *The Fatal Shore* by Robert Hughes, a meticulously researched account of Britain's brutal transportation policy and the birth of Australia as a penal colony.

At the end of the eighteenth century, England's statute book groaned under the weight of over 200 offences punishable by death, including Grand Larceny – the theft of goods over one shilling in value. Amid mounting unease at what would, in later years, be termed The Bloody Code, the law was changed to allow judges to commute the death sentence to transportation.

Between 1787 and 1868 over 160,000 convicts were transported to Australia, a third of them Irish. Fighting for political change in their country, much of which was owned by English 'absentee' landlords, many Irish felons were labelled as dissidents and exiled without trial.

By the mid 1800s, doubt over the effectiveness of The System and Australia's objection to being used as a dumping ground for Britain's criminals saw the beginning of the end for transportation. Finally, in 1867, the last convict ship, the *Hougoumont*, left England and arrived in Western Australia in January 1868.

While the characters in *The Indelible Stain* are fictional, historical references to convict ships, prisoner experiences and Devon court records are all authentic.

For further information and to see the family tree Esme drew up showing the link between the Shaws and the Ashgroves, please go to www.wendypercival.co.uk/theindeliblestainextra.

A message from the author

Thank you for reading *The Indelible Stain*. If you enjoyed the book and have a moment to spare, writing a short review on Amazon or Goodreads (or your favourite site) would be greatly appreciated. Authors rely on the kindness of readers to share their experiences and spread the word.

Join us!

To keep updated on giveaways, special promotions and new releases, and to receive my quarterly newsletter, join the Readers Group mailing list.

You can sign up on my website **www.wendypercival.co.uk**

Subscribers also receive a FREE copy of the Esme Quentin prequel novella:

LEGACY OF GUILT

The shocking death of a young mother in 1835 holds the key to Esme Quentin's search for truth and justice for her cousin.

With the tragedy of her past behind her, Esme Quentin has quit her former career, along with its potential dangers, and is looking to the future.

But when she stumbles upon her cousin in traumatic circumstances, Esme realises that her compulsion to uncover the truth, irrespective of the consequences, remains as strong as ever.

You'll also find me on:
Facebook: www.facebook.com/wendypercivalauthor
Twitter: @wendy_percival

I look forward to hearing from you.